GRISLY GHOSTS

One minute there were barren rocky hills. The next, the same hills were lined with Apaches, who seemed to rise from the very ground like ghosts.

"They're not going to attack us yet," Chance said. "They're waiting to see where we go. About a mile ahead is a place they call 'The Land of the Cursed Warrior.' The few white men who've seen it call it 'Hell's Halfacre.' "

"I'm not going to run because of some stupid superstition," Bradley said sourly. "What's so special about the place?"

"The Apaches believe it brings evil to anyone who goes near it, and death to anyone who crosses it. The Indians are trouble enough. Do we need to go looking for more?"

HELL'S HALFACRE

Brick Killerman

TOWER BOOKS ▮ NEW YORK CITY

To my grandfather.
He would have been a real Chance fan.

A TOWER BOOK

Published by

Tower Publications, Inc.
Two Park Avenue
New York, N.Y. 10016

A Trio of Deadly Sins

1

There was great turmoil and unrest in the South, even eight years after the end of the Civil War. The Southern states, decimated both physically and spiritually, held the victorious North in bitter contempt. The scalawags and carpetbaggers were struggling for control of Southern government through stealthy manipulation. The newly freed slaves, numbering about four million, were hit hardest by the bite of Southern animosity. The Indians were rampaging, spilling blood ferociously; and, with an intensity that almost surpassed the bloodiest battles of the War, were becoming increasingly angry as white settlers pushed westward in their relentless search for new soil to lay claim on. A staggering number of Southern families, reaching well into the thousands, had been left homeless as a result of the havoc wreaked upon them by their Northern brothers. Murder, corruption and mayhem were the elements contributing to the turbulence during this period known as the Reconstruction era.

But the large town of Smiling Sons had blossomed in the wake of this chaos, spreading itself over the fertile plains of north-central Texas, far enough away to escape the sting of Southern defeat. Now, as the sun reached its zenith and baked the frame buildings and surrounding farmhouses and barns, the people of Smiling Sons continued with their daily routines —farming, shopping, browsing—in an air of peace and tranquility. One would never have suspected that for many people this was a rough time.

Riding west from the Brazos River, the grim-faced man atop the black gelding marveled at the sight of Smiling Sons as he walked his mount down the grassy hills, although his impassive

5

features betrayed no delight in the affable landscape ahead. For times were especially hard on the big blond man and he couldn't—either by his own design or fate—revel in the good fortune of others. His large, calloused left hand seemed to rest, either consciously or by force of habit, on the English Colt Dragoon jutting from a well-worn holster tied down to his left thigh. The revolver was old and equally as worn as the holster, but reliable and deadly, as proven on many occasions.

Underneath his low-crowned black hat, he swept his squinting gaze slowly from left to right, indifferently noting the abundance of livestock grazing around their respective farmhouses and barns on the southern and northern outskirts of town. Wheat and cornfields stretched out to the south, shining dully under the glare of the sun. A hot breeze stirred from the Gulf of Mexico to ripple and sway the vast fecundity.

The blond spat, then took out a stubby cigar, and struck a match off his saddlehorn just as he entered Smiling Sons from the east. He sweated little, but flies swarmed about him, causing an irritation which was hard to ignore.

The travel-weary gelding ambled down the dirt street between two rows of brown buildings. The smells of fresh paint, trash in alleyways, animals and brewing coffee wafted through the hot atmosphere. Several people interrupted conversations to stare briefly at the blond stranger, noting with expressions of suspicion and curiosity the rugged handsomeness of his face and the wide shoulders constricted by a dirt-grimed blue cotton shirt, with black Levis equally as filthy. Several of the townspeople noted with particular dismay the Winchester .44/40 sticking from the man's saddleboot.

Guns had once been a rarity in Smiling Sons, and trouble had been almost nonexistent. But lately more drifters had been riding through town to frequent one of the three saloons, causing unrest because of their menacing presence and the reputations which followed them like black clouds. The townspeople spotted the new visitor as a loner, a new breed of outlaw frequently seen after the War. Quite possibly he would bring the trouble this town had so far been able to avert. In fact the blond stranger was a bounty hunter, although his occupation was held in almost as much scorn as the lawlessness of the men he hunted—men who went on mindless killing and stealing sprees; men who were savage animals loathed by the law-abiding people; men they preferred to see brought in by the law dead than alive.

No particular activity was halted for any length of time to inspect the stranger; his presence was merely noticed. The sounds of glasses clinking, laughter and conversation pricked the bounty hunter's ears as he passed horses tethered to the railings in front of saloons, general stores, hotels and other places of business. The sheriff's office, the telegraph office, the bank and a boarding house lined the other side of the street, with a large church at the far west end of town.

Finally he reached that section of town, where he stopped in front of a small white one-story house. After dismounting and tethering his horse to a picket fence, he strolled up the walk, spurs jangling an abrasive tune on the stone. He knocked lightly on the door. Remembering this wasn't a social visit, he grunted, then tossed his cigar into the flower bed to his right, following it up with a large globule of saliva to accentuate the disgust he was feeling. He didn't remove his hat.

The door opened slowly. The petite blonde who answered looked bewildered. After staring blankly for several seconds at her visitor, she asked demurely, "Can I help you?"

"Ma'am," he said, still not removing his hat, his hands held loosely behind his back, his piercing blue eyes causing the woman discomfort. "My name's Neems, Lawrence Neems. I'm looking for a man that you were . . . reputedly intimate with." His thin lips seemed to crack into a sneer.

Neems' rhetoric didn't impress her; instead, it enhanced her amazement at his crudeness. "What do you want? Just who are you?" she rasped indignantly.

"I'm just a man, ma'am, looking for my pot of gold. All I want is some information—call it 'historical reference'—on him . . . my rainbow."

"I don't know what the hell you're talking about; get out of here!" she said in angry contempt, starting to slam the door.

Neems thrust his right foot out, placing it in the quickly diminishing space. The pain he felt when the door edge slammed into the side of his boot further intensified his anger; he pushed open the door violently, knocking the small blonde backward. She kept her balance, fearfully watching Neems close the door behind him in such a calm, natural motion it looked as if he belonged there, it was his home.

7

"I don't have time for a lot of games, ma'am," Neems growled. "He'll be out of prison in less than a week. It's no big secret; his past, his release, you and his other women . . . and the three hundred thousand bucks he hid."

She bolted into the living room, going toward a large cabinet beside the fireplace. Neems strode quickly and purposefully after her, reaching her just as she pulled a gun from the cabinet's drawer. She turned instantly, but Neems wrenched the large revolver from her tiny hands and chucked it across the room, where it landed softly on a red divan.

Lashing out with a vicious backhand, Neems knocked Sara onto her back.

"Bastard!" she snarled vehemently, rubbing her left cheek while tears of pain welled up in the blazing blue of her eyes.

"You're right, ma'am," he said politely, looking at her indifferently. Then he examined six large plates made of chinaware, displayed proudly in a neat row atop the fireplace mantel. "I'm not too chivalrous. And I'm growing less polite all the time, Sara."

She snapped, "How did you get my name?"

"I'm a bounty hunter. It's my job to know things, Sara."

She cringed, deeply repulsed when he used her name. She felt violated, insulted, humiliated.

"I care about one thing—well, two things," he flatly informed her, noticing for the first time the light-colored fabric of her dress, which fitted snugly around a well-proportioned frame. The sweetly provocative scent of her perfume reached his nose and filled his mind momentarily with other thoughts. "You're telling me you don't know anything about anything?"

"I told you I didn't! And even if I did, why would I tell a piece of filth like you?" She immediately realized the mistake she'd made, but she was very angry about the callous hunter's violent intrusion.

"Oh?" Neems said, holding one of the china plates in his hands, scrutinizing the decorations on the hard-paste porcelain.

"Put that down!" she commanded breathlessly, her voice soft but firm. "Those are antiques from Worcester. My great grandmother's!"

"Oh?" Neems flatly replied, flipping the plate toward

Sara's right. She watched in horror, desperately lunging for the plate, but it was just out of her reach and it smashed loudly into pieces on the hard floorboard.

"What are you doing?" she cried as Neems casually threw two more plates to the floor, one to the right, the other to the left of her, both breaking into chunks and myriad fragments.

"You were telling me how you didn't know anything?" Neems asked, picking up two more plates.

Mortified, Sara shrieked, "I told you I didn't! Why don't you believe me? I hate that man! I never want to see him or hear his name again!"

"Hmmm," mumbled the bounty hunter, smashing another plate, then another, this time dropping them at his feet as he glared at Sara. "Of course you don't. Especially if you know where the money is."

"Do you think, if I knew where he hid the money, I'd be hanging around this town?"

"Mmmm-hmmm," was his reply, not indicating whether he believed her or not. "I guess you really don't know anything."

"Why, then? Why did you do this?" she asked, her tone seething with hatred, her eyes alight with malice.

Neems smiled cruelly. "Just checking, ma'am. You never can know too much in my field of work." He took the last plate, examined it, then grunted. "The prison's only a few miles' north, and it's a sure bet he'll stop here first."

She grimaced as Neems looked dispassionately at the smashed pieces of her chinaware. He grunted again, a hoarse, mocking sound, then placed the plate gently atop the mantelpiece.

"Could be back, so hang loose," Neems said, walking from the living room, his boots crunching on the fragments of porcelain.

"Trash!" she hissed. Then, unladylike, Sara spat in his wake, a gesture that might have been comical if not done with the utter vindictiveness she expressed.

"Sorry, ma'am," Neems politely responded, scratching a match off the wall, then meticulously lighting another cigar. "I didn't mean for you to fall all to pieces on me." He headed for the door.

"Go to hell!" she cried in angry despair. "You're nothing but filthy trash!"

9

She wept bitterly as Neems stepped outside into the scorching heat. Flies immediately teemed around him, attracted to his filth and stench, and a sweat that quickly formed while he thought about the rainbow with his pot of gold.

There were four of them. Heading south from the Canadian River into the infamous Indian Territory of southeastern Oklahoma, the four men and their mounts were gray apparitions nearly invisible inside the fierce dust storm sweeping the flat prairie plains. The strong winds blew from the southeast, kicking up the dry soil in such a relentless assault that the thick black bandanas resting just below hooded eyelids and the upturned collars of dark blue frock coats were the only apparel that would allow them to brave the elements. Chin straps kept their low-crowned hats from blowing away. Blinders protected the eyes of their horses.

A short distance ahead, the loud whinny of a frightened horse was barely audible. The storm howled in eerie defiance, steadily smacking its wrath upon man and beast. The horse cried again, and this time the men were closer and able to make out the semblance of a small frame house that looked like a large shack. A smaller structure, where the horse could be heard, was adjacent to the house. The dust had piled halfway up the sides of the structures and might have been the support that kept them from toppling into a heap. Both were decrepit in appearance; both looked grim in their isolation on the desolate landscape, with all openings boarded up for protection against the storm.

But the elderly man they hoped to find here was the immediate goal of the four riders, known as Laster, Stanley, Ridgeway and Mamoreck.

They dismounted and tethered their horses to the porch railing, their movements somber and meticulous. Like pallbearers. Like gravediggers.

As Laster stepped up onto the floorboard the door opened suddenly. A tall, gaunt old man filled the doorway, shielding his eyes with his hand.

"Yeah," the old man growled loudly, trying to be heard over the wind's wailing. Laster ambled toward him, then thrust his arm out, the open hand grabbing and violently shoving the old man by his face.

Laster quickly followed the old man, who stumbled backward several feet until his upper thighs slammed against a table edge. This flipped him onto his back, where he attempted to stop the momentum that would have been strong enough to carry him clear across the tabletop if he hadn't grasped the edge. But when he did grab hold, the momentum was great enough to force him and the table up into the air so that both were canted at an angle. He was paralyzed for a second at the queer tilt, just enough time for Laster to kick the table's edge furiously to complete the old man's flip. The table crashed on top of him as a cup and a plate of food were hurled against the wall.

"Glad I could give you a foot," Laster cracked. His three comrades strolled through the door, the storm following their tall, rangy figures inside.

"Heard your kid's out of prison, Pop. Know where he might be?" Laster asked, watching the old man struggle to his feet, using the wall for support, his features set in an angry snarl.

"He ain't my kid, he's only my nephew!" the old man rasped through clenched, yellowed teeth, as if he were ashamed of the fact. "And I heard he don't get out 'til two days from now."

"We oughta make it by then, don't ya think, Sim?" Stanley asked Laster.

"Yeah. We should."

"Well then, git yer greasy tails outta here and leave me be!" the old man whined, casting surreptitious glances at the Winchester leaning against the far left wall.

"Sure, pop," Laster agreed, "after we help ourselves to a few things . . . . Boys?"

The three began to rummage through cabinets, grabbing sacks and packets of food. Unable to contain himself any longer, the old man bounded forth from his slouch, yelling, "Hey!"

Laster threw a straight right, his balled fist connecting solidly, savagely on the old man's mouth, launching him back to bounce off the wall and crumple in a semiconscious pile on the floor. Blood flowed from a split lower lip as he spat forth chips of bone.

"Forget the heroics, Pop," snarled Laster.

"Careful, Sim," Stanley said, his tone easy and flat, as the three gathered by the door, hands full of loot. "I hear he's good friends with the Injuns round here."

"Ain't that just like an Indian, though?" said Laster, walking toward the door, indifferently listening to the old man's groaning. "Never around when you need one."

Snickering, the four sauntered outside, leaving the door open, the wind continuing to howl and whip dust into the old man's home. They separated their loot, stuffed it into saddle-bags and mounted, spurring their horses into a walking gait.

The old man fell into the doorway, his bloodied features twisted in vengeance, his Winchester leveled. The four men were no more than twenty feet from the doorway. When the old man pumped the rifle's action lever, its distinct metallic clicking whirled the four sideways to their right, revolvers drawn lightning fast and blazing a deadly volley of nine bullets. Four ripped into the old man's chest, slamming him against the doorjamb, where he rebounded as two more blasted open red-gouting holes in his stomach. Another one sliced his inner left thigh and two buried themselves harmlessly into the doorjamb, spraying wood splinters. The old man, dead on his feet, was hurtled backward, bouncing, then sliding in his own blood along the floorboards. Ridgeway and Mamoreck hadn't hit with deadly accuracy.

The horses whinnied briefly, attempting to rear, but their riders brought them under control. Then they continued, heading south, slowly disappearing into the storm that suddenly raged stronger as the eerie howling of the wind became almost a piercing shriek in the wake of death.

Pallbearers of morbid whimsey. Gravediggers in the storm.

Joseph Sterning was a happy man, in love with life. A loyal, devoted husband for twenty-five years and loving father of six children, he had been treated with the utmost kindness by Fate. He had never experienced the brutality of the War between the States, neither during nor after. Nor had he ever experienced any other type of violence or hatred during the fifty-two years of his life. This was something he could never understand, although he rarely reflected on such things as tragedy, pain and death; he didn't have to, they were unfamiliar to him. As Joseph Sterning stood on the steps of the large home he had built with his own hands, he sighed quietly, praising God, admiring the beautiful wheat and cornfields glowing golden under the early-morning Kansas sun rising in the east and promising another hot summer day.

Stepping off the porch, the lanky, gray-haired farmer walked out into a spacious area in front of the house, smiling affably toward the servants' quarters to his left. The servants were a Negro family of six. He paid, housed and fed them well and treated them with the kindness and respect he would show toward any white man, not patronizing them like so many of his Northern brothers did. He believed wholeheartedly in the emancipation of the Negro, abhorring slavery, and not understanding why Southerners held the Negro in such disparagement and rancor, why they were so bitter.

The farmer was joyfully pleased that he had come south after the War and laid claim to this fertile land. The large barn, his home, the servants' quarters, the animals grazing in fenced-off pasture to the east and the abundant crops provided a picture of total serenity. Joseph Sterning was a man at peace with himself and the world. Tranquility was the rule, rather than the exception, that governed his life and the lives of his family. Beauty and love he had rarely been without. He was a God-fearing man who lived according to the Good Book. But today his faith would be severely shaken, tested in a manner that would surpass the plight of Job.

He wasn't the least bit dismayed when a cloud of dust appeared two hundred yards to the west, accompanied by the rumble of horses' hooves as they trampled the tall yellow prairie flowers. The thunderous pounding, as the mounts galloped east, directly disturbed the calm quiet of the morning.

Sterning watched them grow into semblances of men, then walked out to greet them as they reined their horses to a stop, billows of brown creeping up in their wake.

"Howdy, farmer," said one of the six men authoritatively, sitting rigid on his foam-dripping white stallion. He was dressed in the gray uniform of a Confederate general, his black boots nearly a matching gray from the dust. His black-gloved right hand rested leisurely on a saber by his side. His mount was slightly ahead of the others, attributing respect to him and acknowledging his leadership.

"Howdy," Sterning greeted in a friendly but cautious tone,

his gaze flitting over the motley assortment of bearded strangers. Five were in their late twenties to early thirties, but one was no more than a boy of eighteen. The boy's cotton shirt underneath coveralls hung loosely on his slight frame, somehow accentuating the innocence of his grin, the softness of his clean-shaven face and the warmth in his eyes. His saber and the large Colt revolver, holstered and draped at his side, somehow didn't belong on him; they were strangely incongruous with his pleasant demeanor. And the other five, Sterning noted with a stirring trepidation, were grim-faced men with hard, angry eyes and smiles which were more like mocking leers. These five were armed with revolvers, rifles and sabers.

"What have you got for us, farmer?" asked a weasel-faced man with a Spencer rifle canted against his right shoulder, a Confederate flag with a bullethole in it prominently pointing from the barrel, his cowboy garb as torn looking as the flag.

Licking his lips, Sterning gulped hard, looking at the man dressed as a general. The latter was resting his hard stare on Sterning, now tight lipped and somber. "Whatever I have is yours, gentlemen. Feel free to make my home yours."

There was a ripple of soft snickering from four of the men. Sterning didn't like what he was feeling—a cold ball of fear in the pit of his stomach. These men as a group emanated a sinister poison which was both loathsome and chilling.

"Like the way the man thinks, Karl," said another man dressed in Confederate gray.

The general, who was addressed as Karl, flatly replied, "Love it."

"We don't have a lot of time for hospitality, farmer," intoned the cowboy. This man spoke with a slight lisp.

"You see . . . we're renegades, mister," said the general solemnly.

"Pardon?" asked a confused Sterning, beads of sweat starting to form on his brow.

"He means we're outlaws, mister!" the boy gleefully exclaimed. "We're runnin' from the law!"

"Shuddup, kid," growled the cowboy, spitting on the ground. "Don't pay no attention to him, farmer. He's just a smartmouth kid who's tagging along for the ride and the glory of the South."

14

"Hardly wet behind the ears," added another man scornfully, also spitting to the ground, his scowl augmenting the disdain he'd expressed, his accent as clearly Southern as that of his other five comrades.

The boy grimaced, visibly offended by the bantering, his eyes reflecting the hurt as he was taunted into silence.

"Reminds me of Lawrence," the general murmured, briefly scanning the area, suddenly lost in thought.

"He means Lawrence, Kansas, farmer," the cowboy said. "Ever hear of it?"

Sterning shook his head that he hadn't, although he had. Now his fear grew, for he knew what these men were.

"No, I haven't," he blurted.

"We rode with Quantrill. Been about ten years since Karl and some of the boys was at Lawrence. That's all he ever talks about," another man, dressed in Western-style clothes, added, his flat tone not reflecting the pride his eyes indicated when he announced the facts.

(William Clarke Quantrill had been the leader of a band of Confederate guerillas during the Civil War. They terrorized Missouri and Kansas; Lawrence, Kansas was the site of their most notorious and brutal raid, where close to 200 people were left dead in the wake of the carnage.)

"But Quantrill got hisself killed. Our General Nenz is a lot smarter, though," the cowboy gloated. "Hell, we haven't been hardly touched by the law."

Just then, Sterning's wife, two boys and several teenage girls ventured onto the porch. Almost instantly their expressions became ones of curiosity and fright.

"Joseph," said the wife, "is everything all right?"

"Lovin' it," said the general, raising his gloved hand, his eyes still a wide, blank stare as he remained trapped in his void of bewilderment. "Boys?"

"Hot damn!" One of the men leered excitedly, heading his mount toward the porch. "Broads."

"Guess we really don't have time for hospitality, farmer," said the cowboy, his eyes alight with a sick perversion which paralyzed Sterning in horror momentarily as the man steered his own mount toward the women and children. "The general's really lovin' it; and when Stan Krupeck sees some young fluff he just gets beside hisself."

15

The gathered family drew back in horrified revulsion, then dispersed, running wildly in different directions as the Confederate-dressed Krupeck vaulted his mount onto the porch, leaping from his saddle to descend on a shrieking girl like a swooping vulture. He pushed her to the floorboard, savagely slapping her face, his eyes ablaze with maniacal lust, spittle escaping his mouth. The girl's brother ran to help her, but Krupeck straightened up and jerked his prey off the ground before belting the boy in the face, squelching his nose into a blood-spraying pulp. The boy banged off the wall into an unconscious heap.

There were wails of terror as the men galloped their crying mounts in pursuit of the family. Guns were fired into the air at first, and then a hail of lead resounded over the chaos, issued by three of the men, lethally ripping into a boy of sixteen who appeared in the doorway brandishing a rifle. He catapulted backward beneath a blanket of wet red death.

"No! Noooo!" Sterning shrieked in horror. The sound penetrated the atmosphere, tainted gray with the acrid smell of gunsmoke and blood, as he bolted toward the house. He was knocked to the ground, the man with the Confederate flag in his rifle chopping him viciously across the back of the head with the weapon. Then, staggering to his feet, seeing his daughter being ravaged before his eyes and screaming her helplessness under the sick animal's sexual onslaught. Sterning —nauseous from the carnage and defilement taking place, and himself helpless—involuntarily vomited forth a stream of slimy yellow. The hideous apparition of General Nenz appeared before him and smiled wickedly, his cruel, ugly face glowing with ecstasy while he removed his long saber.

Sterning slumped to his knees, his eyes glazed over with tears of pain and shame, his lips trying to form a plea for mercy. But there would be none; the saber was thrust deep into his stomach, the general's face twitching violently, leering at Sterning's agonized features. Sterning yelled, blood shooting forth from his wound, his hands grasping the blade, while a stream of red blasted forth from his mouth to add to the growing pool below him. The blade was wrenched free, the razor-sharp edge slicing open the palms of his hands as he fell face down into a bath of crimson.

The barn was set afire, and the dry timber immediately became a roaring inferno. The man responsible galloped his mount outside, a pitchfork in his right hand.

The boy who had ridden in with the men was frozen in shock and horror, his mind numb as he unbelievingly observed the brutal, senseless orgy of murder and rape.

The Negroes, who had been hiding in fear of their lives, were forced to run from their quarters as a fire was lit and began to rage in swift vehemence.

"Niggers!" cried the man who had started the fire, his expression one of delight and shock. Immediately, he and another man blasted three of the servant children into bloody death with a quick bombardment of rifle fire. They became ebullient with the accomplishment, squealing excitement.

The cowboy prepared to pounce on a Negro woman, but a torch-carrying rider thrust the fire into the woman's hair and in seconds she was a wailing ball of flames, hideously writhing on the ground, waiting for the torment to end while she tried to extinguish the flames.

"What did you do that for?" the cowboy growled, incensed. "I would have done her black ass real good!"

A young Negro raced across the yard, then stumbled over Joseph Sterning's body and rolled onto his back, just as the man with the pitchfork plunged it into his chest. The pitchfork impaled him to the already blood-soaked earth in wide-eyed death, the long handle warbling in grotesque mockery of the slaughter, his dead hands still holding the top of the tines.

"You don't want to touch that stuff. You might get some kind of disease," the rider said.

"Moron," the cowboy replied. He ran down two girls, beheading one cleanly with his saber, glinting metal dripping crimson as he fell onto the other girl and shredded her dress. The severed head rolled on the ground to land beside the cowboy, its eyes wide and glaring at its executioner.

The weasel-faced renegade viciously slapped the young girl beneath him several times. Spittle dribbled down the sides of his grizzled chin and his wild eyes devoured the naked young flesh trembling under his pawing, grasping, calloused hands as he roughly squeezed her smallish, tender breasts. There was a pathetic look of hysteria in the girl's eyes and her mouth was wide in a vain attempt to plead for mercy.

She was no more than fourteen, and the sheer thought of

ravaging such a virgin beauty, of soiling such innocence, of brutalizing and punishing her, as she cried while he mauled her soft buttocks, scratching, digging, filled this renegade rapist with a black fire that could only be doused by ultimately killing her.

Brutally he pushed his enlarged member into the crying girl, forcing her legs wide, finally hurting her by driving deep and hard into her, destroying her maidenhead, tearing the tightness of her vagina, making her scream in horror and pain. Her terror only served to further excite the raw violence within his twisted mind. Several thrusts and he exploded in her, biting her neck and nipples, tearing flesh, grunting like some sick ghoul straight from hell. He would have her again that way before flipping her onto her stomach and penetrating deep into her bowels until blood trickled down her legs.

"Save me a nigger!" the general hollered angrily, before he propelled his horse up onto the porch where the naked girl, after having been defiled, was crouching, hugging her unconscious brother to her, his blood flowing down her exposed breasts. Nenz' horse trampled over her, breaking her back and snapping her neck like brittle twigs. Then the horse leaped through a large window, causing glass shards to cascade upon both bodies.

"Yessir, bossman!" yelled the man who had set fire to the servants' quarters.

In a state of mad ecstasy he ran down the oldest Negro male and clubbed him soundly on the head with the butt of his rifle. The black rolled into an unconscious heap by a large oak tree.

Joseph Sterning was still alive, but too weak to move. His eyes were wide in dying disbelief; he choked and gurgled on his own blood, listening to the grunts of sexual assault unleashed on his wife and daughters, unable to do anything about their gruesome ordeal. He heard the screams, the crying and wailing of his tormented family, making a mockery of his dignity.

"Daddy! Daddy! Help me!"

"Oh God, no! Someone help me!" cried Sterning's wife in despair as her rapist emptied his loins in her, then scrambled to his feet.

"Don't think God's here today, goodlooking," he said, buckling his pants. Then he gored her with his saber, pressing his full weight down on the handle as it pierced her spine and came out her back to stick into the ground. "But if you want to go see Him so bad, be my guest."

Inside the house, Krupeck was finishing his rape of another Sterning girl.

"You scum," Nenz snarled, "you've spoiled her for me!"

Krupeck looked up from his victim's anguished face, his elation turning into terror. The long barrel of Nenz' Colt roared twice and the girl's head disappeared into huge chunks, her brains smearing all over the floor.

"Got your friggin' scum in her!" snarled Nenz.

He spurred his horse onward, forcing it to trample and crush chairs and furniture into piles of rubble as it galloped into the living room and cornered the last Sterning girl. Krupeck was left to gaze numbly upon the headless corpse beneath him, twitching its limbs involuntarily in death throes.

The boy was nauseous, drenched in sweat and horrified into a blank state of mind. He surveyed the carnage—blood-soaked bodies, black and white, male and female, naked, clothed . . . littered in wide-eyed death and mutilation under black billows of smoke covering the orgy's bloodbath. Hordes of flies avariciously gorged themselves on the spilled blood of the dead; the blazing fires were at their pinnacle of strength, scorching the air. The stifling stench of burning flesh, coupled with the last few wails of death as sabers were driven into living flesh and guns blasted deadly retorts, made the boy dismount and gingerly step onto the ground. He couldn't believe this was real. In fact he was hoping, wishing to God that this had all been a nightmare. It had lasted only a few minutes, but it was something he would have to live with for eternity.

The rasping voice of Nenz jarred the boy from his walking coma as the general's horse clopped from the porch onto the ground.

"Did you get me one, Dreyfuss?" he asked.

"Right over here, sir," Dreyfuss responded, kicking the Negro in the ribs.

"Well, string him up," Nenz ordered tautly.

"Hey, a lynching! Great!"

"No," Nenz disdainfully said, heading his mount toward the oak tree. The servants' quarters were now a seething bonfire, causing the horses to snort in their unrest. "Tie the rope around his waist, leaving his arms free. Then get him three or four feet up off the ground."

They quickly did as Nenz ordered, and in minutes had the large black man hanging by his waist. He was fully conscious; they had thrown several buckets of water over him.

"What are we going to do, Karl?" asked Dreyfuss. All of the gang, except the boy, mounted and gathered around Nenz.

"Show these land-grabbing Northern yellowbellies what we think of them and their nigger-loving ways!" Nenz rasped, spitting.

Then he raced his mount toward the dangling black, whose horrified eyes could only watch as the red saber blade was swung viciously. It sliced deep into his huge right bicep and blood poured in torrents to the ground. His agonized scream lingered in the hot air long after the blow had been delivered.

There were grimaces of revulsion, disgust and horror as the man's shrieking continued and intensified, nearly drowning out the roar of the flames nearby. But they reveled in the man's suffering, not just because of their hatred for blacks but because of some mysterious sickness lurking deep down in their wretched souls.

While Nenz admired the savage result of his action and the blood-dripping Negro swayed back and forth, the boy, his face a sickly pale, groaned aloud. The men turned, taking an interest in the boy's presence for the first time that day.

"The kid," said Krupeck. "He's just been hanging around the whole time, watching!"

"Get on your horse, boy; grab a saber and join in," Nenz encouraged. "We'll make a real trooper out of you yet."

It was the first sign of friendship or warmth they had shown him, and they expected him to join in their cruelty eagerly, although they could see he was shaken. It disturbed them that someone who rode with them should be appalled by their actions.

"Well, kid, come on!" Dreyfuss growled, shouting to be heard over the ominous crackling of fire mixed with the screams of the dying.

The boy shook his head and stumbled backward, tripping over the naked body of a dead girl, his face a mask of frightened abhorrence. "No," he croaked. Then he vomited loud and long, spewing his innards over the lifeless defiled, its eyes wide and glaring accusingly at him.

20

"What the . . . . "

"Friggin' candyass pansy!"

"Goddamned fag!"

"A stinking nigger lover!"

Several of the men spat onto the boy's violently retching frame.

"Forget the kid, boys. Let's finish," Nenz ordered angrily.

The men immediately proceeded to ride in line, one after the other, swinging and hacking at legs and arms, grimly acknowledging that chopping their victim to pieces would be the only way to stop the shrill wail continuously penetrating their bones to the marrow.

A dismembered leg and arm thudded to the ground under a bloody fountain that drenched the severed appendages. The boy hugged the girl's dead body, weeping bitterly, then covered his ears to try and keep the screams from bouncing around inside his head.

"Oh, dear Jesus, please!" he whimpered. "Please stop the screaming. Stop his screams!" He knew he was every bit as responsible as the others for the man's suffering, as well as for the total picture of insanity strewn about him. He cursed his cowardice, his inability to stop what was taking place. The screeching continued to be a grisly reverberation inside his skull as he heard the dull sound of appendages dropping on the ground.

Finally the screams ended. The boy sighed his anxiety and grief. The silence that ensued was chilling—an even stronger force more noticeable than the fire's cleansing fury. He heard the men moving toward him. Looking up at their impassive faces, he cringed, as they sheathed blood-dripping sabers.

"What are we gonna do about the kid, Karl? He could put the finger on us," Krupeck said.

"Can't say we didn't give the boy a chance, can ya, Karl," the cowboy said grimly.

"Please, mister," the boy implored, "let me leave—"

"Kill him," Nenz solemnly declared, heading his mount south.

The boy tried to speak, but before he could utter a sound Krupeck had split his skull open with a saber.

"You had your chance to be one of us, boy," Krupeck said remorselessly.

The boy's lifeless body fell face down under a raining torrent of blood and gray brain matter. Thus the men quickly left the massacre with the final blow of death.

Joseph Sterning was barely alive. He stirred and groaned, feeling the intense heat of the fire. The dying farmer had been revived by the incessant animal-like screams of his servant, who had been slashed into a completely dismembered torso that was now just a stump of a human body.

Glancing over at the hanging mutilation, Sterning sighed his last breath as the human stump swayed in the hot breeze, drops of blood falling steadily to the ground. Its wide eyes seemed to glare malevolently. Its mouth suddenly fell open and uttered: "Help me . . . help me. . . ."

A Man Named Chance

2

The heat of midday poured through the open, iron-barred windows, filling the prison's wide corridor without mercy. The shotgun-toting guard's bootheels reverberated softly off the adobe walls as he walked briskly by barred celldoors, his face as grim as death itself. There was no breeze, no relief from the atmosphere rancid with sweat, unclean bodies and the miasma of human excrement seeping through cracks and openings around latrine-hole covers in the cell floors. A perpetual aura of despair filled the insides of these baking walls, an emanation equally as uncomfortable as the heat of day and the chill of night.

A few men stirred at the sound of life, several pairs of eyes peering through the bars, morosely watching the tall, angular guard pass their cages. Flies buzzed and attacked human sweat, gratifying themselves in the fetid surroundings.

A big, burly man with a bulbous nose walked to the bars and, watching the guard move past, gruffly called, "You're not really letting that animal out, are ya?"

The guard ignored him as if he were just another fly, an irritant to which one must grow accustomed. Stopping in front of the last cell, the dark-garbed guard canted the .10 gauge, sawed-off riot gun to his left shoulder. He transferred a neat bundle of clothes from his right hand to under his elbow and locked them against his side while fumbling with a ring of keys. He both liked and disliked what he was about to do. The guard then inserted the key and slid the heavy door open, gazing with a slight sense of trepidation at the lone man in the cell, who was resting on a cot.

A gray Stetson covered the unmoving prisoner's face. His

hands were clasped atop his stomach, his left leg crossed over the right. His attitude could have been mistaken for arrogance if the guard hadn't known him as well as he did.

The guard momentarily observed the man named Chance, wondering what it was about this man that chilled his soul and knotted his stomach. He had guarded this man for eight years and, although he knew a lot of sordid details about this prisoner's past, the man named Chance remained a total enigma to him. The guard couldn't put his finger on any one thing, but there were several factors which dismayed him and caused him to sweat unnaturally in this prisoner's presence. From the first day of his imprisonment he had not spoken more than a half-dozen words, and then only if he had needed something.

Not that sullenness and anger were uncommon here, but some of the men at least developed a form of "comradeship" over a period of time in order to keep from losing all sanity. And even the worst hardcases shared a tacit understanding and respect among themselves in recognition of the other's hope-lessness, or aversion to law and conventional morals. But Chance was, or seemed to be, the hardest of the hardcases. He had always kept to himself as if he despised anyone else's presence. On several occasions, when he was outside his cell among other inmates, he had been taunted about his attitude and loner preference. On these occasions the tall guard had seen him grind the tormentor's face into a bloody pulp with such a relentless, methodical brutality that Chance had to be placed in a cell by himself for his own protection, as well as for the protection of others who might fall prey to his wrath.

Another factor, which had swayed the guard's bewilderment toward awe, was the daily exercises Chance had spent un-broken hours rigorously performing until his muscles became bulging knots, looking as if they were sculptured from stone. The calisthenics should have been unendurable because of the quality of food and the environment, but he seemed to generate energy elsewhere, as if he were fueling off bitterness. Deep-seeded hatred and contempt were all too visible on a one-eyed, scarred face that might unnerve even Satan.

Also the guard's bewilderment about and fascination with this particular prisoner augmented every time he brought Chance the literature he had requested. The books he'd accumulated ranged from pulpy dime westerns glorifying the misdeeds of notorious outlaws of the time, to the widely condemned, diabolical works of the Marquis de Sade; also the Iliad and the Odyssey, Plato's Republic, and works by Hume, Descartes, Aristotle and other great philosophers and men of science. Possibly this confused the guard most, for what connection could there possibly be between reading sensational garbage, as opposed to intellectual works of profound greatness? Was his a twisted mind or just a complex personality? And what added even more consternation to his baffled state were the walls, all three of which were plastered completely with pages torn from the Bible. In bizarre and stark contrast, sections of de Sade's infamous *Justine* and *120 days of Sodom* were sprinkled neatly amid the other papers. Was it a mockery of the Divine, a macabre form of sincere devotion, or lurid revelations of a dark soul consumed by an atheistic hatred of all creation?

It might have been amusing if this man weren't what he was in both character and personification of his life essence.

For this man named Chance had been sent to prison for a series of daring robberies which had netted him a total of three hundred thousand dollars; large army payrolls accounted for much of this staggering sum. But he had hidden the money before being beaten nearly to death by his gang members—the result of a conspiracy initiated by his woman at the time—and pounced upon by lawmen. Everyone but he had escaped the wrath of a justice growing increasingly more austere with those who would make a mockery of law and order.

So, continuing to glance around Chance's cell, the guard concurred that this was a highly intelligent albeit strange, unusual man—sentiments the warden shared after having reviewed a record of Chance's diverse background at the outset of his term. For he wasn't just another criminal, nor a man who had acted simply on impulse, mindlessly satiating sick desires. This was a fact the guard had ascertained years ago, not only out of deference and perplexity, but out of cold fear, because he knew from experience in handling and watching dangerously violent men day in and day out that this was a callous, bitter, calculating individual. Chance's was a face that never betrayed his thoughts. And this perhaps, more than anything else, made him seem evilly treacherous.

Realizing he'd been standing there in dark thought for an unnecessary length of time, the guard scowled, both in embarrassment, and in annoyance with Chance. The latter remained in slumber and had moved only to scratch at the hair on his chest as sunlight beamed through the open, barred window in the cell.

"Time's come, Chance," he muttered feebly, trying to inject authority into his voice while tossing the bundle of clothes on Chance's stomach. "Get dressed."

A few seconds elapsed while Chance remained perfectly still. Then he stirred lethargically, like a man who couldn't be too bothered with anything or anyone, but who knew if he didn't contend with his surroundings they'd just become more annoying. Chance tipped the hat up off his face, revealing a black eyepatch over his left eye and a long scar that ran down the left side of his face from temple to chin. His sinister-appearing features were set in calm repose as his right eye looked at the clothes on his stomach, then at the guard.

The guard shifted his feet nervously, sighed, then tried leaning casually against the bars. "You sure don't act like a man who's been granted a full pardon," he said, an impatient edge in his voice as he watched Chance stand, the muscles of his naked torso rippling in unison with the slightest movement of his body. He looked as if he were encased in a shield of white armor.

Chance stood two inches on the short side of six feet and would have been considered average size. But his one hundred and seventy-five pound frame appeared deceptively larger at first glance because of his exceptionally broad shoulders and large, thick bones. His superb physique made him seem both brawny yet at the same time lean. It was evident that his right collarbone had once been broken clean through, because it had healed in such a fashion that when the bones grew together one slightly overlapped the other. A lump of calcium had grown around the break so it looked as if a jagged rock were trying to pierce the flesh.

"Just how is it I'm supposed to be acting, Rickles?" he cynically asked, his voice distinctly Northern, with traces of perhaps New England origin in it. He finished buckling the black belt around his gray Levis, then pulled a white undershirt over his head, and proceeded to add a light-colored

26

cotton shirt. He rolled up the sleeves. Flies were dipping undisturbed in the film of sweat that had broken out on his clean-shaven face and in the bristles of his short, dark-brown hair.

"Like a free man," Rickles drawled at length, "not like you're getting ready for the Grim Reaper."

Pulling on his black boots, Chance said cryptically, "None of us are free, dude . . . for the reason you just mentioned."

Rickles took this remark with minor dismay and frowned for lack of a retort, causing his mood to go suddenly from anxious to melancholy. He swatted at a fly to give him something to do while he waited for Chance to finish dressing. Finally, when it looked as if Chance was ready to go, he said, "Everything else you had is outside."

"Hey Chance!" yelled the burly man with the bulbous nose, his rasping Southern drawl easily carrying the length of the corridor. "I can't believe they're letting out a thieving, murdering animal like you!" He snorted loud and derisively before adding, "Full pardon! What a crock a' crap."

"Johnson's big mouth?" Chance evenly inquired, smoothly placing his Stetson on his head and tying a black neckerchief around his neck.

"'Fraid so," Rickles answered in laconic mockery, stepping out into the corridor, indicating his desire to hurry and see Chance out. Then, as a quick afterthought, he asked, "What about all your books and other things?"

"Charity," muttered Chance, stepping out into the corridor, as Johnson's harsh criticisms continued to echo off the walls.

"What?" asked the guard, frowning his bewilderment.

"Johnson's founding chairman of the organization."

"Of what?" Rickles asked, impatient and suddenly surly with irritation at Chance's aloofness.

"The severely mentally handicapped of America," Chance replied, brushing by Rickles and heading up the corridor. The barrage of insults diminished slowly as Johnson saw the one-eyed, scarfaced man ambling toward his cell.

"Well, will you look at this guy, boys," Johnson softly rasped, "slicker than spit on a whore's twat."

Johnson's big hands were tightly grasping the bars, his dark eyes balefully glowering at Chance, who had slowed to a stop in front of Johnson's cell. The guard nearly walked up his black in his haste to be free of Chance's presence. But Rickles' nervous fear of Chance outweighed his impatience. Thus indecision took control of the guard's state, forcing him to submit tacitly to the stronger will.

Along the other cells in the corridor several pairs of hands clutched bars, as heads strained awkwardly and eyes peered intently at the newly freed prisoner.

It was no secret that Chance had been scheduled for release that day. The resentment and hostility toward this decision had been building steadily all week. For they felt it a grave injustice that a mandatory thirty-year sentence without probation was suddenly pardoned by the state governor for reasons not publicly disclosed while they had to sweat out the remainder of their sentences or in some cases await death. This angry scorn now reached a crescendo, creating an ominous blanket of tension and ill will that was almost tangible in the fetid heat.

Two men sat behind Johnson and observed the stoic Chance with the same degree of animosity as Johnson did. All three men fitted comfortably in the cell because it was large, like all the south-side cells.

Rickles became visibly nervous and started to nudge Chance onward, but Johnson broke the brief silence, freezing the guard as he growled, "How's it feel to be a free man, Cyclops, huh? How's it feel, you Yankee scum?"

"Feels real good," Chance affably replied, his face impassive, but savoring his situation nonetheless. "I'll be sure to write often." He started to walk away quickly and Rickles quietly sighed relief.

"Hey, I'm not done, Cyclops!" Johnson barked, making Chance freeze abruptly.

Much to the consternation of Rickles, Chance eased back toward Johnson, standing even closer to the cell this time. "Then say what you've got to say, dude," Chance muttered with tight-lipped venom, his lone green eye glaring malevolently up at Johnson, who stood more than half a head taller than he did.

Johnson's cellmates, feeling the renewed tension and sensing something sinister about Chance's tone, stood, then assumed casual stances several feet behind Johnson. They were tall, wide, grim-looking men who remained silent, but

28

whose close, chilling aura only added fuel to Johnson's hate-filled demeanor.

"Live it up while you can, boy," Johnson snarled, his face covered under an evil-glowing sweat sheen, drops of moisture rolling off his chin. Several flies buzzed around his head, and some fed on the salty liquid. "'Cause everyone in this territory knows about that money you hid—and you know that's the only reason they're letting you out, Yank. Pardon, bullshit! You think anybody, specially the law, cares about you?

"Word's spread fast. Yeah . . . everybody who's even read your name's gonna be breathin' up your ass; boys you rode with, and that greaser slut you was pokin' it to, gotta be real sore all this time. And Silas and Kittman? Hell. When you got so-called 'exonerated' for killing them, well that only dug your grave a little deeper. Nobody gives a whore's ass if that judge did rule self-defense! Silas and Kittman don't only got friends in here, boy! I only wish I could've been there when they carved up your face!"

"Then you'd be rotting in hell right now, like they are," Chance calmly said.

His self-assuredness and calm arrogance only incensed Johnson more. "You sure do think highly of yourself, you Yankee bastard!" he viciously rasped, his malice so agitated that his body quivered as he attempted to stifle a rage on the verge of erupting.

"I happened to have fought for the Confederacy, dude."

Johnson sharply interrupted, "It was just a matter of where you was at the time. Nobody's givin' you any points just 'cause you rode for the South. You ain't no Reb!"

"Have you said all you've got to?" Chance easily inquired, looking Johnson calmly in the eye.

"Yeah," Johnson growled, relaxing somewhat, although deeply irritated at seeing that his taunting remarks had apparently failed to rankle the indifferent Chance. "Go kissass to your Mex whore, boy. Enjoy yourself; we'll be out soon enough and we'll be sure to pay you a visit. I just hope you're still alive."

It happened so fast and unexpectedly, Rickles and Johnson's cellmates could only watch in paralyzed horror as Chance—having appeared impassive to the point of sullenness —was suddenly galvanized into a frenzy of violent action, grabbing Johnson by his shirtfront, shoving him back slightly, then smashing his shocked face wickedly into the iron bars. Johnson was out with the first blow, his nose crushed into a blood-spewing pulp. But Chance was livid with a fury which had emerged with such lightning intensity that he pounded his unconscious victim's face into the bars with two more terrible blows, opening up the skin above Johnson's right eye, before he tossed him at his cellmates' feet. There were curses and gasps of angry shock from the other prisoners, creating a tense chorus of low rumbling and helpless excitement, dissension and outrage.

"What the hell!" cried a prisoner in the cell next to Johnson's.

"You didn't have to do that!" raged another inmate.

Chance stepped back, turned, then glared hard at the wide-eyed, slack-jawed Rickles, who had aroused himself from his horror and leveled his shotgun at Chance's chest. Without hesitation, Chance angrily swept the twin barrels aside, smacking them up against the wall. He snarled, "Don't point that damned thing at me!"

Trembling in terror, Rickles tautly ordered, "Well then, move it and get the hell out of here!"

"You're as good as dead, Chance!" screamed one of Johnson's cellmates irately, charging toward the bars. He thrust his arms through and flailed wildly, but Chance was just out of reach as the other man knelt beside Johnson's red-plastered face.

"Just you wait, you son-of-a-bitch! You'll get yours!" the other cellmate threatened.

"Hank! Lenny!" Rickles called down the corridor.

Chance sauntered off as easy and composed as if nothing had happened. Seconds later, keys rattled; then the large iron door at the south end squeaked open on rusty hinges. Two anxious-looking guards of medium size and middle age appeared, shotguns leveled in menacing readiness. One closed the door out of force of habit before they both jogged quickly toward Chance and Rickles, who were moving in their direction. The murmuring buzz of excitement and cursing, coupled with the violent harangue by Johnson's cellmate, continued to plague the corridor.

"What in hell's going on, Lou?" demanded one of the

guards, pulling up in front of Chance and Rickles.

"No big deal," Chance softly cut in, walking by the two guards, who looked at him in angry suspicion, sensing that he was the cause of the sudden unrest. "One of the boys stumbled and banged his head on the bars."

"Lou! What—"

"It's Johnson," Rickles informed irritably, cutting off the other guard, and throwing a curt nod toward Johnson's cell before quickly marching off to catch up with the departing Chance. "Chance banged him up pretty good."

The two men looked blankly at each other, then quickly loped in the opposite direction away from Rickles as the implications of what had happened dawned upon them. Rickles reached Chance where the one-eyed man was waiting patiently at the locked door.

Orders to stand back were issued by the two guards as they reached Johnson's cell and slid the door open. "Good God!" gasped one of the men in revulsion, although it had sounded more like a cry of exasperation—as if this type of thing were commonplace here.

The voice echoed, reaching the ears of Chance and Rickles, who were walking out the door and into the harsh heat of a Texas afternoon. Rickles slammed the iron door closed, drowning out the voices and locking behind the scene of ugly violence as he guided Chance to the left across the baking courtyard. Several rifle-brandishing guards were situated in forty-foot-high canopy towers, watching the two head toward the gate.

"What's all the ruckus, Lou?" one of the sentries yelled down, stifling a yawn.

"Nothin'!" Lou bellowed sharply.

He was more angry with himself than he was appalled by Chance's brutal act, knowing that he could have prevented what had happened by showing some initiative, and knowing also that he might have to answer to the warden because of his failure to do so. But the source of his anger, as well as his lack of exerting force in a situation that had required it, stemmed from a mixture of emotions—fear, awe, and bravado among them—all brought on by the man named Chance. And what he had just witnessed confirmed a week-long nagging suspicion he'd had that this was a dangerous man who by no means

31

should be released. Not that he hadn't seen violence and brutality among inmates before, but what disturbed him greatly was Chance's capacity to hide hatred and other destructive emotions under a veneer of indifference. Thus, malice and hatred kindled the life force of this man. Ugly acts of cruel vindictiveness were the results of sudden explosions of a rage that had lain dormant, and which the guard had felt growing steadily for eight years. So Johnson was merely a tool, a puppet used, Chance's excuse to exercise those dark latent emotions which undoubtedly had boiled his blood lonely day in and long, even lonelier night out as he had been seen sitting in the darkness, wide eyed, looking as if he were lusting to taste the blood of those responsible for his plight and for the lost years of his youth.

They reached the gates quickly. Several rows of adobe-constructed cells running the distance of the high north wall provided a bleak background. The warden, a short, sallow-faced man with grim, hard eyes and stooped shoulders, was waiting by the iron gates. Wearing a dark-gray suit and a broad-brimmed hat, he had the withered yet stern and angry appearance of a man with many unpleasant years, behind him but not forgotten. He looked at Chance with mild disdain, then grunted an order to the guard beside him, who quickly removed the heavy padlock from where it fitted through the loops on the gates, and swung the left one open.

Another guard was slowly approaching the foursome, guiding a fully saddled black gelding by its reins.

"What was all that screaming about, Rickles?" the warden asked, a dark scowl having already creased his face in response to an answer he knew was coming.

Rickles sighed nervously, then blurted, "Chance busted up Johnson's face against the bars."

The guard with the gelding walked it behind the warden and through the gate's opening.

The warden seemed on the brink of outrage. But his eyes fixed themselves on the sinister features of Chance, as if mesmerized by a face that even under normal conditions would not have been considered handsome by anyone's standards. The retort he wanted to issue died in the pit of his stomach, as a cold chill swept his soul under the icy glare of the one-eyed man. A tense pause ensued, for he too recognized something eerie and bewildering about the man. But instead of seeing an indifferent, brooding exterior, as Rickles had, he saw a face that seemed to be etched into a perpetual sneer. The warden had seen many men come and go over the years. Some were better, but most were worse, when they left—which was to be expected from men who could never escape, even if they wanted to, what they had been when they came in.

Most changed one way or another to a certain extent, but he had never seen a man change so drastically in character and temperament as Chance had. He was looking at the result of eight years of silent torment and dark, dark hatred. . . . He was looking at a man transformed, acknowledging to himself that Chance was something less than he had been, a savage, violent man poised and eager for blood. But he was also something more than just a man, because he had forsaken and shed any vestiges of human decency and compassion he might once have had. And it was evident by the evil glint in his eyes that he knew this but believed that he was, and could live, above good and evil.

"I'm glad you could see me off, warden," Chance said, his tone light but biting. "Since you have such a vested interest in me."

"What's that supposed to mean, mister?" the warden asked with angry restraint.

Chance touched the brim of his hat and made a face. As he walked out the gate he said, "Fresh mount." He picked up a gunbelt slung over the saddle and, pulling out the revolver from its holster, opened the chamber and quickly dropped a cartridge into each of the six slots. "My Navy Colt," he said evenly, glancing suspiciously at the warden who stood just outside the prison's gates, his guards directly behind. Chance fastened the gunbelt around his waist, tying the holster's thong around his right thigh before sliding a rifle from its saddleboot. "My Henry. This is all a little unusual."

"Nothing unusual about it, mister. This is Comanche and Apache country. Nobody in his right mind would travel these parts without a weapon!" the warden rasped, unable to control himself any longer as the object of Chance's suspicious attitude and sneering remarks. "That's the only reason you got your weapons back. You just make sure that you use a good deal of restraint, or you'll be back here faster than you lost that eye!''

Chance had been sliding shells into the Henry's breech, pretending indifference to the warden's explanation until he mentioned the eye. Then Chance's head snapped up as if he'd been shot and he glared depthless hatred at the warden, his right eye blazing with a fury which clearly said that he would have killed under different circumstances.

But the warden held his ground in contemptuous belligerence, for he knew Chance was a smart man, not inclined to reckless or irrational behavior unless the odds were on his side, or if it were to his advantage to push a confrontation. Under the present circumstances, they all knew it was not to his advantage, nor was it a situation where he should push his luck.

''I put your spurs and Bowie in a saddlebag, Chance,'' one of the guards blurted effusively, hoping it would ease the tension.

''Shuddup!'' the warden flung over his shoulder.

''You boys are really going to pains to look after your vested interest,'' Chance said caustically, sliding the Henry back in its boot, then mounting the strong-looking horse. ''Tell Judge Martin I said thanks for the pardon . . . but that he won't see one greenback or one gold coin for his trouble.'' Chance heeled his mount into a departure.

''Why that arrogant son-of-a—'' Rickles softly hissed.

''Leave it,'' the warden calmly cut in, somberly watching Chance fade under a curtain of shimmering heat, and head south over a vast scorched expanse of flatland decorated parsimoniously with mesquite and tumbleweed, with rolling brown hills in the far-off distance.

Just then, three men stepped through the open gate to join the warden and his guards, the jingle of spurs acknowledging their arrival. But no one turned to greet them. They were stalwartly built men of medium to tall height, under thirty and dressed in riding boots, Levis, light cotton shirts, vests, neckerchiefs and wide-brimmed hats. Each wore holstered revolvers tied down, and one canted a Winchester leisurely to his right shoulder, puffing on the stub of a cigar. A week's dirt, sweat and dust was ground into their clothing and bristled faces. They had greedy cold eyes and hard angry features.

''Did you catch any of that, Simpson?'' the warden

ominously asked, still gazing straight ahead at the diminishing figure of Chance.

"Caught some of it, yeah," Simpson laconically replied, snorting up a globule of spit, then casually launching it beside his feet. "Don't think this was much of a favor at all for him . . . being pardoned." He snickered softly.

The man with the rifle and the cigar added in agreement, "Nope. Future looks pretty bad for our man Chance." He spat the cigar from his mouth. "He'll be back . . . or he'll be dead."

"Not until after that money's been recovered he better not be," the warden promptly reminded. "And remember, you boys are getting a pretty big cut to bring it back."

"So let's get on with it," Simpson said to his comrades, turning to head back inside the prison.

"No," the warden snapped. "Give him a good hour and a half's head start. He's heading for Smiling Sons: he's got a woman there and he needs money. You won't have any problems picking up his trail."

Simpson quickly admonished, "You forgetting, warden? This has been played up pretty big around Texas. Hell, everybody who'd have cause to—"

"It's been played up for a good reason, Simpson, and that was to make it seem legitimate. Understand? You're to wait. Any freeloaders and tagalongs you'll take care of as you see fit. You've been hired to do a job and you'll do it according to who's stuffing your pants pockets. Your guns won't be worth a damn to me if you go screwing up the job right away and he finds out someone's following him."

"What I meant, warden," Simpson explained, his tone obligingly amiable, trying to cover his embarrassment, "is that a lot of people are going to be after him and his money. He could be dead before we get on his trail."

"Hell," the warden scoffed, looking at Simpson with disdain as he brushed past him to stand in the prison's opening. Then he looked out over the arid terrain to where Chance was merely a small black apparition in the heat haze. His scornful expression suddenly changed to a doleful one as he seemed to be lost in morose contemplation. He sighed wearily.

Slowly he said, "That man's been dead for a long time. In a million years you could never kill what he's already lost."

"Good afternoon, ma'am," greeted a cheerful farmer in dirt-grimed coveralls, tipping his hat to Sara. She gave him a brief but not unfriendly smile as she stepped off the boardwalk, taking great care not to trip over her long, light-blue dress, and turned into the main street.

Holding a large basket of food on her arm, she trudged past the bustling activities of farmers bringing in their produce, children playing, women browsing through stores and conversing in small groups, and men going in and out of saloons where raucous laughter and loud talking were clearly audible over the din of badly played piano pieces. She quickly marched by a line of covered wagons, the families sweating and laboring under the hot sun, paying scant attention to anything but loading supplies into wagon beds in preparation for westward travel.

Wiping a few beads of sweat from her brow, Sara continued her brisk pace, eager to be away from the sun's glare. She finally reached her house, covered the few feet of stone sidewalk to her door, pushed the door open, yanked off her sunbonnet and sighed in relief. She quickly shut the door, drowning the amalgam of noisy activity behind her. The inside of the house would have been uncomfortably stuffy, but the windows were wide so that a slight breeze of warm air moved through the rooms. She never locked the door or windows, believing that if someone were going to break in he wouldn't have much difficulty anyway.

Lethargically Sara started to walk the short distance down the hall to the kitchen. But, passing the living room, the smell of smoke assaulted her nose and alarm erased her weary expression. She snapped her head to the left in panic.

"Hello, Sara," Chance casually said, puffing on a cigarette, sitting on the red divan. "You don't look too enraptured at seeing me."

Her fear had fled. Now she seemed only exasperated. She had expected that he would come here after his release, and had at first been vastly agitated by the thought. But she had eventually accepted the inevitable with bland indifference. Nothing really excited her any more. Though she was still young and pretty, she was quite alone, with no desire to risk reliving a past that had seen much pain and grief. However, she was relieved that the caller wasn't Neems, whom she had initially feared it was. After his first visit he hadn't returned, but she still felt the bite of his cruelty, and his callous intrusion had lingered in her mind. Thus, when she went into the living room his presence might just as well have been real.

"I see you've already helped yourself," she said with soft-voiced rancor, indicating the opened, half-finished bottle of brandy resting on a walnut coffee table by the divan.

The room was small, clean and spartanly furnished, with only a few pieces of furniture.

"My eye was aching," he explained.

"That's too bad," she sneered.

Chance smiled coldly. He shrugged off her comment with a deep, anger-crushing breath. "Didn't see you around town, so I got a room, then thought I'd pay you a little social call." His cold grin smoothed into a leer. "I didn't think you'd let me warm your bed after all these years."

"Well, you thought exactly right," she said without expression, keeping her distance. Then she added coldly, "So you have no—"

"I need some money, Sara," Chance interrupted hastily, laying his cigarette butt on the coffee table, standing, then moving toward a small cabinet, the bottle in his left hand.

"You what?" she asked unbelievingly. "You have real nerve."

"Just a loan, damn it!" he growled, picking up a small framed picture sitting on top of the cabinet. "You'll get it back and much more."

"Yeah, I almost forgot. Your treasure," she hissed, her expression scornful. "Put that down!" she suddenly demanded, striding angrily toward Chance, who was gazing morosely at the picture in his hand. She dropped the food basket on the divan, then snatched the picture from him. She clutched the picture to her chest. In contrast to her angry snarl, her eyes showed deep hurt.

"You look real beautiful in that picture, Sara," Chance smoothly said. His sincere compliment was actually issued out of lust, but it was masked with a dolefulness that escaped her. Sara grimaced, looking in contempt and fascination at the grisly reminders of a horrid past forever marring what she remembered as a handsome man she had once fervently loved.

37

"I take it the soldier's your husband?"

"He was," she mournfully replied after a moment, still holding the picture as if it gave her courage and incentive to continue the conversation. "Apaches killed him three years ago in Arizona." She gazed into his catlike green eye, seeing that he received this with haughty indifference. There was a strange emptiness about him, and it was unnerving.

"Sara," Chance said, his breath reeking of liquor, his right hand slowly reaching out and gently clasping the side of her neck.

"Uh-uh, mister," she said with brusque softness. She left his hand on her neck, as if daring him to force a play. But her audacity was fleeting, because his touch was unnaturally cold, matching an expression totally devoid of warmth or sincerity, and this caused her to shudder involuntarily. She lightly brushed his hand away. "It will never, never happen again. When you left me for that Mexican slut and your life of fun my love died . . . and it died quick," she spat vehemently. Dredging up the past had overcome her with an intense fierceness.

Chance easily sensed this feverish enmity and remained impassive out of bitterness, knowing that what he had done would foreshadow exactly the type of response he was now getting. But his pride forced him to try. His earnest attempt was shallow, a thinly veiled plea from a man incapable of genuine, decent emotions.

"Sara," he implored lightly, "there's three hundred thousand dollars out there. Me and you could—"

"So go get it," she interrupted with resolute stoicism. "Just as 'they' want you to do. Because you're living on borrowed time, Chance. You might have been something once; you could even have been a decent man if you'd wanted. But you use things; you use money, violence, power over others; you use women especially. You used me as easily as you would spit on the ground."

He put the bottle down hard, the gesture augmenting his spite. "Was he that much more of a man than me?" Chance asked, his face taut with controlled anger. He had spat the words.

She became rigid, holding her chin high in arrogance. "Yes, he was; he made me forget you easily. He was the way a man should be. He was loving, gentle, respectful, loyal."

Change nodded slowly. "No wonder he got killed," he caustically cracked.

With disgust, Sara glared hard at him. "Your arrogance is sickening! But I can easily see you've changed to something far worse than what you were when you left that day. And your attitude could be expected. You're a repulsive man."

There was a brief pause, Sara's last remark having a deep and bitter effect on Chance. But he saw the futility of his vain attempt. He grunted. Then, with an edge to his tone, he asked, "How about the money?"

"Oh, sure!" Sara blurted, her voice trembling as she flailed her arms in exasperation. "Waltz right in like you own the place, help yourself to a drink, stink up my home with your cigarette, ask for money!" She brusquely stepped past Chance, opening the drawer to the cabinet in a frenzy. "Get out of the way!"

"Fifty should see me to Arizona," he said, watching Sara scrabble through the drawer until she found a small brown box. "I'll make sure you get ten times as much back."

She scoffed, "How can you be sure it's even there?" But she took a key and opened the box, her agitation subsiding.

"I'm not; in fact I doubt that it is. But I have to make sure. And if Maria snatched it I'll have to go into Mexico after her." He watched her unravel a roll of bills. "I know she has some family living in a valley southwest of here near the Pecos."

"So why don't you go there?" Sara asked, anxious to be rid of him. "Why go all the way to Arizona?"

"Because, like you said, I'm living on borrowed time. And whether the money is or isn't there, I'll need that stretch of land to shake off any unwanted company."

"That reminds me," Sara said harshly. "There was a man here earlier this week, said his name was Neems. He told me he was a bounty hunter. He slapped me around and broke five of my porcelain plates."

"So?"

"So?" she snarled, her tiny hand crumpling the wad of bills in anger. "He thought just because I once knew you that I knew where you'd hidden that money."

"Describe him," Chance flatly requested, suddenly intrigued.

"Big, blond—six-two, two hundred pounds. Dressed in black. You couldn't miss him in a crowd. I haven't seen him since."

Chance sighed, his face perplexed.

"Here!" she said, thrusting the bills at him. "Take them and get out."

He took the bills, smoothed them out, and pocketed them. With conscious emphasis he repeated, "You'll get back what I promised."

"I don't want your money, Chance," she said firmly, with a calm dignity which made her words even more powerful. "Just don't come back. Never."

"I'm sorry it had to be this way, Sara."

"No you're not. You'll do just as you damn well please, like you always have. The only person you ever cared about is yourself. And that's the only person you'll ever care about."

He nodded morosely. "I guess you're right." Heading for the door, he mumbled over his shoulder, "If I don't . . . nobody else ever has."

"Chance!" she called suddenly, as if a desperate afterthought had come into her mind. He stopped abruptly, turning halfway. She felt foolish, timid. "I won't be at your funeral."

"Nobody will, Sara," he said, a trace of sadness in his tone. "Nobody will."

A tear rolled down her cheek as he disappeared around the wall. She heard the door open and close quietly. Suddenly she felt totally alone, swamped with a grief she didn't want but had felt slowly coming on.

Weakly she muttered, "I hate you."

Chance quickly put Sara's house behind and headed up the street into the welter of activity, slowly dissipating into late-afternoon lethargy as women walked homeward to prepare evening meals, some with children at their sides, others with husbands leaving various shops and stores. Some men begrudgingly left saloons to be with families after their brief respite from a long, weary day's work in the fields. A blacksmith's hammer clanged against an anvil.

The smell of sweat and liquor hung in the hot air, and as Chance stepped up onto the boardwalk, this unpleasant combination seemed to enhance the irritation caused by his bitter encounter with Sara. His face was set in an angry scowl, and people passed him by quickly, giving him plenty of room as if he had some dreaded disease. They cast him surreptitious glances, making conscious efforts not to stare at him for fear he might look their way. Several children gawked at the one-eyed, scarfaced man, only to be yanked rudely ahead by apprehensive parents.

As Chance continued to head up the boardwalk, a girl trudged out of the general store to his left. Awkwardly holding a large sack of flour in her arms, she cut in front of Chance, unmindful of his or anyone else's presence. The sack was obviously too heavy for her, but she strained defiantly and fought with it, her long black hair and strikingly beautiful face wet with perspiration.

"Mary," called a male voice from inside the store, "wait a minute and I'll help."

Briefly, Chance stared at her as she plodded past him, going toward one of the covered wagons lining the street. Her ridiculous struggle was what had caught his attention at first. But now his attention was riveted on her as a woman, and he raked her over with a squinting, cursory lust. She was in her early twenties, tall and lean, with what appeared to be a well-proportioned frame hugged tautly by a long brown skirt and a white blouse. From where Chance stood he could see the contour of ample breasts riding up and over her upper arms, because of the way she held the sack to her. His angry disposition eased. He smiled seductively, in a way he hoped was warm and pleasant.

Chance stepped toward her preparing to help, but she stumbled suddenly and cried out in alarm, knowing she was going to fall down the boardwalk steps. Chance's right hand shot out immediately and he grabbed her by the back of her blouse, scrunching the cotton fabric, roughly snatching her back just as the sack hit the street. It burst open where it hit a large stone, and a cloud of white powder swept outward and upward. While keeping her from falling, Chance had accidentally torn her blouse at the right shoulder and popped one of the buttons free.

"Mary!" cried the man who had been inside the store, dropping two brown sacks and rushing toward the tall, dark-haired girl. She was breathing heavily in relief and gazing at Chance

41

with a mixture of horror and fascination, unaware that her lips looked as if they were trying to utter either thanks or a scream.

Several other people had quickly converged on the scene from inside the store and the other wagons. They had baffled looks as they huddled around their source of consternation; a few of the men became suspicious, then angry, seeing her torn blouse and the way Chance was grasping her shoulders.

"It—it's all right, everyone," Mary quickly said, her voice strained and tense. She appeared mesmerized by the lone eye of Chance, and was not struggling from the grasp of the man who'd come to her rescue. "Thank you," she breathed, flushing crimson, still staring intently with wide blue eyes at a face that struck her as both gruesome yet handsome at the same time. She was wrenched free of his grip by the man who had come to her side.

Some of the tension and impulsive hostility had subsided now, as the crowd saw what had happened and that no harm had been done.

Ignoring the perplexed faces and the cool resentment, Chance smiled slyly. "You have to be careful with how you do things these days, ma'am."

He touched the brim of his hat, then brushed through the huddled pioneers. The men reluctantly stepped aside, glaring resentment at the departing one-eyed man for his timely interference and the long look—which they had taken to be a leer—he had given Mary. Perhaps they were even more disturbed and angry that Mary had held his look with something akin to infatuation or lust on her own part.

The voices of questioning concern, and Mary's explanation, became distant and faded. Chance put the scene briskly behind him and out of his mind entirely, his immediate future becoming rapidly of grim concern. He was in trouble and he knew it. Everything that was said between him and Sara had been the biting, naked truth.

For everything had been too easy, too convenient, too well arranged. He figured the law was getting desperate in their eagerness to recover the money; it was too large a sum to be let go. So now they were playing their last hand and making what they thought was their smartest move. But Chance was no one's fool. He didn't know who they'd send, or how many; it didn't matter. Getting to the money would be every bit as difficult and dangerous as getting rid of whoever chose to be his bad company.

On his way to Smiling Sons he had been wrapped up in a maelstrom of emotions: vain hope that Sara would be willing to bury the past and take him up on his offer; bloodlust for the men and the woman responsible for putting him in prison. His blood boiled with bitter contempt whenever he thought about the members of his former gang. He had also been excited in anticipation of finding the money, but nervous as well, fearing that it might not be where he'd hidden it. It was a gamble; both he and the men who had set him free were taking a dangerous gamble that would most likely result in monstrous bloodshed. For Chance had made up his mind that there was no way in heaven or hell he was going back to prison. He was more than happy to be given this gamble. It was a grim opportunity, and life or death would be the ultimate results. But freedom tasted very good, and the prospect of becoming rich and getting lost in Mexico after he'd recovered his stolen wealth, crushed any fear of the unknown into a forgotten pulp. Greed does strange things to a man. He knew this all too well from bitter experience.

Chance unhitched his gelding from the railing and walked it to the livery stable. Numbly he ambled through the next fifteen minutes, dark thoughts racing through his mind.

The stableman was somewhat aghast when he had named an exorbitant rate for feeding, watering, cleaning and reshoeing the gelding, and Chance had accepted the fee of four dollars and fifty cents without a word or even a scowl. Almost all his other customers normally did. But it was obvious to everyone Chance encountered at this time, from the stableman to the gunsmith to the general store clerk, that he was lost in deep thought.

Now, his Henry canted to his right shoulder, with a saddlebag draped over the barrel, Chance walked across the street. He was unaware that he was being watched by the bounty hunter Neems, who stood by a window on the second floor of the hotel.

The big blond man was partially concealed by drapes, but the thin fabric was unable to hide totally the stark blackness of his clothes. Smoke from his cigar drifted out the open window. Squinting eyes peered intently from behind the gray cloud

43

upon the man he'd been so eager to see, as Chance sauntered toward a hotel on the opposite side of the street far to Neems' right.

"Chance!" growled a man, freezing Chance in his tracks. Cautiously, he turned around, looking for the source of the voice that had a familiar raspy tone he instantly recognized as the sheriff's.

"Sheriff Burch," he curtly greeted with mild disdain, eyeing the man coming at him with long, arrogant strides. "Real pleasure."

"Knock it off," he rasped. The sheriff pulled up two feet from Chance. He was six feet tall and his one hundred and ninety pounds were spread out over a broad, thick-boned body. His hair was sandy brown and his face was deeply tanned and weathered. His flat-crowned plainsman's hat did little to mask the harshness that the sun and the other elements had wrought over forty-five years of hard living. His hard, icy-blue eyes were bitter reminders of these tough years—which had lately softened, as evidenced by a beer belly constricted uncomfortably by his holster, fitted with a brand-new Colt Peacemaker. His favorite color seemed to be light brown, for he was dressed from shirt to boots in light-brown apparel.

"I heard you were getting out and I figured you might make this your first stop before heading out to get what I sent you to prison for." A gold toothpick dangled precariously from his lower lip. Whenever he spoke it was something akin to a miracle that it didn't fall off, for his Texas drawl was like a spiteful grunt blasting forth disdain along with vile-smelling breath.

"Yeah?" Chance snorted.

"Yeah? Well, let me tell you yeah, mister!" Burch mocked, taking out his toothpick and pointing it defiantly at Chance. "A few boys you know rather well are in town: Hayes, Morris, Niklinson and Benson. And I'm sure it's no coincidence they're here the same day you're out. I told them the same thing I'm going to tell you: any trouble and I'll bounce you into jail and make you eat the key."

"Do I look like trouble to you, Sheriff?" Chance asked, smiling wryly.

Burch relaxed, put the toothpick back in his mouth, and grunted victory. "Word's written all over your face as clear as

44

day, Chance," he disdainfully said. Then he took his tooth-pick and started pointing it at Chance again, this time lightly poking Chance's chest with it in arrogant contempt. "Just remember what I told ya! You're walking a tightrope anyway."

"Sheriff," Chance snarled, his left hand shooting up, his index finger flicking the toothpick from Burch's hand, "don't ever point your toothpick at me again." He turned, stepped up onto the boardwalk and left Burch looking at his empty hand in angry surprise.

"You best watch yourself, mister!" Burch vehemently warned, pointing an accusing finger at Chance. "I won't put up with your crap, you hear me?"

"Sounds like you got Burchy boy a mite steamed," chortled the hotel's desk clerk as Chance crossed the threshold into the lobby. He was a withered bald old man, stoop shouldered, with only a few teeth left. He continually blinked, longer and harder than necessary, as if it hurt his eyes to keep them open for any length of time. But his disposition was pleasant enough. He took a key and slid it toward Chance, who was signing the register.

"Yeah," the clerk garrulously continued, "ole Burchy boy don't like it none if someone starts makin' waves on his turf. Nope, likes it best when everyone's kissin' up to him. But lately there's been a lot of mean-lookin' fellers driftin' through and he's been catchin' lotsa flack. Hear the town council's pushin' for an ord'nance against guns bein' carried, but he says he don't go for that none; that this is bad territory for a man to walk around without no protection. Meanin' not only outlaws but Injuns. He says you can't rely on the damned cavalry no more when they start makin' generals out of longhairs. But them red devils been quiet for awhile. . . ." He cut himself short, seeing Chance had grabbed the key and started up the stairs for his room. Then he cried out timidly, "I'm sorry 'bout earlier, Mister Chance. But house rules says you have to put down room and key deposit ahead of time."

"That's all right, pop," Chance flung affably over his shoulder. "I had to scrounge up some bucks anyway. And I wouldn't want to get Burch boy on you."

When Chance opened the door to his room, stale air bit at him like a rattlesnake. He dropped his rifle and saddlebag on

45

the single brass bed, then threw open the window. A draft of warm air floated through the room but did little to relieve the stuffiness. He closed the door, then pulled a table and chair over by the window, where he put his revolver, rifle and saddlebag on the table.

So they're here, all except two, he thought, looking out over the street, taking his revolver, opening the chamber. Then he removed the cartridges. From his saddlebag he took a small can of oil, bore cleaner, a wire brush, a cloth and some saddle-soap, then went to work cleaning the single-action Navy Colt that he had gotten during the war. It was an old-style 1851 model, converted to fit .44 cartridges, and it had always proven reliable when plinking at targets. After his medical discharge he had spent countless hours learning the gun and the draw, and adjusting to a whole new world until he became confident of his ability to use it. He surprised himself by how good he'd eventually become.

The only men he'd killed had been during the war in an all-out, maniacal frenzy where men kill or die; and just before his capture, when he'd knifed two men to death in self-defense. Now it was totally different. Now he was hunting men, seeking them out to kill them in cold blood. Retribution in its most heinous form against those who cared nothing for his life, only for the money he'd hidden? It could only be done with swift remorselessness.

Deep in dark thought, he continued his chore. The gun appeared to have held up fairly well over the years it was out of his possession. He disassembled the revolver, then bore cleaned the barrel and cylinder with nitro solvent. He was pleased that there were no signs of rust.

He felt unusually calm and relaxed, quite unlike the bitter hatred which had agitated him whenever he thought of the treachery and beating inflicted upon him by the men who were now here. Eight years had passed since, and quite frequently that treachery had plagued him in nightmares. Judgment Day? The occasion had arisen. He would handle it, or attempt to, as he had envisioned it.

Looking out the window, where evening was creeping over the quiet town, Chance froze in the act of wiping down the now-assembled Colt. His one eye blazed wide as he recognized the familiar forms of Warren Hayes and Bob Morris. They were across the street, stepping from a saloon, apparently making the early-evening rounds. Morris was tall, lanky and fair skinned. Hayes was several inches shorter, but stocky and built like a bull. They glanced around the street before they walked slowly across to the other side.

Chance watched them disappear under the canopy, grunted quietly, then checked the cylinder pawl to make sure it lined up with the barrel, spinning the cylinder around several times. It met his standard of perfection. Then he finished wiping down the revolver with the soft cotton cloth. He did likewise with the Henry, after which he rubbed down the top of his cutaway holster with a thin layer of saddlesoap. He put his spurs on. Then he put his gunbelt on, and the sheath with its Bowie knife, picked up the rest of his possessions, went downstairs, checked out under a garrulous barrage by the old man, then went to the livery.

At the livery Chance had to wait fifteen minutes while the stableman finished reshoeing the gelding. Then he saddled his mount quickly, ignoring the man who was feebly protesting that the horse hadn't really needed to be reshod, as if the extra work had taken ten years off his life. His whining tone indicated that he expected a little something extra, but Chance left him with his hand empty, swatting at the air in annoyance.

The clinking of poker chips and the low rumbling of inter-mittent conversation greeted Chance's ears as he pulled up in front of the You're Welcome Saloon and tethered his horse. The smell of woodsmoke and the aroma of cooking food were strong in the air. The red sun was beginning its descent into the western horizon.

There were only a few people out now. One of them was Neems, casually leaning against a beam, rolling a cigar around in his mouth as he observed Chance from the opposite side of the street. He had not a care in the world—or so it appeared.

A cold chill swept the one-eyed man after he had pushed through the batwings. He stood momentarily inside the doors, quickly taking in the smoky setting and its patrons. It was decor typical of most of the saloons he'd been in, except this one was cleaner than most and there wasn't a fancy-dressed whore to be found. There were no rooms upstairs. The long mahogany bar, with shelves of bottles behind it, lining the front of a mirror with fancy wood trimmings, was the only sign of opulence.

A dozen men besides the bartender were scattered among the tables and chairs. The place smelled of beer, whiskey and sawdust, and would have been almost pleasant if the heat didn't stifle the air.

They were mostly farmers, family men. Chance noted that only a few were wearing firearms; four of these were to his right, just beside a large window. He looked blankly at the foursome, who had set cards down on the table amid bottles, shotglasses, chips, greenbacks and gold pieces. Hayes and Morris looked over their shoulders at Chance, smiling arrogantly, as if they'd been expecting him. Niklinson and Benson eyed him with apprehension.

There was a mournful atmosphere about the place, the dullness having an almost stupifying effect. But now heavy silence descended as more heads turned. People recognized the one-eyed man instantly; he was as well known for his past deeds as he was for the scars he bore.

Sweat broke out on several foreheads as Chance moved slowly, lithely toward the foursome's table like some predator. His face was hard and grim enough to raises the dead from hell. The tension became uncomfortably tight, and the quiet jingle of Chance's spurs was like a loud death rattle disturbing the otherwise constricting silence. The enmity radiating between the one-eyed man and the seated four was menacing, almost unbearable for the other patrons. But no one moved, both from fear and from a macabre expectancy of certain confrontation.

Chance pulled up two steps away from the foursome's table. They were a bristle-faced, shaggy-haired bunch with saddle-tramp stamped all over their sweat and dirt-grimed hats and denim clothing. Seated in a semicircle, all four faced Chance— Hayes and Morris slightly to his right, with their backs against the wall, Niklinson and Benson directly in front of him, closer to the window. All four men's hands rested in their laps.

It was so quiet Chance could hear men swallow in the background; drops of sweat hitting a hard surface. He could feel men holding pentup breath. He cautiously took out the makings and rolled a cigarette. Then he took a match—his one eye slowly flitting back and forth over each man—and scratched it on the tabletop in front of Hayes, who watched each movement of his hand with suspicious contempt.

Casually Chance dropped the match in front of Hayes. Then he moved back two steps and to his left, where he could easily keep the four in his vision and also see any sudden movement anyone else might make to his right. No one was directly behind him.

"This is all pretty unnecessary, don't you think, Chance?" Morris softly asked, his tone indifferent yet belligerent, his voice like a cannonblast in the eerie silence.

Chance replied, "I don't think so, Morris. I've had a lot of time to think about it." He inhaled on the cigarette, his left hand hooked inside the back of his belt, his right hand loosely behind the gunbutt. "Where's Bradbury?"

"He split from us long ago," Morris said tautly.

"Too bad. I kind of wanted to wrap this up real neat."

"We only want our rightful share," Morris quickly countered with irritation. He continued to be softspoken, but bloodlust was written in eyes barely discernible between narrowed eyelids. But his greed was an immobilizing factor, an edge he unknowingly gave away.

"Just like that night you boys nearly killed me?" Chance sourly asked. He was wary of Morris the most, having seen him set up several men in the past with his calm, undaunted aplomb, then gun them down. He knew that Morris was the fastest and the meanest of the four, and that he would have to be the first to go. Hayes was nearly as good on the draw as Morris, but tended to be hasty and thus often inaccurate. Usually he relied on his comrades to pull him out of a tight spot. Niklinson was just a "squirrel," slow to act and having little intelligence to act with. He and Benson had always followed Morris' lead in anything. Together they were a vicious, deadly lot, but singly they didn't amount to much more than wornout saddletramps with a grudge against the world.

"Then when you'd found out I'd hidden the money," Chance continued, "you dumped me off at the sheriff's door in exchange for a little amnesty action."

"You don't forget things too easy, do ya?" barked Niklinson, his eyes nervous, his face glistening with sweat.

"Things like that I don't, dude," Chance snarled through gritted teeth. His cigarette smoke had produced a gray cloud that lingered over their table. "But it seems you boys still haven't figured it out."

"How's that?" asked Morris with tight-lipped anger.

"Didn't you ever wonder why Maria lit off afterward? She was with me that day I hid it, but she didn't see exactly where. And she probably has it. But you boys always did sit on any brains you might have had. It always came out in the form of gas."

"Then I guess we'll have to find the greaser slut," Morris rasped.

"Uh-uh, dude," Chance said. "It's one-man-band action these days."

The implication was fully understood by everyone in the room. No one even breathed. The brief silence was broken by Hayes scoffing, "You've never shot anybody I know of, pal. I've never even seen you fire that thing."

"It'll be a cold day in hell before a one-eyed loser guns down the four of us," Morris arrogantly snarled.

Chance took one last draw on the cigarette, blew the smoke out, tossed the butt at Morris. "Then go see for yourself."

There wasn't time to think about anything, not even dying. Chance didn't allow them but a split second. He lashed out with his right foot, connected with the underside of the table and drew and cocked his Colt as the seated foursome lunged for revolvers. Hayes, Morris and Niklinson started to jump to their feet. Chips, money, bottles, liquor flew over the four startled, angry men. The upended table crashed on the half-risen Niklinson and knocked him back against the wall. Benson froze momentarily; Hayes and Morris stumbled while Chance's Colt quickly roared twice, pumping bullets into their chests, flinging them off the walls and dumping them on the littered floor to their deaths. Glass burst off the wall as Chance immediately turned the gun on Niklinson, who had raised himself erect. Niklinson was pinned between the wall and the heavy table; Benson was bounding up from his seat, gun starting to clear leather. Chance shot through the table and splinters rained the air as Niklinson slammed off the wall, spinning toward the window. The bloodstained table was thrown forward, where it swept through the thick smoke and bounced on the floor. The Colt turned and blazed death right into Benson's horrified face, exploding the top of his head, hurling him backward just before he had leveled his own weapon.

Niklinson had spun around, his weapon drawn and cocked, blood gouting from his mouth and chest, only to have Chance blast him out the window. Huge shards of glass followed him out, cascading his lifeless body to the boardwalk. In a blur of speed Chance whirled, and men dived for the floor in horror and panic, overturning chairs and tables in their haste.

The bartender was bringing a long double-barreled shotgun from beneath the bar, and was within a hair's breadth edge of leveling it at Chance. But the one-eyed man fired his last round and the bullet caught the bartender in the shoulder. The twin barrels roared harmlessly upward as he was thrown back into the shelves of bottles.

Outside, feet were pounding the ground, then the boardwalk. Chance holstered his gun and crashed through the bat-wings, instantly spotting the enraged face of Burch to his left, bounding over the wide-eyed corpse of Niklinson, his gun drawn. A rifle-brandishing deputy was behind him. Chance gave Burch no time for decision; he bolted like a charging bull directly at him and grabbed the sheriff's shirtfront. Viciously Chance pushed him aside, where he hit the railing with a tremendous thud, flipped backward and was dumped into the trough. Great sprays of water splashed up on the horses tethered near by.

The deputy was swinging his rifle down at Chance, but Chance also snatched at him. This time Chance grabbed the gunbarrel and, making sure the muzzle was behind him, strongly whirled the frightened deputy in a half circle. He used the momentum perfectly, timing an open-palm punch with his left to the deputy's chest, so that the force of the slam combined with the swing drove him over the low railing. The deputy also tumbled into the trough, but his head smacked against the edge and he slid, unconscious, alongside Burch, who was flopping around in rage, trying desperately to escape the slimy water. But the weight of the deputy's limp body forced Burch to stay in long enough to give Chance the few seconds he needed to untie his gelding, mount, draw the Henry, look for any immediate retaliation, then race off, leaving behind a trail of dust and hordes of people flocking apprehensively to the scene of sudden upheaval.

Chance was low in the saddle, furiously spurring his mount

onward, using as much care as possible to avoid digging into the animal's flanks with his spurs. He thundered past the line of wagons, the shocked and horrified pioneers instantly recognizing him. He nearly trampled Sara, who had run out into the street, and would have if he hadn't steered the gelding away at the last possible second.

"I want a posse! I want one now! Quick!" screamed Burch in hysterics, flailing wildly as he finally clambered from the trough, soaked and dripping water. Then he dragged his deputy from the trough under the noses of the panicked mounts, and dumped him on the ground. The sheriff's face was crimson with maniacal fury as he beat water from his hat, whipping it against his leg.

Wan-faced men stepped from the saloon timidly, dreading that the fight wasn't over.

"It was cold-blooded murder!" gasped a redhaired man.

"They didn't stand a chance!" roared another incredulously.

"He shot Sam, but he ain't dead!" added another in somewhat horrified relief.

A crowd of men, women and children had gathered in the streets and on the boardwalks. Their faces were locked rigidly in terror and revulsion. This was the first blood ever spilt in Smiling Sons. And most were paralyzed by the sight of the bullet-riddled, bloody corpse of Niklinson.

Neems was perched against the same beam he'd been supporting before Chance went into the saloon, smoking the same cigar, his face the same picture of serene indifference.

"Is he dead?" cried a man, indicating the deputy with a trembling finger.

"No!" growled Burch, as if the man had asked a stupid question. "I want every man who owns a gun mounted up in ten minutes! We're—"

"Sheriff! Sheriff!" hollered a man with a black visor, as he ran from the telegraph office, frantically waving a telegram, his eyes bulging in sheer fright.

"What is it?" bellowed Burch, appearing to be violently agitated because his wild harangue had been curtailed by the interruption as the man with the telegram thrust it at him.

The ragged breathing of the operator was sharply loud in the silence. The townspeople watched Burch with keen interest while he read the message.

"Oh my God," Burch murmured, the color in his face having suddenly changed from red to ashen. His jaw was slack as he gazed ominously at the operator. "Oh my God," he repeated, then stumbled from the crowd, which was buzzing with disturbance and bewilderment. Questions hit him from all sides. He quickly loped toward the telegraph office, the operator hurriedly trailing in his wake. "Somebody get my deputy up," Burch tightly ordered over his shoulder, before both he and the operator disappeared into the telegraph office, slamming the door on the now agitated crowd.

Neems quickly assumed a position by the beam in front of the office. Several citizens headed his way, faces registering dark concern. The bounty hunter caught several eyes with a quick, menacing gaze.

"Uh-uh, people," he said softly, his hand draped over the butt of his Dragoon. "Go about your business; go home."

"And who are you to order us around, mister?" demanded an angry man from the safety of the crowd.

"A law unto myself, feller." Neems treated the outspoken townspeople to a steady, steely gaze, and in it each and every person saw the look of a man ready to kill. They saw unbounded malice and callousness. "And my justice is always swift and sure, feller."

There was low-voiced grumbling of angry discontent, but Neems' point was made and they slowly dispersed, moving away from where he stood, casting him venomous glares, but not wishing to instigate any more violence. Wives forced restraint on any husbands wishing to pursue the matter.

Neems had obtained what he wanted, and that was some room and quiet in order to pick up any pieces of conversation he could from inside. In his trade you never could know too much.

"I don't give a damn if you've got to ride all the way to Fort Sill, Concho or even Fort Meade yourself," Burch angrily spat. "You get some troopers here from somewhere, and fast, Martin!"

"But Sheriff," Martin whined in a trembling voice, Burch's threatening demeanor forcing him down into his chair by the telegraph equipment. "Every available man from Sill, Griffin and the other military reservations near here is up north. The

Comanche and Cheyenne are putting up one last murderin' fight!'' Martin was petrified by Burch's temper, but more so by the news he had received. ''You read the telegram: Apaches ambushed and slaughtered nearly every man at Concho, and the wire to Worth's out. Them red devils must have cut it down.''

Burch backed off. He was past the point of horror, shock or anger; now he was just numb with disbelief and indecision. He released pentup breath. ''We've got real problems, Martin,'' he said, looking as if he were going to faint. ''Unless you can get some of that sad-ass bunch we call a cavalry, we're in serious trouble like you never seen.''

''I'll try, Sheriff,'' Martin cried. Then hastily he added, ''But I can't promise nothin'.''

''You hit every place you can think of, mister,'' Burch rasped authoritatively, heading for the door, his mood once again sour. ''And if you don't come up with anything . . . you'd better grab the nearest rifle.''

''Sounds like you've really had your share of problems for the day, feller,'' Neems said laconically as Burch came through the door and slammed it behind him. Neems rolled the cigar around in his mouth, impassively watching men working on the deputy, and the throng of curious bystanders milling about.

''What the hell are you supposed to be, mister?'' snarled Burch, while several men studied the two from across the street. The bodies of the dead were being hauled unceremoniously from the saloon to where a buckboard wagon had been drawn up in the front. A grim-faced, black-garbed mortician scrutinized the bloody remains of the deceased and shook his head in slow, somber appraisal.

Neems flicked ashes from his cigar at Burch's feet. He didn't take his eyes off the scene across the street. ''I am who am, feller. Bounty hunter.''

''Bounty hunter,'' Burch scoffed derisively. ''Where were you five minutes ago when that maniac was shooting the place all to hell?''

''Right here,'' Neems said calmly. He turned his head to the right, glancing up the street to study three riders coming from the east.

The sheriff was about to issue a retort, but he also saw the three men coming down the street. It was Simpson and his two comrades, heading toward the huddled mass of confused, horrified humanity as if they owned the town, the President, and God.

"Name me a price, feller," Neems said, his eyes fixed on the menacing trio. "And I'll sing you a sweet tune."

Contemptuously, Burch said, "What are you talking about, bigshot, who can't even lift a finger when five men are getting gunned down!"

"I'm talking about Chance. I thought we both were."

"I got more problems than Chance right now."

"I'm well aware of your problems, feller. What makes you think you're going to be able to round up a posse, much less assemble a decent fighting force from among these farmboys? You must think there's roses up a whore's asshole."

"Watch your mouth, mister!" Burch rasped, incensed. "I'm not even sure those red devils will come near here."

"Knock it off, feller. You believe that about as much as I do. Apaches are on a rampage, on a wildass tear that would shake the fat off your belly if you ever saw it." Neems' arrogant stoicism was having an infuriating effect on the sheriff. But he remained silent, mostly because he knew that what Neems was saying was glaringly true, and also because he was curious about what he was getting at, and he was full of anxiety and indecision at the moment. "I've seen it happen before," the hunter calmly continued. "This time it looks like they've come east, swept south and will head back west into New Mexico, making sure they hit every place they even think a white man's under rock. You can bank on it that this town is ripe for red death. And you, Sheriff, don't have a whole lot of time." Neems dropped the cigar butt on the boardwalk, ground it out with the toe of his boot, then fixed Burch with a steely, chilling gaze as if he'd just handed him an ultimatum.

"And just what are you suggesting, mister?"

"Like I said, name me a price."

"On Chance?" Burch softly growled.

"Who do you think we're talking about, feller?" Neems said in exasperation. "I've never been offered money for an Indian."

"I could use you a lot more here than I could sending you after Chance."

"Mind's made up. What'll it be? I'll deliver him to the law alive or dead; makes no difference to me."

Burch grimaced visibly when Neems had used the word law as if he'd already buried Smiling Sons and written off the sheriff. After a brief pause, Burch offered, "Fifteen hundred. I'll have to get an okay from the territorial marshal or judge, but—"

"Two thousand," Neems countered, once again preoccupied with watching the trio, who had stopped in front of the You're Welcome Saloon and were surveying the horror of the fight's aftermath.

"Fifteen hundred, and that's final," Burch said. "I see right through you, bigshot. You don't think I know about Chance's money, hidden somewhere out there in the desert? Uh-uh, mister. You're just looking for a gravy ride, some traveling money for your trouble. You bring him in and we'll talk business. If you understand my meaning . . . feller."

Neems looked closely at Burch, squinting disdain and suspicion. Finally he asked, "Then we got a deal, I take it?"

"Yeah," Burch grimly assented, "we got a deal."

Neems grunted what sounded like approval, then turned and headed back to his hotel.

"Where you headed now?" barked Burch in bewilderment. "Get on it!"

"Gotta catch a little shuteye, feller. Long day ahead of me tomorrow."

"What, sleep? Tomorrow?" howled Burch incredulously.

"His tracks will still be there tomorrow," Neems irritably explained. "The way he was beating that horse out of here, he's going to have to stop soon anyway."

"Hell, by that time—"

"Hell nothin', feller. I'll be on it in a few hours. Besides, I have a pretty good idea where he's headed," Neems said. He glanced once more at the trio across the street, who were asking questions. Children pointed frantically, explaining all that had happened with wild histronics, then were hauled away by parents who had seen enough to satisfy their morbid curiosity. "Looks like I might have a little company," Neems quietly called down the boardwalk to Burch. "Company's always good for a man's soul; keeps his reflexes honed."

Burch guffawed scornfully, then spat into the street—

gestures which were clear indications of the total frustration, humiliation and anxiety he was feeling. "I could really care less about your company, mister," he scoffed. "I've got hell on earth."

Neems nodded agreement, looking as though he was immensely enjoying Burch's predicament. He said, "And then some, feller." He disappeared through the doorway as Burch muttered a curse in his despair. "And then some. . . ."

The stream was as brisk and refreshing as the night air. Chance wet his face and hair, then unsaddled his exhausted horse, took a jar of salve from his saddlebag, and guided the gelding into the shallow stream. While the horse drank, Chance washed it down quickly, then rubbed the salve over several cut areas on the horse's flanks. There were three wounds, all superficial. But Chance rubbed the greasy ointment vigorously over a large area, nonetheless, to prevent any possibility of infection.

Several times the gelding neighed softly, starting to protest, but Chance soothed its anguish with expert skill, using gentle strokes along its mane, and soft words into its pricked ears. Then he wiped down the horse with a towel.

The quiet was ominous, and the outstretched barrenness, marred only by hilly belts, looked hostile and every bit as uninviting as the people Chance had left behind hours ago. But if he was worried it didn't show. For his grim visage was as hard as ever as he pulled the animal from the stream and tied it to a cottonwood, where several clumps of curly mesquite were easily accessible for the hungry animal.

There would be no cooking fire or sleep tonight. He would rest, but his mind would not drift off into deep slumber. Although he had put close to forty hard miles between himself and Smiling Sons, and was now sure no posse was in immediate pursuit, from here he would have to exercise every bit of animal cunning, savagery and caution he was capable of.

He grabbed his rifle and bedroll and his saddlebag, and walked upstream several yards to where several large rocks lay scattered at the base of a low hill. Quickly, but carefully and thoroughly, he checked the area for snakes or scorpions. Finding none, he spread his bedroll a few feet from the stream's bank behind the cover of rocks.

There was a quarter moon but the sky was sprinkled with only a few stars. The darkness was thick and eerie. This was as good a place as any for cover and for bedding down for a few hours.

He took out a hard biscuit, some beef jerky and a bottle of rye whiskey. After he had lost his eye in the war, he'd taken up drinking hard liquor, but only occasionally, when his eye socket hurt so bad that it made his brain feel as if it were going to explode. Now his eye ached and his head pounded without mercy. He felt like screaming, but gritted his teeth instead and took a long swallow of whiskey.

He wondered what it would have been like if he had just gotten as far away from the southwest as possible when he'd been let out. It was a fleeting vision and an impossible dream. Now it was too late. His greed and ruthlessness had dictated the path he was now pursuing, and fleeing from. He was both hunter and hunted. He could almost have predicted this, because he was constantly calculating and premeditating, always planning his next move and anticipating the reactions of others. That, he knew, was the only way he could survive. And although luck had played a hand back in town, his utter ruthlessness and coldbloodedness had given him the vital advantage. He was alive while others were dead; that was his only consolation.

The visions of the four men he'd killed flashed briefly before his eyes: their shocked, angry faces. Their greed and smugness, and their hope that the past could be buried, had buried them instead. Was he avenged? He didn't feel any different.

He laid down in pain, shut his eye and sighed.

The Good Samaritan

3

Laster prodded Ridgeway with the toe of his boot, tautly ordering, "Get up. Get up." He was annoyed, and his grizzled face was set hard in anger. "Supposed to have been up before dawn!"

Ridgeway stirred, pried his eyelids open, and made a face as the early-morning sun growled at him from the east. Laster's gruff tone had also awakened Stanley and Mamoreck. They muttered discontent, but pulled themselves from under bedrolls and blankets nonetheless, stifling any further comments.

They were inside the Texas-Oklahoma border, camped underneath a cottonwood grove several miles south of the Red River. The level land which reached out in every direction was dispiriting, and no one was eager to mount up. But the intense heat which would soon prevail over the prairie was aggravating motivation, causing every man to settle into states of tacit rancor against the harsh elements.

"Why are you in such an all-fired hurry, Sim?" Mamoreck asked as the men were busy gathering camp and tying bedrolls to saddles.

Laster unhitched his roan mare from a cottonwood. "Because," he barked, spitting, "we've been loafin' and slinkin' around the last day and a half like cathouse bitches! I wanna get to Sons and pick up his trail before he gets lost in New Mexico or some damned place."

Ridgeway pulled a slab of ham from his saddlebag, but just as it reached his cracked lips Laster swatted it wickedly from in front of his face. It landed in the dust.

"What'd ya do that for, Sim?" Ridgeway cried angrily, looking at his empty hand, then at Laster, as if he'd been branded by a hot iron.

"We'll eat on the way!" Laster said harshly, mounting. Then he sneered, "Either mess around and whine like some snotnosed kid, or get on your horse. I want Chance, and I want that money, a helluva lot worse than I want to eat." He moved out, as a murmur of anger escaped Ridgeway's lips. The other two were also disgruntled with Laster's sudden surliness. But they quickly mounted, trotting to catch up with him.

Ridgeway's expression had become apologetic. Diffidently he called out to Laster, "Damn, Sim, I didn't mean to get you all keyed up."

"Shuddup!"

Nenz and the others forded the river, climbed the low, grassy embankment on the south side of the Washita and continued somberly across the flatlands of south-central Oklahoma.

Since their barbaric slaughter of the Sterning family and the Negro workers, they had ridden many long, hard miles, crossing the Kansas border to leave their gruesome escapade far behind, but not forgotten. Although they had left no witnesses, they still feared the outside possibility that someone along the way had spotted them. And when word of what had happened to the Sternings spread, suspicion would quite probably point an accusing finger at them.

The knowledge of the atrocity seemed to be smeared all over their filthy, bearded faces, and their clothes, caked dark brown in spots, tainted by their victims' blood. Their sabers had long since been wiped clean.

"What have you got in mind, Karl?" asked Krupeck, downing a swallow from his canteen, as Dreyfuss did likewise.

Grimly, Nenz replied, "There's a town less than a couple hundred miles south—Smiling Sons. Ever hear of it?"

"Farmin' town, ain't it?" asked Dreyfuss flatly.

"That's the place," Nenz answered. Ever since the slaughter and rape of the family, the men had noticed that Nenz' mood had become morose, as if the incident had drained his spirit. He had been mysteriously taciturn, his eyes having a constant faraway look. Few words had he uttered since. It was a relief to the men when he did talk, and they listened intently. "Big town," he continued, his mood suddenly alive. "But it's a dull place; dull people. No whores; little gambling."

"A real nice family environment, eh?" chirped the man with the Confederate flag in his rifle. His name was Thompson, and his ugly weasel face and slight lisp had earned him the nickname "weasel."

The last man's name was Reynolds. He was dark skinned and dark haired. He fancied himself a comedian, ladies' man and philosopher, although he rarely said anything remotely humorous, touched a whore only once in a great while when he had enough stolen money, and never said anything close to profound. He was simply a buffoon and a braggart.

"Then what are we heading there for, Karl?" asked Reynolds. "Need a little rise to get the ole juices flowing."

"Not now we don't," Nenz said firmly. He spat, but some of it caught in the gray whiskers on his chin and lay unnoticed, except by a roving fly. "We'll pick up supplies, then get lost out west for awhile and let things blow over. We won't pull anything in Sons 'less we have to."

"You think they'll be able to pin what happened back in Kansas on us, Karl?" asked Krupeck rather cryptically.

Nenz shrugged. "Hard to say. But we've done worse and gotten away with it." He spat again, then delicately touched the saber dangling by his side. His eyes lit up and an eerie smile creased his weathered, prunelike features. "Just have to keep our eyes peeled, won't we?" he said gravely, reflecting back on the savagery of almost two days ago.

The sun was now drawing sweat from his pores as it became more intense. It beat disdainfully upon the five, making them well aware of the heat which would follow them like a curse.

At first, they didn't know whether to be outraged at Sheriff Burch, or horrified by the news he'd just sprung on them. A sea of men, women and children were huddled together up and down the main street, countless faces expressing shock, anger, fear, sullenness, bitterness, irritation. All of it was directed toward Burch, who was standing tall and arrogant atop the canopy over the You're Welcome Saloon, addressing the throng as if he were Moses delivering the Ten Commandments. Or at least that's how he struck the vast majority of townspeople.

Arms akimbo, Burch was trying desperately, by haughty

and contemptuous glares, to squash the resentment being directed at him. The townspeople weren't so much angry at the news of a possible Apache attack—although they were scared and horrified—as they were deeply embittered by the fact that Burch had waited until this morning to inform them of the grim possibility. And they grew even more furious about his lame excuses, and the manner with which he addressed them, as if it were their fault.

"So now what are we supposed to do, Sheriff?" growled an irate man.

"After you wait all night and morning before telling us the Apaches are on the warpath!" another enraged citizen chimed in. A loud murmuring of discontent started.

"Goddamned red bastards will slaughter us all!" screamed another man hysterically.

"Watch your mouth, Cook!" Burch vehemently bellowed. "There's women and kids here!"

"Won't matter none before long, Burch!" snarled another man, waving his fist in futile rage.

The deputy was standing close by, to the left of Burch, holding his rifle in the crook of his arm. He was a medium-sized man with pale skin and weak, almost feminine features. He always appeared tired looking, but right now he was clearly anxious, and whiter than usual with unconcealed fright.

"I was afraid there'd be a mass panic," Burch tautly explained. The past twenty hours had taken their toll on Burch's nerves and his tolerance was frayed dangerously thin. He was doing his best to hold his temper, and he accomplished this by being arrogant and surly. "I didn't want everyone stampeding all over each other to get out of here."

"Well, you sure weren't worried about that bounty hunter we heard you sent after that murderin' son-of-a-bitch!"

"I told you to watch your mouth, Cook!" Burch viciously snarled, his voice booming like thunder.

"Go to hell!" Cook retorted.

A ripple of scornful laughter passed through the crowd.

"If we had known last night we'd have left with those settlers!" informed another citizen indignantly.

With deep loathing Burch said, "You telling me all you men, who probably outnumber that Apache warparty four to one, are afraid to make a stand and protect your families and

this town you've worked so hard all these years to build?''
There was a chilling silence. Burch's glare raked over the
crowd with accusing contempt and incredulous spite. "Is that
what you're telling me?" he boomed.

"We're not telling you nothin' of the sort, mister!" hollered
a man. He received weak confirmation from some of the
crowd.

"Cavalry's supposed to be for protection against those red
savages!" informed another irascible citizen.

"Well, the cavalry's gone, people!" Burch retorted, saying
the word cavalry as if it were a bad taste in his mouth.
"They're out chasing the Comanches, Cheyenne, Kiowa and
God only knows what else! And those Apaches have slaughtered every soldier at Concho and even pulled off an ambush as
far as Peterson's place near the river! Now it looks as if they'll
be heading this way back into their happy hunting ground. So
you either live with it . . . or die with it." Another eerie silence
ensued. This time several gasps emphasized the grim audacity
of the sheriff's last words. "It's up to you, people."

"What if we all leave town and seek cover in the hills?" a
man timidly inquired.

Burch's reply was quick and mocking. "Then I won't even
look at you, pal." He paused, letting his disdain soak in like
cold rain. He snorted, then spat on the canopy. "Because
you're not even worth piss."

"Watch that mouth, Burch!" snarled an outraged man
from deep in the crowd. "I don't need my wife hearing that
kind of language!"

There was angry grumbling up and down the street. The
people were using Burch as an outlet for their fear and venom,
being unable to cope with the harsh reality of the unpleasant
situation. They were hardly able to bear the grim prospect of
dying a horrible, violent death, without wild frenzy. They were
now close to that.

They had been smug and secure too long. Their problems
had always been taken care of by the Army—as incompetent
as it was sometimes—or by the law. Their hands were clean
and lily white.

Burch had feared just this type of response because he knew
these people well; he knew their character and temperament,
knew there were a lot of jellyfish backbones and hypocritical

moralizers. He had postponed the announcement as long as he could in the hope of getting help from elsewhere. But he had found out that the message they'd received had come from a dying man at Concho. They were isolated from any help; even if it could be reached, it would probably be too late. Thus he had come up emptyhanded. But he wouldn't be shamefaced again, after yesterday. He was determined not to bear the blame for recent events. He had lived his life tough, hard, and he was a proud man not used to being humiliated, as Chance had done, or put on the spot, as the bounty hunter had done at first, and now the town.

"So what are we supposed to do?" was voiced almost in unison from several people. Some small children had started to cry in the background and the commotion was too much for fragile nerves.

"Stay here and fight, if necessary," Burch said quickly, with supreme confidence. "If you run into the hills the Apaches will easily run you down. At least here we can all band together and use the town for cover. We have the numbers; we have the weapons. If we become disorganized we'll all surely be slaughtered. And we might as well hand our scalps over to them personally."

There was minor rejection of Burch's proposal, but most recognized the truth of his words. Nevertheless they admitted the utter futility of the situation and cursed silently to themselves, cursing the thought of death—not realizing that what most were really cursing was their cowardice, the notion of leaving the good life and the idea of risking their town, their homes and their possessions to destruction. It was indeed frightening, but few options were open. They had everything to lose and nothing to gain, whereas the Indians were at the opposite extreme.

The sea of faces was now moribund. A grim atmosphere hovered over the town. Most were no longer irritated by the late-morning heat or Burch's words. And Burch, realizing he'd exhausted their feelings with his perilous warnings, finished in an almost morose tone, saying, "Go to your homes, your businesses; do whatever you have to do. Those of you who wish to flee of course are free to do so. Those who wish to stay and make a fight of it, come back with your families, and every kind of weapon you can lay your hands on, in no more than three hours. I honestly don't know what's going to happen; I can't say.''

His voice abruptly stopped, letting the people know he was finished. The throngs then dispersed slowly, quietly.

The deputy watched the crowd thinning, as people went off in every direction. Burch also watched, but with doleful eyes, as if he were observing people he'd never again see in this world.

In a trembling tone the deputy asked, ''What do you think's going to happen, Sheriff?'' He waited, looking at Burch with wide expectant eyes.

Burch turned his head slowly. His face had an ominous look to it. He looked at the deputy with a faraway gaze and remained silent for a brief moment. Then he left the deputy standing there alone.

The deputy shivered. Never before in his life had he seen a look like that. He quivered convulsively again, knowing that those eyes had given him the whole answer. They had seemed to look right through him and into the future—a red future.

For the past three hours Chance had noted that the terrain had been rising slightly, changing gradually into more rugged, rocky landscape. The lowlands were now giving way to the High Plains. This immense, flat desert, known as the Llano Estacado, rose to more than two thousand feet above sea level, its desolation devoid of water or trees, with only patches of dried grass growing on the gravely surface. It was a land loved by the snakes, the lizards and the buzzards. For things tended to die here with noticeable frequency, as evidenced by the dried-out bones of buffalo, cattle and other fauna of the region.

Now, from a quarter mile away, Chance had spotted the three vultures circling high over the rocky hills he was now approaching. It wasn't too hard to spot their familiar black shapes against a cloudless blue sky. It would have been easier later in the day, but the sun was now climbing to its strongest pinnacle of glaring anger, and it shrouded the flying predators in a haze, just as it did anything which dotted the barren flatland.

As Chance stealthily eased his gelding along the foot of the hills, his hand was draped over the Colt's butt. Whatever was ahead, man or animal, was in the act of dying, or had just recently expired, and now the vultures were upon it. Chance reached the end of the hill, where several large boulders were piled at its foot, and climbed up a jagged limestone escarpment.

The man seemed to appear out of thin air, silently catapulting forth from behind a boulder, knife clamped between his teeth, as he fell from twelve feet. He landed hard on the startled Chance, knocking the one-eyed man violently from the saddle. Both thudded to the ground. But Chance landed on his back, the air whooshing from him, while the other's fall was cushioned by Chance's body. He rolled away due to the momentum, while the frightened gelding trotted away from the sudden explosion of action.

Chance saw stars, paralyzed for a second. His stomach and chest felt as if they'd been caved in. He groped for his gun, but it had been thrown free of its holster and was decorating the ground near his hat. He started to pull himself erect but a hand suddenly clamped under his chin, forcing his head back and up. He stared into the sweat-sheened, leering face of the man who'd jumped and who was about to kill him with a gleaming butcher knife. The blade reflected the sun as it swooped down toward Chance's pulsing jugular in a mockingly slow arc. Chance's right hand shot out, grabbed the man's right wrist, and forced the blade to sweep by his neck mere inches from the skin.

Chance was on his knees, the attacker standing behind. Instantly Chance twisted, driving his left elbow up, deep into the man's groin. Chance felt the tip of his elbow slamming into the man's testicles, producing a horrid shriek which pierced the air and echoed inside Chance's skull.

Now it was the attacker who was paralyzed with numbing agony. He made a long, eerie, sucking sound, as if he were drowning. He gasped for air, his eyes nearly forced from their sockets.

Leaping to his feet as he sensed his opportunity, Chance grabbed the attacker with both hands by his long hair, then flung him to the ground at the hill's base. The man had held onto his knife, and Chance realized, after he'd thrown him through the air, that the man could have stabbed him easily when he had grabbed him.

"Want me to plug 'im, Bobby? Huh? Huh?" yelled a man standing behind the high boulders, brandishing a .56 Springfield rifle.

"Shut your face and stay out of it," croaked Bobby in unconcealed misery, his eyes tearing under immense pain, yet blazing with a depthless hatred. He clambered slowly to his feet, holding the long, thick-bladed knife low at his side, pointed slightly upward.

Chance backed off stealthily, arched slightly up on the balls of his feet. He gave both men intent glances, sizing them up, his sweaty, bristled face becoming frigid with evil intent as he unsheathed his Bowie.

The one called Bobby, and the other with the rifle, spoke with accents which placed their origins in either Tennessee or Kentucky. They were both dirty and shaggy; only their wild eyes offset otherwise nondescript features. Bobby wore black boots, buckskin pants and no shirt. The other wore matching buckskin pants and a shirt with frills along the edges. A coonskin hat was perched at a rakish angle on his head.

"What if you can't do 'im like ya done the other?" cried Springfield, his voice strained, his eyes scared, as Chance and Bobby slowly circled each other, crouched low, knives flashing and ready. "Been awhile since ya done 'em! Might've lost yer touch!"

"I said to shut your face, Brad!" hissed Bobby. "I'll take this one-eyed asshole as easy as the other," he boasted forcefully, his teeth gritted in pain and savage hatred. He limped slightly, gingerly, circling with Chance, feinting strikes. "You dirty son-of-a-bitch! I think you cracked one of my nuts!" he snarled.

"Kind of a bum rap, huh, feller?" Chance snickered evilly, taking cruel delight in the other's torture. "Ought to be more choosy about who you jump. Stick to small kids and little ole ladies." His teeth were also clenched tight.

They watched each other's blades with sharp intensity, parrying, testing each other's speed and agility. Chance was lithe, fluid in his movements; Bobby was slowed somewhat by his misery. His legs felt heavy, his body awkward as the sun continued to beat down relentlessly, sapping strength and energy without regard for the men's attempting to inflict brutal death on one another.

It was a skilled, lethal exhibition. Each man was aware of the other one's adeptness, detecting the other's experience and deadly knowledge with an innate sense common among predators, among those who live by the sword. Blades continued to sweep up and across in slashing motions; short jabs were aimed at midsections, neither man leaving himself exposed to counterattack for longer than a split second.

But Chance was in better shape. He knew that he could possibly wear down Bobby's softer, less developed body in a few more minutes under the blazing sun. So he stayed back, looking for an opening, playing off Bobby's hatred and pain. He let Bobby think that he had the offensive, and the latter, his state clouded with emotion he couldn't crush, didn't realize Chance was setting him up for a cut of death.

Bobby jabbed at Chance's midsection. Chance continued to retreat and Bobby came at him, taking two vicious swipes at his stomach, then two at his face and head, as Chance ducked under quickly. Coming up, he scored then, slashing his blade across the right side of Bobby's exposed ribcage just before Bobby could lunge out of the way.

Chance had drawn first blood, and Bobby stood still momentarily in outraged disbelief and fear. The red gore flowed freely from the ugly slice extending from the upper stomach to just under his right arm, causing Bobby to shake briefly in panic. Several of his ribs were obscene in their naked, gleaming white horror. He knew he was going to bleed to death if he didn't end the fight soon. But his hatred for the one-eyed man who had caused him such pain and humiliation was a more overwhelming factor, spurring him onward.

Chance eased back, content to let his adversary bleed and have to come to him. He could see the terror in Bobby's eyes. The fight wasn't over yet, but he found himself feeling confident, and possibly too brazen. He was sure of his skill with a knife, having fought and killed two men with one nine years ago. But a knife fight was also how he had been hideously scarred for life.

Chance and the profusely bleeding, raggedly breathing Bobby moved in tight. This time only one would walk away.

Bobby switched hands, throwing the knife casually into his left. Then, faking a swipe to the face, and starting to drive Chance back, he drove his right foot into Chance's left thigh.

The one-eyed man started to buckle and his adversary's knife swung in a long, continuous lash, a killing blow.

Chance let himself fall to his left knee, leaning back just in time. But it was not quite far enough, because the blade ripped through his shirt and sliced open a three-inch gash across his right shoulder. Wasting no time in useless worry over his wound, Chance galvanized off his haunches. Bobby was unable to bring his knife back in time or to retreat, as Chance swiftly whipped his blade backhand over Bobby's face, opening a grisly slice from right to left temple and taking his eyes out in the process. Bobby shrieked, dropped his knife, and threw his hands over his blind eyes, blood showering his face and body in torrents.

Brad froze in shock and horror, his mouth slack. Then, as Chance thrust his Bowie savagely into Bobby's chest to end his wailing, Brad leveled his rifle, trembling in terror. He aimed and squeezed the trigger. But Chance had grabbed Bobby's lifeless body by the hair and held it in front of his as a shield. He hoped to confuse Brad and throw his aim, knowing that the heavy-caliber bullet could just as well kill him with or without the protection.

The bullet, tearing into the outer left side of Bobby's back, ripped away a large chunk of skin, muscle and bone, then grazed by Chance, who tossed the mutilated corpse aside. He was drenched in blood, both his and Bobby's.

The distance between Brad and Chance was twenty feet. Brad had no time to react again, for Chance was a blur of motion, slinging his Bowie through the air. The knife flew up, end over end, then thudded deep into Brad's stomach. He dropped his rifle, clutched the Bowie's handle and tumbled down the incline, his face etched eternally in astonished horror as he bounced and flopped grotesquely over large rocks and jagged protrusions, his skull cracking open, his neck snapping before he lay motionless at the foot of the hill, torn to bloody shreds by the fall.

Quickly Chance retrieved his gun, then the knife, after wiping the blade on Brad's shirt. He found his gelding around the corner of the hill. He also found two men, one with his throat cut, the other shot in the back—victims of highway robbery. Everything, from boots to gunbelts and hats, had been stripped off their bodies. All clothing and valuables were piled by four horses corraled around several rocks. The corpses were already swollen; they'd been dead for some time. Faint traces of rotting flesh were beginning to infest the scorched air. Before long Chance knew that the heat and the buzzards would turn the vicinity into a cesspool of stench and dripping innards.

Chance wasn't certain how they knew he'd been coming, but it was a good ambush point. Rocks jutted out, piling on top of each other up the leveling incline. An ambusher could position himself behind large boulders on either side of the hill's face and be hidden from the view of a man coming toward him from east or west.

The one-eyed man sat down in the shade of the hill, removed his shirt, took some whiskey and poured it on his wound. He wiped it clean and examined it, the alcohol burning his whole arm, then reaching every nerve and sinew in his body as if he'd been set afire. Relief swept through him, seeing it was nothing more than a superficial wound. Any deeper and it would have been serious. The bleeding was starting to stop. The arm stung badly, and he knew it would cause him great discomfort in the days ahead. He took some salve and rubbed it over the injured area, then tied a towel around the shoulder and under his arm to soak up any more blood. He put his shirt on and mounted, willing the pain to subside from his mind.

Chance glanced up at the vultures, now circling lower in greedy anticipation, the added deaths having increased their wantonness. Grimly the one-eyed man raked a sweeping gaze over the carnage, then heeled his horse into a walk, muttering, "Rest easy, boys. The Good Samaritan's here to take care of you."

The Fires Of Gehenna

4

Grimaces of disgust were partially hidden under black neckerchiefs, for the stench of death was a merciless assault on the warden's hunters. From as far away as a hundred feet, Simpson and his two comrades had noticed the malodorous stench of putrefying flesh. As if they were being sucked into the very pits of Sheol, they drew closer to the foothills, while the vile miasma grew stronger and more repulsive.

The mutilated, bloated corpses of Bobby and Brad greeted approaching life, the scavengers helping themselves to unfeeling flesh, remaining busy and unconcerned, viciously ripping out chunks with beaks and talons until the men were right on top of the quagmire of death.

Then several of the vultures spread their large wings and flapped off, squawking annoyance, talons clutching dripping innards. The remaining predator took to flight as the trio dismounted. Savagely it plucked the eyes from Brad's corpse before joining its brothers of hungry death.

Holding his mount by the reins, Simpson examined Bobby's corpse while the other two men, known as Snake Eyes Logan and Bloody Brand, combed the area.

As Logan moved around the right bend of the hill, brand flatly asked Simpson, "Chance?"

Simpson grunted. His scowl was one of perplexity and concern. Matching Brand's laconic tone, he replied, "Who else?"

"Matt, Bloody," called Logan from around the corner.

The two immediately headed in his direction, hearing more buzzards squawking off in anger before seeing their ominous black figures ascending skyward.

71

"Them jokers must've been having a real field day before Chance came along," intoned a grim Logan, staring at the two remaining dead, greedily ravaged by the buzzards' devastation. His two comrades came to a halt alongside him. "These two been dead a helluva lot longer."

"How far ahead you reckon Chance is?" Bloody Brand inquired, coughing briefly from the nauseating odor.

"Hard to tell, what with this heat and the buzzards," Simpson replied. "Say at least half a day, maybe. We played hell picking up his tracks at first."

"Yeah," Logan said, somewhat irritated. "We wasted good time back in Sons, fooling with that damned warden."

"And that jack-off sheriff who made us wait to use the friggin' telegraph," Brand caustically supplemented.

"Yeah," growled Simpson, shaking his head in bitter acknowledgment. "So let's go close the distance. Now we know we're headed the right way."

"If Chance continues leaving a trail of bodies like he has, we won't have much trouble following him," Logan said.

The trio made to mount, but Simpson froze abruptly, pausing, his right foot in its stirrup. Hastily he added, "Almost forgot; must be this damned stink. You boys see anything you want?"

"Hell with it, Matt," Brand said, mounting. "Ain't nothin' this garbage got interests me—not when I think about what we're headed for."

"Damned straight," Logan chimed in, also climbing into his saddle. "Let's go 'fore I puke my guts, Matt."

Reluctantly, and somewhat annoyed by their rejection of his indirect proposal, Simpson joined the two. "Yeah," he said, jerking his kerchief from his face, then hacking and snorting up a globule of spit to launch on one of the nearby dead. "Let's get the hell out of here. I can almost taste that bastard's money."

Much to the delight of the vultures circling high overhead under the sun's late-afternoon glare, the trio gladly left the carnage behind. As the vultures swooped down in their gluttony to once again make ravenous feast out of the dead, Simpson muttered over his shoulder, "Happy days will be here again."

Beginning its descent in the west, the early evening sun seemed a bored spectator, its red-orange eyeball watching the somber souls of Smiling Sons massing in the main street. From the surrounding farmhouses the few remaining families morosely plodded toward the huddled humanity, men brandishing rifles and pistols, women holding small children close to their bodies. Fright poured out in sweat. Tension rose in the heat. All that was needed now was a death knell. For, as Sheriff Burch began barking orders, black smoke ominously hovered over the corn and wheat fields to the south, then wafted skyward, orange flames shooting and licking after black clouds of smoke, the dry crops in their brittle states becoming consumed rapidly before chilling warcries pierced the air.

Every head in Smiling Sons seemed to jerk in unison; countless horrified faces peered southward. A wave of feminine shrieking resounded through the air, intensifying the angry warcries as more than a hundred Apaches stormed forth from the foothills in the east, while another hundred or so left the flaming fields behind and raced their ponies for the shocked townspeople.

"Oh my God!" cried a woman.

"Nooooo!" shrieked another citizen.

"Aaaaah!" screamed a terrified woman holding a crying baby.

"Savages! Monsters!" gasped a rifle-toting man.

"Must be the whole Apache nation!" bellowed Burch in horrified disbelief.

"Bloody Christ! Death to the heathens!" raged another man.

Clad in buckskins and breechcloths, the first wave of warriors descended on the several petrified families on the southern and eastern outskirts of town. Heavily armed braves made a quick and easy massacre of these few whites.

In their sudden panic, the townspeople crowded in the main street bolted in different directions, most heading for the cover of buildings. Blindly the horrified whites pushed and shoved in their haste. Many were trampled to death, the snapping of bones and crushing of flesh drowned out by the screams of

73

anguish from those being pounded to bloody pulps underfoot. Generally it was women and small children who were snuffed out in the initial pandemonium.

While rifle fire cracked—the whites retaliating, as men climbed atop canopies and rooftops, others crashing through doors—the warriors converged on the main street from the east and west ends, and up through the south-side alleyways, making an instant slaughterground of the street. Dozens of arrows flew through the air, thudding into white flesh and toppling men from their perches. Their corpses smashed down on the living still seeking shelter.

In the alleyways, several braves were blasted from their barebacked ponies, blood and chunks of shredded flesh following their death descents into piles of garbage. A white stuck his head around the corner of a building, firing his rifle at the rushing Apaches, shooting two into bloody death before a war ax flew through the air and split his face and skull wide open.

Although the Apache warparty was large in number, the whites had them severely outnumbered. But sheer force of numbers presented no problem for the savage warriors, who continued to butcher the townspeople relentlessly, their dark faces twisted in barbaric hatred. Ferocious, high-cheekboned, sweat-sheened faces bare of war paint, for it was not the custom of the warriors of their nation to daub paint on their faces.

Bloodcurdling screams hung in the air as flaming arrows were shot into the sides of buildings, through windows and into several unfortunate whites, who were turned into wailing, short-lived balls of fire. It was during these minutes that dozens of braves became enthralled with setting fire to as many buildings and victims as they could.

Through the smoke-filled air, bullets flew, arrows whistled, lances and tomahawks were blurs of lightning death. A nine-foot feathered lance impaled a rifle-brandishing citizen to a beam in front of the You're Welcome Saloon and held him upright in wide-eyed death.

Those Apaches who were armed with rifles blasted whites to death in the street and on the boardwalks. Brief fusillades of bullets hurled several townsmen through storefront windows, the crashing of glass shards adding to the grotesque chaos. Other braves fell from ponies, blood pumping from chest and head wounds. Warriors galloped ponies up onto the body-littered boardwalks, trampling several women and children beneath unshod hooves. Others crashed mounts through storefront and saloon windows, but shotguns boomed in unison and the few warriors who had attempted this frenzied charge were flung violently backward onto the boardwalks with gaping red holes punched through their exposed torsos.

There was nowhere for the whites to run. They were trapped. Continuous screams were issued not only out of agony and horror, but also out of despair, for swift, bloody death seemed inevitable and brutal.

Bullet and arrow-riddled corpses were dropping everywhere. Tomahawks and war clubs with stone balls split open white heads, the cracking of bones preceding the rain of blood and gray brain matter. Several buildings were now immersed in flames. Soon both sides of the bone-dry wooden structures would be consumed. There was little choice between fighting or cowering inside. But the majority of those who bolted forth from the burning hell were greeted by death and the vicious leers of red faces.

As of yet there was no looting or raping. It was a joyless, vindictive slaughter, the carnage heaping in merciless vehemence. No one was spared the wrath of the red man. It was as if all the pentup hatred and anger of hell itself had escaped its tortuous abyss and was being released through those who were sick of what they felt was a severe injustice done to them by white invaders.

Those citizens who escaped to the outskirts of the fiery hell were quickly run down, shot to death by fusillades of bullets and arrows. Some were hacked to pieces, or beheaded by tomahawks and large knives already dripping with crimson. Those braves who had chased after fleeing whites sliced off scalps as trophies of prey. Then they searched the surrounding houses, and, finding no one, set fire to the dwellings. Almost instantly, dozens of structures became roaring infernos, adding to the expanding area that was already ablaze.

Wails of the dying were heard in every direction, sounding even more hideous as they mixed with the roaring crackling of fire. Corpses roasted and the stench of melting flesh was trapped underneath thick clouds of black smoke, which rose in grim harmony everywhere.

With arrows protruding from his right shoulder and left thigh, Sheriff Burch leaned against a beam in front of his office, a large revolver in each of his hands. To his left on the boardwalk, his deputy was furiously pumping the action lever of a Winchester. Both men wore maniacal expressions of rage and hate as they made their heroic stand, blasting Apaches from mounts and into the sea of dead, the vast river of bedlam and blood.

But their valiant fight soon ended, as a hail of arrows and rifle fire was directed at them. The Apaches were now concentrating their assault on the few remaining groups of whites left fighting.

While the deputy shot two more braves to death, eight arrows plunged into his torso, another drilling through his right eye and deep into his brain. Looking like a red pincushion, he was hurled backward, where he slammed through the window behind. Three more arrows immediately ripped into his groin.

Shielded partially by the beam, Burch escaped most of the salvo of lead and arrows. But then several bullets tore into his side, and an arrow stabbed into his left bicep and pierced all the way through his arm. Shrieking horribly, he stumbled back toward an open doorway, where he loosed several more rounds before another arrow caught him high in the chest. Covered in red gore, he fell inside, toppling over his desk nearby.

Within several more minutes the fighting was finished. The last of those whites marked for death were pounced upon, and, as the screams of the dying faded under the mountainous flames, those dead whites untouched by fire were scalped. The air was now thick with the sounds of the dead being mutilated further, ravaged for prizes.

Sara had tried in vain to run from, then fight, the short, heavily muscled brave now ripping the clothes from her body. Her house lay in shambles from her violent struggle with the Apache; furniture and glass were smashed everywhere.

Violently tearing her dress down the middle, the brave,

straddling Sara, feasted his eyes first on her breasts, then on the light-colored triangle of hair covering the object of his cruel lust. Slowly, looking as though he were in a trance, the rapist ran his hands over the white woman's large, soft breasts, cupping, squeezing, rubbing. Then, his mind inflamed with the sight of Sara's tender, beautiful whiteness, the brave felt the lips of her vagina, brutally sticking two fingers into her, then withdrawing those fingers and, lifting his hand to his face, smelling her, as if seeking to learn something.

The Apache leered. Sara was numb with terror. Chuckling evilly, the brave said, "I will have white squaw many ways."

Sara's terror, humiliation and helplessness causing an overpowering sickness in her head and stomach, the next few minutes, as the brave drove himself into her, deeply and with a terrible vengeance, grunting, cursing and laughing, were like some half-remembered nightmare. Sara saw everything as if in a white light, with the bile threatening to erupt from her gut, the nausea swimming in her head and building with pressure.

Hundreds of corpses—men, women and children, white and red—littered the street and the town limits. There were myriad heaps of twisted bodies, and the dead were also slung over railings and windowsills. Already the flies were gorging on spilt blood and lifeless flesh. Overhead, shielded by rising black clouds of smoke, a half-dozen vultures circled, having been almost instantly attracted to the gory massacre.

A large section of canopy on the north side collapsed under the fiery assault. Soot and ashes mushroomed skyward.

Seemingly unperturbed by the nauseous stench of blood and burning death, the warriors, whose numbers had been depleted to almost half, grouped near the west end of town. Their belts and lances were decorated with the grisly, blood-dripping trophies of white scalps. Now all eyes were staring down the sea of death, as an Indian chief, who looked as old as time itself, lethargically steered his black stallion through the smoke.

The silent expectancy was suddenly pierced by the loud screams of a woman.

"Nooooo! No! Just kill me!" she pathetically moaned.

All heads turned and saw one of their own dragging a blonde woman from a small house untouched by flames, her face stained with blood and tears.

The group slowly headed toward the scene, while the warrior, having shredded Sara's clothes to tatters, pounced on his victim's nakedness and started to defile her. In her abhorrence and helplessness, Sara retched curses.

The Apaches crowded around the picket fence and watched for several seconds with grim dispassion. The lone warrior was unaware of all the eyes cast upon him; he was too enraptured with and consumed by his sick lust.

Then a warrior in front of the line of braves raised his rifle, as did a dozen others. They fired a ragged cacophony of bullets which ripped Sara and her rapist into mutilated death. With bitter hatred and contempt, one of the warriors spat onto their still forms.

The large group then turned and faced the old chief, faces etched in somber pride as the Apache leader raked a slow gaze of intense scrutiny over the warriors assembled before him, his craggy face bitter and angry even in repose. Though autonomous rule was the Apache way, and though there was no principal chieftain among their tribes, it was clearly evident that all the warriors, young and old alike, held the eldest warrior among them, Swift Vengeance, in awe. His was an undeclared leadership, but the Apaches looked up to him and followed his every utterance as indisputable wisdom. They recognized that his leadership was just and that his every intention was for the best interests of his people.

One of the braves spoke up, his voice loud enough to be heard over the din of the raging inferno behind Swift Vengeance. "He chose disgrace by dirtying himself with a white woman, when you forbade such a thing."

At length Swift Vengeance nodded slowly, grimly. "Let us then leave," he said softly, his voice strong and resonant for someone so withered, weatherbeaten and shriveled as he was. "All the white eyes are dead, but so also are many good Chiricahua Apache."

"Your vengeance is indeed swift, Swift Vengeance," said another warrior of high rank, proudly sitting straight and angry on a saddled gelding he had stolen from a dead soldier. Several of the other Apaches also had saddled mounts, and rifles, which had been taken from victims too. "Your name will be feared," continued the high-ranking warrior, "and the white eyes will shake when it it mentioned. And as for those dead warriors, they will be avenged."

There was no immediate vocal response from Swift Vengeance, who merely grunted quietly. His face appeared mournful as he turned his eyes from his warriors to stare briefly at the dying sun that was now inching below the horizon in the west, as if it were glaring accusation at the warriors, yet attempting to hide from the macabre, brutal scene of tragedy.

"Perhaps," he muttered softly, "there has been enough killing."

His voice was drowned out by the almost deafening anger of the all-encompassing fire, as he slowly headed away from the heinous carnage with his warriors trailing respectfully in his wake.

On the western outskirts of town a large wooden sign was staked into the ground. While the warparty moved onward, slanting on a southwesterly course, a brave stopped, read the sign, and, taking an arrow, shoved a scalp through the tip. He then fired the scalp-ornamented arrow into the sign, where it thudded angrily into the wood, warbling briefly as if mocking in grotesque sarcasm the inscription, which read WELCOME TO SMILING SONS, A TOWN OF LOVE, PEACE AND GOD ALMIGHTY.

"I think we've lost him, Matt," said Brand. His tone revealed that he was disheartened, yet a note of annoyance also escaped.

"Got to agree to that, Matt," Logan chimed in, equally dejected and irritated.

"Damn," Simpson muttered, rubbing his jaw, staring intensely into the glow of the dying flames of their campfire, feeling the chill of night air edging through his tired body and disturbing his sour reflections. "Damn," he repeated, this time gritting his tobacco-stained teeth, then looking sharply at his two comrades.

In the faint glow of the fire it was easy to see their faces against the surrounding black background—faces strained with exhaustion from hours of long, hard riding. Uncomfortable, unhappy and unlucky faces.

Like leeches, dust and dirt clung to clammy skin, rough bristles and clothing damp with sweat. The dirt was vastly irritable and noticeable after the scorching heat of the day.

With underlying anger, Simpson noted his comrades' morose disenchantment. His stare was icy and his tone became hard. "We backtrack, then head south."

"What?" cried Logan incredulously.

"How the—" started Brand.

"It's the only thing he could have done," Simpson interrupted with resolute bitterness, turning his eyes toward the fire, then spitting into the flames.

Feeling astonished and indignant, Logan and Brand exchanged blank stares, searching the other's face, as if locking gazes would help them comprehend what Simpson was thinking.

Logan finally broke the silence, saying, "In all these gorges and arroyos Chance could be hiding anywhere. It ain't hard to lose a man in this part of Texas."

"I agree with that," Brand tersely added, his tone weary, yet strong with spite. "And I think we should split up, flush him out and make him take us the rest of the way to the money."

In silent contempt Simpson glared at Brand for several seconds, regarding him as he would a piece of trash. "That's stupid," he spat in deprecation. "And he ain't stupid. Even if he was doing that, and you go out there peeking under all those rocks like you was looking for a sidewinder, he'd blast your ass into a million stinking pieces!"

"Maybe he spotted us," Brand countered defensively, as Simpson returned to gazing into the fire. "Maybe he figures he'll hide out for a few days and let us pass on by till we're way ahead, and then he'll be following us!"

"He didn't see us," Simpson flatly replied with adamant confidence. "We were a good half day behind him. How the hell could he have seen us? He ain't no damned Indian; he can't stick his damned ear to the ground and hear us goddamned comin'!"

"So just what are you thinking, Simpson?" asked Brand, his tone edging toward caustic. "You're supposed to be the big-time hunter with all the brains."

Sourly Logan added, "And so far this half-blind scumlicker has left ya with your ass in your hands."

"You two assholes listen to me real good," Simpson acidly started.

He separately fixed each man with eyes filled with cold fury and malicious contempt. For hours he had been chiding himself, and he knew it was unprofessional to do this. Yet in his self-admonishment he knew, from the fear and uncertainty clawing the inside of his stomach, that he was hunting prey that was not only vicious, but smart—possibly smarter than he was. And the fact that Chance was desperate only enhanced the growing apprehension inside Simpson. For he had often seen, and hunted, the results of savage desperation. Thus he tended to act very cautiously, his desire to win being ferocious but his desire to survive being even stronger. And he was unsure of the two men with whom he had just recently teamed up. He didn't know exactly how they would perform if confronted with adversity. This, he grimly acknowledged to himself, was the most dangerous factor of all.

Brand's mouth hung open in rage, ready to hurl a retort. But in the brief, tense pause, a voice called forth from the darkness behind Simpson, "No. You three assholes listen to me."

Instinctively their hands reached for revolvers. But the distinct clicking sound of a revolver being cocked discouraged any further movement. "Don't do it, boys," warned the flat voice mockingly. Knowing they were easy targets because of the firelight, they were paralyzed, uneasily aware of the fear generating inside them as they unsuccessfully searched the darkness for a figure.

"Who's there?" called Simpson.

"Show yourself," snapped Logan.

"I see what you were getting at, Matt," the voice slowly said. "Pretty good deduction."

"Who the hell are you?" growled Simpson. "Chance?"

"No," the man said. He stepped closer, but all the men could see was a tall dark figure, barely discernible some thirty feet away. The clouds which were rolling north covered the moon completely. "If I was him I probably would have killed you by now."

"Then what do you want?" Logan asked.

"Talk about Matt's analysis," the man replied.

"How did you sneak up on us without us hearing you?" Simpson asked.

"Took off my spurs. But with all that mouth going back and forth, it wouldn't have been too hard anyway." The man paused and took another step forward. "Pays to be careful in my business, fellers. You ought to know more about caution than what you've shown, Matt; you been a hunter for years. But I guess amateurs like Logan and Brand will ruin this business soon enough. I mean, any man who would call Chance a 'half-blind scumlicker' doesn't know too much more about the real world than that greenbacks are green and whores have sewer tunnels."

"Forget them," Simpson snapped, feeling the enmity radiating from his comrades at having to bear the insults of the mysterious stranger looming in the dark. He had the uneasy feeling that the man was trying to taunt either Logan or Brand into gunplay. "What about what I said?"

"About backtracking, then heading South? The thought had crossed my mind, but I wasn't sure if he'd do that . . . until I lost him too."

"So why are you telling us?" Simpson inquired.

"Just one professional to another one is all, Matt," the man affably replied. Then he continued, "See what you think about this: Chance backtracks through the canyons and hills east of here. Then he heads south for the easier traveling on the plains, with one idea in mind. And what do you think that is, Matt?"

Simpson grunted. Then, as if he had known the answer the whole time, he said, "The wagon train from Sons."

"Exactly," said the stranger with supreme arrogance.

Confused, Logan cut in, "Why would he do that?"

"Them wagon trains usually got army escorts," Brand added knowingly.

Simpson looked over his right shoulder, snorting disdain at his two partners, finally admitting to himself that he was stuck with amateurs. He realized that the stranger had the situation read perfectly, either out of intuition or knowledge. He also realized they wouldn't leave the campsite alive. But if he could keep the stranger talking, and if Logan or Brand didn't do anything impulsive out of recklessness and fear, then he might have a chance for a surprise play.

"They don't have any escort, feller. Every soldier around Texas that can be spared is being used to put down a massive Comanche and Cheyenne uprising," the stranger tautly replied, his tone bordering on exasperation. "And I wish you two amateur scumlickers would kindly butt yourselves out of the conversation."

"Why you son-of-a—" Logan started.

"Shut your face!" Simpson vehemently interrupted.

"Thank you, Matt," the stranger said politely.

Peering intensely into the darkness, trying to discern more of the stranger's form, Simpson continued saying casually, "So you also figured that he's gone to link up with those settlers, huh? For protection maybe?"

"That, and to confuse anyone who might be following him. Without any bluebellies I'm sure he won't have much problem persuading those people to let him ride with them."

"Yeah. I guess Chance can be pretty persuasive," Simpson said glumly.

"A little too slick for those boys with you," taunted the stranger.

Logan and Brand were on the verge of uncontrollable rage; their hurt pride and anger were getting the best of them. Simpson knew the situation was quickly getting out of hand, and he also knew now for sure that the stranger was looking for an excuse to gun down the three of them. The palavering was just a preliminary, a way for the stranger to confirm any uncertainties he might have about Chance.

Hastily, Simpson asked, "You think Chance will find that outfit?"

"It's logical. There's a trail near the Divide, a day and a half out of Sons—or the closest thing to a trail around here. Oxbow's been unused for years, and the Jackass Mail is even worse. Besides, both of them are too far south. So I figure it's safe to assume Chance will run into any outfit on the trail."

Simpson nodded. "Reckon you got it all figured out, Mister—?"

"Neems. Lawrence Neems. And you reckon pretty good."

"Hunter?" Simpson asked.

Neems grunted affirmation.

"Thought maybe I was supposed to know you," Simpson said.

"Maybe you do," Neems responded evenly. "It could be you do, feller."

"So now what?" asked a belligerent Logan, his sharp tone indicating that his dignity had been severely injured.

"Up to you, scumlicker," the hunter said from the darkness, taking another step forward. "I'll watch Matt here hogtie you two scumlickers to your saddles. Then me and your boss can talk some things over."

"The hell you say!" rasped Brand, rising slowly to his feet, his face flushed with anger and venomous challenge.

"One more word out of you, halfass scumlicker, and I'll blow your kneecap off," Neems threatened softly. Then he ordered, "You two get up nice and slow. Matt, you tie these boys up, like I said."

"You're not going to do what he says, are ya, Matt?" asked a worried Brand.

Simpson's face was a picture of complete bewilderment. He looked dispassionately at Logan and Brand, not sure what to say or do. There was something peculiar about Neems' tone and manner, something sinister about his words and demeanor. Simpson was frozen with confusion and nervousness.

"Sure you are, Matt," Neems encouraged, his tone suddenly cold and sardonic, causing Simpson to jerk his head toward the hunter. "Me and you will be riding high and mighty, with Chance's money filling our pockets, while these two sorry scumlickers dangle from their horses, cursing their lack of brains and guts."

There was now a scornful, caustic tone to Neems' voice that chilled Simpson with horror. He knew Neems was trying to frighten his already enraged, confused partners into going for their guns with his taunts, and it was working. Both Logan's and Brand's faces were slowly twisting with hatred and angry contempt.

"This guy talks like he knows you, Simpson," accused Logan, with acid loathing in his voice, both fearful and indignant.

"What the hell's goin' on here, Simpson?" snarled Brand.

"Don't you see what he's trying to do?" Simpson countered stubbornly. "He's talking like that to make you mad so you'll go for your guns!"

"C'mon, Matt," Neems chided. "You can do better than that. Me and you had this all planned out."

"He's lying! Don't listen to him!" Simpson cried in horror, his eyes going wide as Logan and Brand reached for their revolvers, faces wild with hatred. "Don't, you crazy bastards!" But it was too late by the time he'd shrieked his warning. And he knew the only thing possible would be to try for his revolver and hope for a lucky shot at the treacherous Neems.

Yet when Simpson whirled for his chance, his hope literally died, for he turned to face certain death, already blazing blue-orange flame from the blackness of night. Smoke belched forth and roaring gunshots sounded like cannonblast as they penetrated the brittle silence.

Neems' first shot from his Colt Dragoon tore through Logan's sternum, ripped his heart into mush, then lodged in his spine. While Logan fell backward in death, his mouth agape in terror and shock, Brand took the hunter's second bullet in the lower portion of his left lung, where it then glanced off the sixth rib and made a bloody exit out his back.

Crouched low, Simpson had his .36 Remington cocked and leveled at Neems. But as he swung toward Neems, Matt Simpson took a hurricane of four successive bullets in the chest, stomach and side. The first one blasted into the left side of his chest, jerking him upright as if he'd just knocked heads with a buffalo. The second one opened his stomach and twisted him violently sideways and back, his feet dancing a jig of death. Blood from his wounds sprayed with a crimson shower the dead strewn near his feet. The last two heavy-caliber slugs shredded the back of his left arm, cutting through the tricep, splintering ribs, lodging in his lungs and throwing him viciously backward. His tattered corpse slammed to the crimson-soaked ground as if a boulder had rolled him over.

Neems opened the cylinder, dropped the spent shells on the ground, and quickly put in six fresh cartridges. Fully loaded, he holstered the Colt Dragoon.

"Amateurs, Simpson," he said, a low guffaw escaping his throat as he turned and became one with the darkness. "They'll be the death of us all."

The Redemption

5

Crawling toward the western horizon, the late-afternoon sun glared hellfire down upon the settlers, its hostility nearly equaling that of the land over which the caravan rolled. The line of sixteen mule-drawn wagons trundled up the pass. The rock-strewn incline gradually led from the far-reaching prairie of the north-central plains behind the caravan into the higher elevation of the great plains. It was more of the same brown desolation, except that the treeless terrain became more obdurate with rock. Now travel would become harder and more dangerous.

The caravan, with pack horses and several head of cattle flanking its sides, was making its way up the trail toward a pinnacle of rock when a hot breeze stirred dust from the west. The wind brought with it a rancid odor which suddenly enveloped the first few wagons; and slowly the miasma's invisible cloud reached the others.

The lead wagon came to a halt, causing a chain reaction of stopping the great canvas-covered worm.

Under a babble of coughing and gagging, the man driving the lead wagon called out to the wagonmaster, "Damn, Frank! What in blazing hell's that stink?" His prune face was nearly covered with unkempt muttonchop sideburns. He was a burly man in his late forties with virtually no neck; instead, a large head rested on a thick stump. His hands were large and calloused, the right grasping the reins to his team, the left holding a bullwhip. His wife, holding her hands over her nose and mouth, sat beside him on the seat, grimacing her distaste. Their three children peeked apprehensively between their parents' bodies and over their shoulders.

"Can't rightly say until I check it out," replied the wagon-master atop his brown gelding, a black kerchief now over his nose and mouth. He was a large, broad-shouldered man of forty. He wore brown denim pants, black boots with spurs, a dark shirt and a matching wide-brimmed hat. He also wore a holstered Colt .44, like many of the other men.

Galloping his mount from the rear, the assistant wagon-master made his way to the front. As the result of pumping hooves, clouds of brown dust settled over the families huddled around the fronts and sides of their wagons.

Pulling up alongside Frank, the assistant anxiously inquired, "Got somethin' dead over the rise?" He was blond, with a long, lanky build. His skin was smooth, and the hardness he tried to set on his face was almost comical. His bright blue eyes, which always appeared frightened, revealed his lack of experience and ability to control his emotions. He was not quite in his midtwenties. "What do you think, Mr. Jenkins?" he asked, clearly deferential toward the older man as he hacked, spat, then pulled a kerchief over his face.

The animals were becoming as uneasy and uncomfortable from the stench as were the settlers, who were now milling about and grumbling in tones of fearfulness and confusion.

Jenkins grunted perplexity. As his blond assistant unbooted his own Winchester .44/40, Jenkins instructed in a loud tone to the families, "Everyone sit tight. Me and Bob will go have a look. No need to worry; it's probably just some dead cattle."

They turned their backs on the caravan and quickly guided their horses up the incline, disappearing over the crest of the rise within seconds.

"What in the name of. . . ." gasped Bob, jerking his gelding to a stop.

Statues of shock and grim dismay, both wagonmasters gazed out over the flat rocky plateau. Straight ahead, a little more than a hundred feet, a stagecoach lay battered on its side. Yet their horror had been immediately riveted on the scene of carnage related to the overturned vehicle.

Then their eyes fixed on the lone figure of Chance, who was mounted and sitting thirty feet in front of the massacre, his Henry resting against his right shoulder, pointing skyward.

"It's him," muttered Bob, his tone one of apprehension. "The one who murdered all those people back in town."

Ignoring the obvious revelation, Jenkins spurred his mount toward the unmoving one-eyed man.

There were ten visible corpses altogether, strewn in various attitudes of death in and about the red-and-black Concord coach. All were mutilated to some extent. All had been scalped. Six were riddled with arrows. And one man, possibly the driver, had been shot to death with as many as twelve arrows. He lay on his back, outstretched across the right front wheel.

Another dead body lay half in and half out the side window, its severed head resting on the ground beneath. This corpse, like three others, had been a soldier escort. The soldiers' bodies had been ravaged the worst, and their blue uniforms, caked with dried blood and dirt, were nearly shredded from brutalized bodies.

It was evident they had been dead for some time, although the heat of a Texas summer caused decay much faster than normal. The eaters of death only enhanced the decaying process. The vile stench of putrefaction was an all-encompassing, cloying misery, and it intensified twofold as Jenkins and Bob closed the distance between themselves and Chance. Now, as close to the dead as they wanted to be without losing their senses to nausea, both saw clearly the vicious wounds—genital mutilation on both males and females, severed appendages, gouged eyeballs, sliced throats and skulls split open.

The teems of flies were so great they seemed like tattered rugs moving over the dead. Here and there scorpions could be seen joining the macabre feast. A large buzzard was digging for the juicier remains of a female body. Evidently his brothers had already gorged themselves earlier, judging by the shredded clothing and the chunks of flesh missing from the corpses.

For several long seconds Jenkins and Bob stared in amazement at the picture of stoicism Chance presented. His Stetson was pulled down low, and a black kerchief, damp with sweat, covered the lower portion of his face, resting well up on the bridge of his nose. One squinting eye, eerie in its somber appraisal of the living and the dead, was all that could be seen.

Jenkins found himself uncomfortable in Chance's presence. The one-eyed man's silence rankled him, and was almost as chilling as the brutal scene of death about their feet.

At length the wagonmaster, for lack of anything else to say, asked, "Indians?"

Chance continued to study the man coldly for a second, then nodded perfunctorily, as if a dark thought of his had been intruded upon. "Would appear that way," he muttered. "Apaches."

"How do you know they're Apaches?" Jenkins asked. "This is Comanche territory too."

Chance shrugged easily. "Mainly because there's a few dead Apache braves scattered behind the coach."

The note of condescension in Chance's tone escaped Jenkins, who exchanged a worried look with Bob while Chance remained silent and stone still, out of both private thought and exhaustion.

He had ridden hard and almost constantly since late afternoon of the day before. He knew of the trail out of Sons, and after the self-defense killings of the murdering thieves Bobby and Brad, a plan of action had formed in his mind—a safer and more elusive course to follow than the one he had originally forced himself into.

Timing and luck had played a hand in his long ride south in order for him to intercept the westward-bound pioneers. Just as he had seen the wagon train coming toward him from a mile or more out on the flat prairie atop his vantage point on the rise, so he had spotted from atop a hill the trio of hunters following him near the Llano Estacado. Then he had gone through twisting arroyos and gorges, able to cover his tracks in the rocky soil, making it hard—if not impossible—for his pursuers to track him. Using no campfires, covering whatever trash needed disposal, as well as burying excrement—both his own and that of his horse, when possible—he was able to lose them while he waited and rested for several hours in a cave-pocked gorge.

Several hours ago Chance had come across the aftermath of an Apache massacre. Since then he had waited for the arrival of the wagon caravan he hoped would pass by the unexpected scene of death. This might help him persuade the settlers to let him ride along as an extra gun against any trouble, and as a guide who was relatively familiar with the country ahead. For not only was he seeking to circumvent any quest for his capture by either lawful or unlawful means, but he was running desperately low on water and supplies. Yet his money was enough to pay for any provisions he took. And in this hostile, barren land, a man without water soon became a sun-bleached skeleton.

"What are you going to tell the others, Mr. Jenkins?" Bob asked, stifling a fit of gagging he felt trying to overcome his nervous agitation.

"The truth," Jenkins sternly replied. "What else can I tell them, boy?"

"That you've got a free gun," Chance flatly injected.

Jenkins turned hard eyes on Chance. "How's that, mister?"

"Just like I said it."

Dark eyes studying Chance suspiciously from behind narrowly cracked eyelids, Jenkins asked, "You mean we let you ride with us in exchange for your gun?" His attitude was caught between a sneer and confusion.

"I know the country you're going to be traveling," Chance supplied with resolute confidence. "I could scout and guide."

"That's my job, mister, and I'll lay money that I know these parts better than any man around," Jenkins emphatically declined. "Besides, I already have me an assistant."

"Him?" Chance asked flatly, staring at the assistant, who eyed Chance with defiance. "He's nothing but a kid," Chance proclaimed. His comment was not meant to be derogatory; he was merely stating a fact. But Bob tensed, drawing rigid with unconcealed anger, feeling a severe affront to his manhood because of Chance's words, and ready to issue a retort. Chance quickly added in a placating tone, "I have nothing against the boy. It just so happens I know Apaches, and I know you've got real problems ahead. Another gun couldn't hurt."

"Yeah," growled Bob, sensing his opportunity to lash back at the callous one-eyed stranger, "we know your gun's good, mister. After seeing those men you murdered back in town, nobody will doubt your word on that."

"I didn't kill anybody who didn't deserve it, kid," Chance

said. "A long time ago those men I shot nearly killed me. It usually helps if you know what you're talking about before you open your mouth. That way you don't end up looking like someone else's ass, kid." Chance quickly shifted his attention to Jenkins, leaving Bob slackjawed with mounting rage, then continued before Bob could respond. "So how about it, dude? I'll pay for whatever I need."

Out of indecision and exasperation, Jenkins sighed. "What about the law, mister?" he rasped.

"The law may or may not be after me. If they were then I've probably lost them. A wagon train would be the last place they'd suspect. But if the law or any bluebellies show, and you feel you've got to turn me over, then tell me well ahead of time so I can get a jump."

Chance's voice was hard with ice and underlying menace. Yet his strong tone appeared to have a convincing effect on Jenkins who, even though he knew there were ulterior motives to Chance's proposal, sensed honesty underneath a cruel-looking exterior. That this man was indeed honorable, he wasn't certain. But Frank Jenkins had always been one to give a man the benefit of the doubt. Thus he found himself believing—or wanting to believe, due to the veracity of the one-eyed stranger's analysis of a grave situation—the sincerity of Chance's words.

Young Bob Howard, however, was just the opposite. He felt an ugly bitterness toward Chance steadily growing inside. His blood rushed, and, much to his dismay, he found his heart pounding uncontrollably with fear. He felt threatened and insulted. Yet what he hated most was not just the presence of Chance, but the fact that he had to acknowledge to himself the uncomfortable tension stirring within. His pride was damaged, tainted with shame because of the wild fright surging through him. Chance, the threat of possible Indian attack, and his first close encounter with brutal death combined to create his irritation and terror.

After looking long and hard at Chance, Jenkins assented, somewhat perfunctorily, "Personally, I don't think it would hurt if you rode with us. But it's not up to me."

"You're the wagonmaster, aren't you?"

Even with the kerchief concealing most of his face, Jenkins

could tell Chance was scowling.

"Yeah," Jenkins replied. "But Mr. Bradley's in charge of this outfit."

Seeking to escape most of the repulsive odor, the settlers were gathered near the last few wagons of the caravan in a tight cluster. And when the figures of Jenkins, Howard and Chance appeared over the crest and came down the trail toward them, all eyes watched the trio expectantly. But when they drew nearer, gasps of surprise and alarm filled the air, seeing the stranger with the black eyepatch and recognizing him as the source of the trouble which had erupted back in town.

The prune-faced, burly man showed no fear as the trio reined to a halt in front of the assembled pioneers. "What's going on, Frank?" he growled, looking up at the mounted men, coldly acknowledging Chance's presence without surprise but with obvious dismay. Standing, his bulky, two-hundred-pound figure almost attained a height of six feet.

The three pulled their kerchiefs off almost simultaneously. Howard sat slightly to the right and behind Chance, glowering at him and brooding silently. Jenkins flanked Chance's left, and appeared either embarrassed by or frightened of what he had to reveal. The wagonmaster sighed softly, snorted, then scratched his nose, while Chance, giving the entire outfit a cursory assessment, remained somber.

"Might as well lay all the cards out for everyone, Mr. Bradley," Jenkins said. Most of the group studied Chance apprehensively, but gave Jenkins their undivided attention as he continued. "Looks as if a stage coming down from Fort Union got ambushed by an Apache warparty."

"Apaches!" cried a small, red-haired man with a shaggy beard. His consternation was echoed by others, now restless and horrified. "I knew we shouldn't have left home without a soldier escort! Damn it to hell and back, Bradley, this land is full of them red, scalping, raping bastards!" the man whined.

"Watch that tongue, Bugler!" Bradley viciously snapped, turning and staring the man down into silence. "Pretty soon you'll have the women and kids using that filthy language, damn it! And you're getting everybody lathered into an uproar!"

"Sorry, Mr. Bradley," Bugler muttered feebly. A mixture of emotions were directed by everyone toward the sniveling Bugler, the angry Bradley, the menacing and sudden appearance of Chance and the news of the Indian ambush. "I only—"

"You only what, Bugler?" Bradley said, his tone condescending. "You only expected a gravy ride?" Then he directed his words toward everyone, hoping to reassure them with calm words of strength. "We all knew it wasn't going to be easy. It's a long way to California. And we've come this far from Louisiana, so I really couldn't see the sense of anyone's turning tail because of a few miserable Injuns—if that's what any of you are thinking.

"You asked me to organize and lead this outfit. I know most of ya as friends, neighbors and relatives, and most of ya know me. And you know I've never been one to run from anything in my life. I sure as hell is hot ain't running from a few lathered-up redskins. We got enough guns and ammunition and manpower to hold off trouble. Be nice to have the Seventh Cavalry or whatever the frig, for Chrissakes. But we ain't got it, 'cause I felt we could fend for ourselves. . . . Now," Bradley finished, turning and facing the mounted trio again, looking briefly at Chance with hard suspicion, "what's he want? Running from the law, ain't ya, mister?"

"Like you said, dude," Chance said flatly. The enmity in his nature was expressed by the penetrating ice of his lone green eye. "I've never been one to run from anything in my life. Now I'm only trying to stay free. Those men I killed back in town almost beat me to death nine years ago. I've been in prison for eight. I paid my debt to society, and they paid theirs to me. The law doesn't have anything to do with what concerns me and you."

Under normal circumstances Chance would have offered no explanation for his actions. But, although his motives were obvious to him, they were not to the settlers. It was necessary to clear the air before Bradley launched himself into another monologue, if he was to obtain what he wanted.

"He wants to ride with us, Mr. Bradley," Jenkins supplied hastily, giving Bradley an excuse to tear his scowl from Chance and peer quizzically at his wagonmaster. "Said he'd give us his gun and help. I figure that's worth something, especially in the light of this new development. He also said he'd pay for whatever he needed."

"I'm only going as far as the New Mexico-Arizona border," Chance informed, his tone still easy, but his attitude and the knowledge of his lethal capabilities having an unsettling effect on Bradley and the others.

Bradley's scowl turned into angry confusion. "I don't think it's worth something except a pain in the butt, Frank. Law finds us harboring a fugitive, we're all in trouble." Bradley had an odd way of speaking. One moment he used simple words and vulgar expressions, and the next he seemed almost scholarly.

"He said he'd pull out if we spotted any law or soldiers," Jenkins quickly pointed out. He considered the presence of Chance's gun an asset, even if Chance was helping for purely selfish motives. "I think we could use him, even though he's using us for cover. And we won't be hitting any military outposts until we're close to Arizona territory."

Grunting irritation at the truth of Jenkins' statement, Bradley frowned at Chance. "All right, mister," he reluctantly assented, looking at Jenkins, then back at Chance. "My wagonmaster's a good judge of men, and a good handler of 'em, too. You do like he or I tell you to, don't cause any trouble and stick to your word, and you can ride on with us. You understand what I just said, mister?"

"It's as clear as where we stand, dude," Chance slowly replied, a small grin creasing his lips.

Briefly Bradley was baffled by the one-eyed man's remark, but he accepted it with seeming indifference although he felt he was either being ridiculed or scorned, or both, by the enigmatic response. And his dislike for the stranger was enhanced as a cold chill bit at him when he looked at Chance. "Your name's Chance, right? Least that's what I heard the sheriff call you."

"That's my name, Mr. Bradley."

"Kind of an unusual name, ain't it, mister?" Bradley asked.

"Not for the kind of life I've had," the one-eyed man replied, bringing forth a low grunt of disapproval from Bradley.

95

Bradley turned to the settlers, his face hard with determination. "Fine with you folks if the stranger rides? I hope it is, because it looks like we could sure use him. If he causes any problems I'll send him on his way."

At the moment, most were too stunned by the new development of the Apache threat to be concerned with Chance. Some were leery about accepting the stranger, but most nodded and shrugged agreement with Bradley. And Bradley, satisfied, turned to face Chance.

"All right, Mr. Chance," Bradley tautly said. "You act right and everything will be just fine. Tell him what you want him to do, Frank. But first we got to get away from this stink." Bradley turned toward the settlers. "Everybody hop on! We're movin' out!"

"Don't you think we ought to bury the dead?" asked a woman, in a tone of amazement and dismay, as if she had just been awakened from a nightmare.

"I guess we could," said an annoyed Bradley. "What do you think, Frank?"

"It would take awhile. I counted the bodies, and Chance says there's a few Apaches behind the coach I didn't see."

"Forget the redskins," grumbled Bradley. "We'll just bury the whites and save time."

"That's a gross attitude to take toward other human beings, Ben," called an astonished woman standing beside Bugler. Suppressing her consternation caused her thin, cracked lips to tremble.

"I agree with Martha, Brad," said Bugler, his tone lacking conviction. He didn't care; he was seeing only his opportunity to strike back at Bradley in the aftermath of Bradley's disparagement toward him.

"You want to bury them red, scalping, raping bastard heathens, like you called them, Bugler, then be my guest! In this heat it's going to be an unpleasant, dirty job anyway. But it's a decent thing we're doing, burying our dead comrades. So let's get it done and get out of here!"

As Bradley brushed past the horses and headed toward his wagon, the crowd slowly dispersed, hesitatingly resigning themselves to the situation out of fearful vacillation. Yet they were determined, because they had willingly accepted the

96

venture westward, to appear in control of themselves.

Spotting the woman he'd helped back in town, Chance remained unmoving in his saddle. Catching her eye, he felt, and saw from the bewildered look on her beautifully sculptured, high-cheekboned face, and from the infatuated beam glowing in her uneasy blue eyes, that she had been intensely watching him the whole time. He smiled at her, out of the lust he felt stirring within, aroused by the fact that it had been quite awhile since he had caused such a reaction in a woman.   He was proud of it, and suddenly found himself wanting to pursue her.

She in turn accepted his look with a smile, yet her smile was warm and inviting. She was fascinated by the one-eyed stranger, who, she knew, would be a fine-looking man without the brutal reminders of a grim past.

"Chance!" Bradley barked in annoyance.

The one-eyed man slowly turned from his eager appraisal of the woman and faced the surly Bradley, who was pointing his brown Stetson at the mounted man as if emphasizing his displeasure with the overall situation. "Don't just sit there! Grab a shovel and follow me!" He turned, stalking off, but stopped almost immediately and added, "And since you want to prove yourself so useful, make it the biggest shovel you can find!"

"Certainly, Mr. Bradley," Chance softly said, a wry smile twisting his face into a sneer, as Bradley once again strode up the rise. "To follow you I need the biggest one I can find."

Dusk was like a black band of mourning settling over the charred rubble of Smiling Sons as Laster and his astonished men scanned the nearly leveled remains of the town, with its surrounding farmhouses, from two hundred feet afar to the north. Now, more than a full day after its total annihilation, the fires had nearly died, leaving only wisps of gray smoke that drifted skyward from the scorched earth, which was blackened for hundreds of yards in nearly every direction. Only a few buildings were left, though even these were ablaze and ready to fall to the ground at any moment.

It was a grim, awesome picture of death and destruction, and to take it in in one eyeful was impossible. The four men sat rock steady in their saddles, their mounts snorting and swishing tails in unrest as the sickly-sweet odor of burnt flesh and rotting death combined with the heat and the pungent smell of small fires burning themselves out on spilt blood, assorted corpses and the few wooden structures still intact. The odor assaulted their senses mercilessly because of a slight breeze which had suddenly kicked up from the Gulf. The low humming of the wind, and the crackling of fire and glowing embers from the smoldering tomb, made an ominous requiem for the slaughtered townspeople in the otherwise chilling quiet.

"If he was here, Sim," Mamoreck somberly said, "then we can best forget that money."

Laster offered no immediate response. Instead, he continued to gaze solemnly forward for several seconds. Then he heeled his mount into motion, saying gravely, "Let's check it out."

Mamoreck shrugged indifference, while Ridgeway and Stanley moved out to join Laster. Then he spurred his horse onward behind them.

Black kerchiefs pulled up over their noses, the four men slowly turned their mounts up the east end of the main street. Blackened bodies of men and horses, some untouched by the ravages of fire, littered the street from side to side where the buildings had once stood. Now were only heaps of ashes, soot being blown around in the breeze and greeting the riders. Black shapes of scavengers could be seen digging for food, as well as a lone dog that rummaged through the debris.

Spreading out sufficiently in order to make their way around the dead, the men continued to guide their nervous animals up the street. Disturbed by the presence of life, the vultures spread wings and flapped skyward, squawking irritation.

The smoke was thick enough to sting their eyes, and the heat from several fires was strong enough to draw beads of sweat from morbidly curious faces. Under the kerchiefs the faces were stubbled with thick bristles, their eyes even more expressive of the weariness their journey had produced.

Ridgeway's horse cried loudly and reared when the bottom half of a burning structure to his right crumpled to the ground, along with a short section of canopy. A cloud of smoke and soot blossomed upward and halfway across the street, covering Ridgeway and Stanley in a thick gagging fog.

Noting the arrow-riddled bodies, split skulls and missing scalps, Stanley said grimly, "Hard to believe a handful of Indians could do all this."

Laster had dismounted. Holding his mare by the reins, he toed several of the bodies, examining them apathetically. "I'd say more than a handful wiped this bunch out," he murmured, as another burning structure near the west end toppled into the street.

"Hell," Mamoreck exclaimed, "all we been hearin' for months is how the tribes are all on the warpath."

"They Comanche or Kiowa, Sim?" Stanley asked.

"Neither," Laster called across the street, opposite the others, examining several buckskin-clad braves with black bandanas wrapped around their heads. "Apaches."

"Sim sure knows his Injuns, don't he?" muttered a mocking Ridgeway, chuckling to himself, drawing blank stares from Stanley and Mamoreck.

Ridgeway's sarcasm reached Laster's ears. He looked over at the others, bringing himself erect just as a loud moan came from behind the smoldering ruins to his left. Drawing and cocking his Army Colt, Laster took several steps toward the charred debris. Where there had once been an alleyway was now filled with burnt wood and ashes from the buildings which had flanked it. Here the piles of black debris were five feet deep in spots.

Hearing the consistent moaning and scrabbling sounds of the person on the other side attempting to climb the pile of rubble, the men quickly fell in by Laster's side, revolvers drawn.

Their curiosity was immediately quelled as a figure, that they could only determine was a man because of the amount of soot covering his body, clambered over the pile.

The groans of torment and grief escaping Sheriff Burch's mouth were more than enough to inform the four of his plight. For several seconds Burch gasped horribly, his eyes glazed over as he studied the foursome through blurry, pain-wracked vision. He held a Winchester loosely in his right hand. His left arm was held unnaturally close to his body, limp and useless. Now the arrow that had rendered his left arm ineffective was

99

jagged at both ends from where he had unsuccessfully tried to pull it out, only to break it in the attempt. Other arrows in his right shoulder, left thigh, and high in his chest were broken off in similar fashion. His clothing was torn in the places where bullets had shredded material and flesh. The soot stuck to his sweat and blood in black patches.

Burch managed to raise himself to his knees before his rifle fell from his hands into the side of the pile. Then his eyes rolled back in his head and he toppled slowly forward, sliding sesveral feet down the rubble. He rolled up at Laster's feet face down.

Uncocking and holstering his revolver, Laster quickly bent down toward Burch, felt for a pulse, and, finding one, ordered over his shoulder, "Give me a canteen." He then rolled Burch on his back. "Looks like we got the sheriff here," he said, holding Burch's tin star between his fingers, then turning his head and grabbing the canteen Mamoreck was holding toward him. He doused Burch's blackened face with water.

Seeing this didn't immediately revive him, Laster snarled softly, snatching Burch's shirtfront and slapping him several times until the sheriff moaned and forced his eyes partially open.

After shaking Burch roughly, either out of anger that Burch wasn't responding quickly enough to satisfy him, or anticipating frustration that Chance might be dead and the money lost, Laster harshly snapped, "Sheriff! Sheriff! What happened here?"

Burch groaned miserably and his eyes fell shut. "Apaches. Hun . . . dreds. . . ." He grew stiff and heaved forth blood from his mouth, groaning in pain. Some of the red gore landed on Laster's right arm.

Fearing that the sheriff was slipping away into death before he wanted him to, Laster lashed Burch across the face again. "Sheriff! Chance!"

"Keep slapping him like that, Sim, and you'll lose him too quick," Stanley chided.

"Shuddup!" Laster rasped, holding Burch upright, pouring more water over his head and face, then shaking him violently, his teeth clenched in venomous anger. "A one-eyed man, sheriff!" he growled loudly into Burch's face. Then he eased up as he saw the sheriff stirring and opening his eyes. "The one-eyed man Chance—was he here? Did he leave before the Apaches came?"

"Left," he stammered, almost incoherent. "Killed men . . . left. . . ."

Laster jolted his head around toward the others. His crooked nose, long chin and knitted eyebrows made him as ugly and sinister looking as a gargoyle. His expression of triumph blazed an evil grin across his sweat-sheened, sooty features, made him appear even more ferocious, in a macabre way, like a candle stuck inside a skull.

Even Laster's partners were unnerved by the fiendish expression of mindless greed on his face.

Burch sighed his last breath. Laster turned and looked at the sheriff distastefully. Grunting mock sympathy, he shoved Burch into the ground, then quickly rose to his feet.

"Well, that's just fine, Sim," grumbled Ridgeway. "But which way's he headed for?"

"No problem," Laster replied, sounding irritated by the question. "I knew some clown who used to ride with him. It's somewhere in western New Mexico territory or eastern Arizona. All we have to do is hurry and pick up his trail."

"Lotta country to cover, if you ask me," muttered Ridgeway.

"What about that Apache warparty?" Stanley sharply inquired.

Laster snorted, spat, then climbed into his saddle. "I'm willing to risk it. Hell, boys," he said placatingly, "we've ridden these parts all our lives. And we've been able to turn back a few Indians when we had to."

"Yeah—a few," Stanley sourly said. "But the sheriff was muttering something about hundreds."

Solemnly Laster nodded, while coldly eyeing each man. "You're not going to chickenshit out on me, are ya, Tod?" Then he shrugged. "Well, if you do that'll just be more for me and whoever decides to come."

Laster tugged on the reins, turned his mare westward and moved away from the fearful, undecided trio.

"You know I'm no chickenshit!" Stanley angrily called

after Laster. Then he climbed into his saddle and headed to catch up with Laster. Ridgeway and Mamoreck fell in behind silently.

It was as if they were trying to prove their worth as men to Laster, as if he were constantly challenging their manhood.

Laster pulled his kerchief down and spat on a charred corpse. "Then shut your face and follow me out of this stink-hole."

There had been no incidents since the burial of the dead, nor had they encountered any more evidence of the Apache uprising. Now, more than seven hours later, with roughly seventeen miles' distance from the scene of slaughter, the Bradley outfit was settled for the night, though vigilant for any sign of trouble.

The spot chosen for the journey's recess was excellent from a defensive standpoint. The flat, barren tableland which stretched out in every direction around the corraled wagons provided those assigned first sentry duty outside the circled encampment with easy surveillance of the terrain's perimeter. Aided by the light from a half moon in a cloudless sky, it was almost too easy. Yet all were aware that the protection afforded them now was strictly an accident of geography. For soon the earth would become treacherous, with rugged mountain ranges, broad desert basins, lofty canyon walls and wind-eroded arroyos. The safety of the plains would be only a memory. And the threat of death, from both nature and man, would loom ever more imminent with each step, with each trundling turn of wagonwheels toward some of the most hostile and virtually unexplored desert land known.

Walking from his bedroll toward a water barrel hanging from a wagon's side, Chance sucked in the cool night air through his nose. Somehow he was enjoying the tired ache in his body, possibly from the knowledge that he was relatively safe for the time being.

Nearing the barrel, the sounds of the animals herded and grazing outside the wagons, and the crunching of the guard's boots on rock, grew stronger to his keen hearing. His ears detected noise louder and more sharply than a normal person's might have. Because of having only one eye, Chance had made himself learn, over the years since the eye's loss, to use his other senses to their maximum. Thus he rarely noticed the hindrance unless the occasional fire inside his skull made him painfully aware of his handicap.

In his hours with the pioneers Chance had learned a few things about them. Most of what he'd learned had been through a short evening conversation with Jenkins, with whom he had built something of an affinity. A tacit deference had formed because each man was aware that the other was capable of handling difficult situations and experienced in the hardships of long travel over harsh country.

He'd learned that there were nine families in all headed for the Pacific Coast—the Bradleys, Meltons, Carlsbads, Deegans, McMeeleys, Jacknells, Smiths, Buglers and Thorntons—fifty people including himself. They were traveling at their own risk; it was a small outfit consisting of, for the most part, poor farmers, a tough-minded lot banded together, for the most part, courtesy of Ben Bradley's savings over the years. His financial status as a farmer had been slightly better than that of the other travelers, who were all now on a loan from Bradley. He often reminded them of that fact, though never reminding them of the high interest rate he'd connived them into.

There were two mess wagons loaded with food, extra water barrels and other supplies. The two largest families—the Carlsbads, with seven members, and the Smiths, with eight—had wagons to themselves. Another three wagons were also bulked with supplies and various items of necessity to ensure the safe completion of a journey that would cover close to twelve hundred miles and last more than two months. It was a journey that had begun more than a month ago; a journey, most were aware, that was filled with risk not just from man and nature, but from cholera. More than likely not a civilized soul would be encountered until they reach their next stopping point, Fort Bayard.

Chance had also learned that Bradley didn't know as much about Apaches as he had so facetiously boasted earlier.

The burly leader of the outfit had been furious when the others insisted on burying the dead Apaches, back at the ambush site. He had made it perfectly clear his main philosophy on Indians was that "The only good Injun is a dead Injun." Hardly an original thinker was he, but Chance sensed a bitter hatred inside Bradley for Indians, Apache or otherwise. And underneath Bradley's surly veneer Chance saw a man who would seize an opportunity to unleash his hatred to kill, or torture, any red man, possibly at the jeopardy of other lives. Thus, Chance was leery of Bradley's ability to lead or to remain levelheaded at any sign of possible danger.

And, due to Bradley's false belief that Indians would not attack at night—an error in judgment common among whites, usually dead ones—Chance had had to argue rigorously for more guards than just the one Bradley was going to post outside the campsite. This advice had been met with resentment by Bradley. But Jenkins backed Chance, and Bradley had begrudgingly resigned himself to Chance's will. This caused a mounting friction between the one-eyed man and the leader of the outfit, who felt his judgment had been tested. Because he had acquiesced in front of some of the others, he knew his competency was now being weighed, though they freely admitted that Bradley was chief financier. Thus his authority in at least one area was recognized as powerful.

But the most interesting, or aggravating, information had been presented to Chance by way of an unspoken warning. This had nagged him relentlessly for the past several hours. Jenkins had spotted Chance eyeing Mary Thornton with unmistakeable lust, several times during the day and evening. In a low tone Jenkins spoke about her to Chance, while acknowledging his own desire for her by saying she was the best-looking female he'd ever seen this side of the Appalachians. Chance didn't doubt that for one moment. Jenkins related also that several young men riding with the outfit sought to win her affection—another fact Chance didn't doubt for one moment because during the trip so far he'd witnessed several of the men, including Bob Howard, vying for her attention and approval. Not only that, but her father, Dick Thornton—a brawny, hard-eyed, mean-mouthed Protestant farmer—was extremely protective of her, occasionally scowling away a potential suitor, much to his daughter's dismay. Mary seemed terribly embarrassed by his harsh attitude and unrealistic disapproval.

Chance sullenly dwelled upon this particular fact for several seconds as he poured himself a tin cupful of water and slowly drank. Yet the potential hazards and the trouble the situation could beget only enhanced his desire to possess Mary Thornton.

Thinking about this development, he grinned sheepishly, pouring himself another cup of water. Chance glanced briefly around the solid phalanx of wagons abutting one another, seeing several dying fires burning down the remainder of buffalo-chip fuel, and women and children preparing to bed down for the night.

It was brazenness which made him decide to walk toward the Thorntons' wagon. He slowly ambled past several wagons, looking around intently, pretending to ensure security while trying to think of an excuse he could use to sneak in a word with the Thornton girl. He was feeling somewhat foolish about emotions he hadn't known in years.

If it was sheer lust to possess her body, then he could cure those feelings with a bout of sex and become wholly himself again. That is, if he could get her away from everyone, and if she consented, and if he didn't have to punch somebody in the mouth because of her.

To make himself appear legitimate, he became stern looking as he peeked into the back of a wagon. "Everything all right in there?" he asked in a solemn tone.

"Aaaaah, I'm undressed!" cried Mrs. Deegan, from the candlelit inside. "Of course everything's all right, you Peeping Tom!"

His face flushed crimson in embarrassment, Chance hurriedly tipped his hat in sincere apology. He stepped quickly away from the back of the wagon and the flaps slammed after him. "Sorry, ma'am," he called gruffly, his expression angry as he turned to face several grumbling men huddled around a fire.

Briefly Chance glowered challenge at them, offering no explanation, covering his discomposure with cold venom. This caused the eldest Deegan boy to stifle a curse he was about to hurl at the one-eyed man. Yet his dark scowl indicated to Chance that this was an incident he wasn't going to forget.

Within several seconds those who had been alarmed enough

to stick their heads out of the backs of wagons or peer across the campsite returned to their own business, realizing the mistake for what it was. Chance quickly shrugged off the incident and put it behind him, noticing with concealed delight that Mary Thornton was sticking her head through the canvas flaps, staring at him in surprise and mild concern.

As Chance pulled up behind her wagon, he touched the brim of his hat, wearing a somber expression. "Miss," he greeted quietly, sounding aloof, but hardly feeling indifferent.

"What's all that noise out there, Mary?" called a worried Mrs. Thornton from inside.

"It was nothing, Mother," Mary replied softly but firmly, eyeing Chance with the same interest she'd shown toward him earlier. "Go back to sleep."

"I was just checking to see if everyone was in, miss," Chance explained, suddenly at a loss for words.

Mary continued to eye Chance with quizzical infatuation. "Why are you doing this, mister?" she asked evenly, her tone clearly expressing her puzzlement.

Chance found himself surprised more by the strength in her voice than by the question. She seemed totally unperturbed by his scars and the fact that she must have known he was a killer. "Why am I doing what?" His tone had an edge. His face became uncontrollably hard with instinctive suspicion. Yet he was more at ease now that he felt impersonal.

Mary's grin was wide, happy. To Chance she appeared childlike. "This." She rolled her eyes and head from side to side, indicating the wagons. "It's a way of saving yourself, isn't it?" She said this with a trace of disappointment, not questioning concern.

Momentarily Chance considered this, holding her gaze with emotionless scrutiny. "Atonement?" he suggested at length.

"What?" Mary frowned, not sure of what she'd heard.

"Maybe," he slyly continued, "I'm destined to perform some magnanimous deed."

"To have me?" she bluntly inquired. Then she smiled demurely, mockingly, erasing the coldness her face had shown just a second ago. Now she was enjoying the look of foolish confusion the abruptness of her remark had left on Chance's face.

Chance quickly made an effort to appear unaffected by her boldness. He smiled, playing along with the insinuation, drawing hope from an audacity he had thought could never be possible from her. "That, Miss Thornton," Chance replied with sincere admiration and eager desire, "would be a truly magnanimous thing."

After he'd said it, he feared a negative reaction from her. But Mary seemed pleased, an odd look of wonder and fright playing on her features. Her mouth fell open and she was going to respond, just as the large figure of her father stepped from the darkness behind Chance. And Chance, seeing the look of concern as she stared past him, smoothly but quickly turned.

"You got any business here, mister?" rasped Dick Thornton. He was six feet three inches, two hundred five pounds of solid muscle and thick bones. Angrily he pulled up face to face with the considerably smaller one-eyed man. The size difference made him feel more confident that he could take Chance if it came down to a physical confrontation.

In suspicious outrage, Thornton fumed great gusts of air through his flared nostrils. "Besides trying to cheapen my daughter with your filthy mind?"

"Father!" she cried.

"Quiet, girl!" Thornton harshly commanded, turning his scowl on his daughter to assure her silence. Then he lowered his voice as he spoke to her. "This cheap trash is a murderer and God above only knows what else. And I hardly want him riding along with us, much less trying to dirty you with his impurities."

"I was just checking to see if everyone was all right, feller," Chance laconically injected. Thornton turned furious dark eyes on Chance again at the aloof sound of his voice.

"You sure do have a funny way of 'just checking,' mister," he sourly growled.

By now most of the men and women who weren't asleep had started to converge on the tart exchange between Thornton and Chance, although they could all easily tell it was Thornton who was the source of the heat. Several men yawned, while others grumbled curiosity as Bradley pushed his way through the group, rudely clearing a path for himself.

"What in blazing hell's going on now, Dick?" griped Bradley. In a white nightshirt and a cap with a fuzzy ball, he looked like a paunchy court jester. "Some of us are trying to get some sleep, damn it!"

Thornton glared at Bradley, waggling an accusing index finger at Chance. "I caught this scum of the earth you're letting ride with us leering at my girl like he was going to jump on her any minute."

"He was only talking to me, Daddy," Mary explained in disgust, having grown bitter with her father's austerity. She explained this for the benefit of Chance, who was the center of contemptuous attention. Howard and several of the others looked as hostile as a pack of starving wolves ready to devour prey.

"I said to stay out of it, Mary!" Thornton barked. "I know what this filth was intending!"

Only Bradley and several of the elders remained unconvinced by Thornton's cruel accusations about Chance and his intentions, for they knew the iron hand with which Thornton ruled his family, in particular his daughter. These men wanted to bring the conflict under control, and were irritated by the sudden disturbance, knowing the ridiculous impulsiveness upon which Thornton often acted when suspicious of anyone's intentions regarding not only his daughter, but anything else.

Bradley made a snicker of annoyance. The leathery skin twisted on the left side of his face in a frank show of displeasure. "Chance, what the blazing hell's going on?" he griped.

"Just going round to see if everything was safe," Chance explained, with some exasperation creeping into his even tone.

Mockingly, Bradley smiled at Thornton, looking at the man as if he considered him a pestilence. He waved off Thornton with a deprecating hand. "That's good enough for me, Thornton," he snorted, turning and walking quickly away. Several of the others did likewise.

"What?" bellowed Thornton, staring at the departing Bradley with indignation. "Just like that you're gonna—"

"Go to sleep, Thornton! Next time you cry wolf we're gonna stuff your mouth with a dead rattler!" Bradley rasped over his shoulder, amused with his own grim words of warning. "Damn it to hell and back," he grumbled under his breath.

Thornton turned on Chance. For a stretched second they considered each other, Chance coldly eyeing Thornton, tensed and ready to act if the bigger man moved on him; Thornton seemingly stumped by the contemptuous reaction by most of the others. He had expected Bradley to chime in with abuse, or get rid of Chance.

Out of astonishment and shame, Mary had disappeared inside the wagon.

Before the elder Thornton could start another harangue, Chance silently brushed past him, feeling Thornton's fumes of angry breath on his neck.

Jenkins stepped alongside the grim-faced one-eyed man, who walked several more paces, then stopped just long enough to scowl threateningly at him. The wagonmaster tersely growled, "I didn't think I'd have to come right out and warn you about Mary, mister."

"Shut up!" Chance hissed between tightly clenched teeth. He waited to see if Jenkins would issue a response; when he didn't, Chance left the rankled wagonmaster feeling futile anger. The look in Chance's eye and the tone of his voice hit Jenkins in the pit of the stomach like a cold ball of ice, stifling any taunt the wagonmaster might have made.

But Chance wasn't to be left alone so easily. Bob Howard and several other young men sauntered up behind him. He was not more than four steps from the slack-jawed Jenkins when Howard, his face torn by jealousy at the thought that the stranger who had so swiftly put him down earlier was pursuing the woman he himself desired, dropped his right hand on Chance's left shoulder and started to spin Chance around to face him. But Howard didn't have to force Chance to meet him.

Just as Howard's hand touched Chance's shirt, it was as if a tornado had blown by and over Howard. That was how the petrified bystanders viewed the incident, as Chance whirled smoothly, but not so fast that those watching were amazed by his speed. It was the suddenness and the calm, deadly violence with which Chance turned and dropped Howard flat on his back, with a bone-thudding right roundhouse, which startled them and held them frozen in astonishment and terrified deference.

The maneuver was flawless in technique: a graceful turn, with the blow that had landed on Howard's left cheek and jaw and jolted his head grotesquely to the right amid flying spittle from his open mouth, already on the way.

His right hand instantly covering the butt of his revolver, Chance stood upright, daring someone to pull a gun. But no one even breathed except for Howard, who moaned softly and writhed on the ground, his mind fogged with pain and the edge of unconsciousness.

Adrenalin surged through his heated body, but Chance eased up, seeing that no one was up to challenging him at the moment. Howard clambered to his hands and knees. Then, after a laborious effort to raise himself off the ground, Howard stumbled back into the supporting arms of the eldest Deegan son and a Smith son whose pimpled complexion stood out luridly even in the dim firelight.

Howard heaved several deep gasps of breath, viewing Chance with depthless hatred through glazed eyes.

"Don't ever try something like that again, kid," Chance softly warned in an ominous tone, "or I'll kill you as fast as I dropped you on your butt just now."

Howard's lips curled in brooding venom. His breathing was ragged with uncontrollable fury while he watched Chance turn and walk away with easy, undisturbed calm. This only compounded his malice and agitation as his right hand snaked downward for his revolver.

If it hadn't been for Deegan's hand of strong restraint, Howard might have pulled his weapon and shot Chance in the back.

"Don't be stupid!" Deegan muttered vehemently near Howard's right ear. "That'd be coldblooded murder. How was he supposed to know what you were going to do? You're lucky he didn't kill you."

This only added more humiliation to Howard's predicament. He seemed on the verge of wrenching free of Deegan, but he became aware of the presence of the other bystanders as they gathered uneasily around him, and his fuming subsided. He was forced to accept the facts.

Most of the bystanders who had seen the incident seemed caustic about Howard's plight. Most of them were able to interpret for themselves that the lanky assistant wagonmaster had instigated the scene. The look on his face before he had grabbed Chance and been belted to the ground, gave them full warning of what his intentions had been. Deep down, they admired the swiftness and deadliness with which Chance had acted, knowing now that what they had suspected was true. They had taken into their company someone capable of doing what he was supposed to do, and in Chance's case that was to help protect them from the Apaches. His ability to act had been proven to them, as many others had learned the hard way on just such occasions.

The pimply-faced Smith picked up Howard's hat, and Howard, snatching the hat, continued to glare malevolently after Chance, who had lain down in his bedroll.

"I'm going to kill him," Howard grumbled with hate, delicately touching the bruised cheekbone and jaw, already swollen black. "Mark my words."

Howard stumbled away from Deegan and Smith, who stared dourly after him, then fixed each other with disconsolate looks. Somehow they feared they might have more to worry about than just Indians.

The Most Deadly Sin

6

Gray sky of dawn yawned forth from the east, promising another day of blistering Texas heat. As Dreyfuss, Thompson and Reynolds searched charred and mutilated corpses, and rummaged through rubble in search of undamaged loot, they sweated profusely. Every so often sharp coughs would blast forth from underneath neckerchiefs in response to the foul stench of death.

Had they been familiar with the Old Testament they might have compared the blackened ruins of Smiling Sons with the destruction of Sodom and Gomorrah. But of the five, Nenz was the only one familiar with Scripture. He remembered vividly his Sunday School lessons as a boy.

Having digested many passages from the Bible, Nenz had at one time found himself greatly intrigued by the wonderful stories and beautiful philosophy. But later he came to believe the stories of the Old Book ridiculous and the ideas of the New One absurd, as he discovered he enjoyed things quite contradictory to what he'd read and was supposed to behold as the righteous way of living. And the notion of a God who hurled those who didn't adhere to the words of this book into a lake of eternal fire was to him repulsive. Thus he spurned any belief in a Higher Power than man, than himself.

For what was life, Nenz surmised, but death and destruction? There is beauty only in death and utter chaos. A brutal proposition indeed, but Karl Nenz and his men thrived on things of death and lived off negative emotions. Their only life was the mental and physical torment of any who fell in their paths to destiny.

His bristled face barren of protection against the stench, Nenz sat straight and tall in his saddle, leering and sniffing. He enjoyed the smell. And as he watched Krupeck join in the looting of the dead, he imagined the roaring flames which had toppled this town. Recreating the scenario in his dark mind, he heard the screams of agony; he saw the killing blows and the human torches flailing as they could only await their deaths. He admired those—even though he feared they were Indians, whom he despised—who had committed the atrocity.

Within several minutes the men realized the hopelessness of their chore. Their pillaging had been for naught; nothing worth the effort had been taken. Even in the surrounding remains of farmhouses, which they had just inspected before venturing back onto the main street where the general awaited them, nothing had been saved—no food, no weapons, no money or other valuables. Few revolvers or rifles remained, for after the annihilation the Apaches had seized undamaged firearms and gathered ammunition. Apparently they had also confiscated the town's surviving horses—a thought that angered Nenz, because they could have used fresh mounts.

The disappointed men mounted—except for Reynolds, who walked forth from the debris he'd been going through, his brow wet with perspiration and blackened by soot. A brown kerchief over his mouth and nose, Reynolds held a tomahawk in his right hand and a black Apache headband in his left. Both possessions seemed to be undamaged.

"Hey, Karl!" Reynolds called excitedly, sounding gleeful as he placed the headband on his head triumphantly and displayed the tomahawk to the others. "Check this!"

Nenz and the others peered blankly at Reynolds, who was grinning absurdly at each one in turn, making sure he had everyone's undivided attention. Then Reynolds launched himself into a mock rain dance, bringing his knees up and down quickly, stamping the ground and clumsily moving in a circle. "Got a new routine!" he howled, enthralled with his ridiculous imitation dance. "Song-and-dance gunfighter!"

"Song-and-dance jerk," growled Nenz, balefully eyeing the dark-haired, dark-skinned Reynolds.

He added singing to the performance but his singing was horribly off key, and he stumbled over many words, obviously making them up as he went on. And went on he did, much to the dismay of the others.

Nenz snorted contemptuously, then turned his back on Reynolds and guided his mount several paces up the street, away from the idiotic scene.

Reynolds stopped long enough to search for a response. "What do you think, boys? Karl, what do you think?" He started his routine again under a barrage of scornful laughter. This reaction only made him more enthusiastic; he believed it was appreciation, viewed it as applause, feeling he could do no wrong in the eyes of those with whom he rode. So enraptured was he with himself that their jeering comments escaped him entirely.

"Yeah, Reynolds," Nenz flung over his shoulder, scoffing, having halted his stallion to survey the rubble with the same sadistic entrancement he had shown before the interruption. "You ought to be in show business."

"Maybe you can be like that organ grinder and his monkey we seen in 'Frisco," scoffed Krupeck, his raucous laughter fading into chuckles and snickering. "You could form a team somewhere. Could be the start of something big for you."

"Yeah!" howled Dreyfuss. "But who's gonna crank the organ?"

"No good," Thompson chimed in. "He don't step well enough to make a monkey's ass look good."

Reynolds was oblivious to their sardonic remarks as he continued singing. "Injun, 'Pache Injun coming home/Redskin bucks ain't much on their own."

"Must've been something," breathed Nenz in astonishment.

Krupeck, Dreyfuss and Thompson gathered around the general, trying to escape the inane display that was still going strong.

"Oh, Injun, 'Pache Injun, clean his breeches/Oh Injun, 'Pache Injun got him six smelly beetches."

"Bigger than Lawrence, Karl?" Krupeck solemnly asked, stopping alongside the general.

"Much," Nenz murmured.

"Looks like an army marched through here," injected a muttering Dreyfuss.

"Must've been some army," Thompson grimly

supplemented.

"Must've been some show," countered Dreyfuss.

"Had to be better than Reynolds," cracked Krupeck, waving a deprecating thumb over his right shoulder.

"Only wish he could've been here," Thompson softly growled, grimacing in annoyance as Reynolds' song-and-dance routine continued to assault their ears painfully. "Bet that warparty wouldn've really thought it was hysterical."

"Just makes me uncomfortable knowing it was Indians," intoned Dreyfuss in somber unrest.

"I remember what Atlanta looked like after General Sherman left," Krupeck related with an edge to his voice. "Hardly compares. Never seen anything quite like this in all my life."

"Gehenna," Nenz suddenly said, his tone ominous.

"What?" asked a confused Krupeck.

"Gehenna," the general repeated with more emphasis. "For some reason I thought about a book I used to read."

"What are you talking about, Karl?" Thompson inquired, wearing a dark frown of perplexity.

"Sheol, Tartarus, Hades—ever hear of those names?"

The three mumbled that they hadn't.

Nenz gave a grunt, his dark eyes growing wide and cold. They seemed empty, devoid of life. But now they held a peculiar hardness; it was as if he were seeing a vision which held him captivated.

"The Bible," he stated as an answer.

"What the hell's that?" asked Krupeck gruffly.

"A book," growled Nenz, caustic toward Krupeck's ignorance. "Any of you ever read it?"

"Naw," Krupeck snorted. "Course not."

"Never was big on books," Dreyfuss humbly murmured, as if embarrassed by this admission.

"Reading hurts my eyes," Thompson sneered. "Rather be drinkin' and whorin'."

"Illiterate bastards," Nenz acidly grumbled. Then he spurred his stallion away from them, heading it for the west end of the ruins. Angrily he called over his shoulder, "Tell Reynolds to saddle up or we'll leave him!" The general continued setting the pace. He spat, snarling with the sudden distaste he felt for the others. "Friggin' uneducated trash!" he rasped to himself.

Though they shrugged skeptical encouragement to each other, Thompson and Dreyfuss were seemingly undaunted by the general's remarks and suddenly unfriendly manner as they started their mounts after him.

"Come on, Pocahontas!" Krupeck sardonically snarled at Reynolds, then heeled his mount and headed for the departing trio.

Seeing his comrades suddenly leaving, Reynolds instantly curtailed his routine. He stuck the tomahawk inside his belt, and, making sure the headband was fitted snugly on his head, mounted. "Wait up, gentlemen," he called, trying to sound diplomatic.

"We will," growled Krupeck with soft-voiced sarcasm, "if you spare us the encore."

"Hey, Karl," Dreyfuss said, interest in his tone as he addressed the general, upon closing the gap between them. "What about this book you read?"

"What about it?"

"I want to hear some more about it," Dreyfuss said. "I never knew anybody who'd read a book," he added.

"I got nothing to tell you," Nenz growled savagely. "'Cause I don't read it any more."

"Why not?" inquired Dreyfuss in a bewildered tone. "How come you don't read it no more?"

The general set a quicker pace. "Because it makes me angry!" he rasped.

They were a disconsolate group with little conversation and no movement other than what was necessary. The earth coughed up no water and the atmosphere offered little friendship; both took all they could get while giving nothing in return.

Over the barren tableland, under the relentless glare of the watchful orange eye set at its culminating point in a cloudless blue sky, the caravan trundled toward the line of demarcation separating Texas and the New Mexico territory. But this was only the great plains of northwestern Texas running into the great plains of southeastern New Mexico, and nothing unusual would tell them of the transition. The arid landscape was as

116

level as the barrel of a rifle, and the flat desolation seemed every bit as threatening as a gun.

Dust was at a minimum as animals and children flanking the wagons plodded over the sandy loam soil, stubbled here and there with rock, mesquite and tumbleweed. On occasion a lone butte or mesa, or a series of low brown hills, would loom on the horizon, but it felt like an eternity before they were reached.

Maintaining their assigned sections along the train, Chance assumed a position at the rear right of the caravan, while Jenkins rode front and center, with Howard in the middle flanking the left.

Breaking the routine, a Carlsbad son suddenly strode up to the one-eyed man, having made his way from the front. He was in his early twenties, short and stocky, with a sort of nondescript handsomeness to his face. Even with the Winchester rifle he held in the crook of his right arm, he would have gone unnoticed by most people.

"Hey, Chance," he called none too politely, falling in beside the one-eyed man's gelding. "Mr. Bradley wants a word with you."

His grunt and solemn-faced acknowledgment produced a scowl on Carlsbad's face as Chance pulled away and headed up the line.

Passing the wagons, Chance could feel the animosity directed at him by several of the settlers. He chose to ignore the sweaty faces which emanated hostility toward him. He did not even look at the woman indirectly responsible for the incident the night before, as he moved quickly by the Thornton wagon, feeling the glowering eyes of Dick Thornton on his back.

Chance pulled up by Bradley's immediate right, slowing his pace to match that of the lead wagon's.

Holding the reins in his hands, Bradley was slouched slightly forward on the seat, his wife to his left. His face was set in a morose expression, while his head remained stationary. He didn't bother to acknowledge Chance's presence for several seconds, as if making Chance wait was a display of his power and ability not to be intimidated. Then he sniffed and scratched the bridge of his nose with a dirt-grimed finger.

"Saw the results this morning of what you did to Howard." Bradley spoke slowly, distinctly. He was now attempting to use his "cultured" tone.

Jenkins was more than a hundred feet ahead of the Bradley wagon. Bradley's young son walked ahead and to the right of the horses, while the two older Bradley daughters were hunched behind their parents' backs, sweating profusely in loose cotton skirts. They waved hand-held fans in front of their faces.

From underneath her blue sunbonnet Mrs. Bradley threw surreptitious glances toward Chance. She had a tight, almost pained expression; obviously she was uncomfortable in the presence of the one-eyed man.

She remained tense, while her husband, receiving no immediate response from Chance, showed the faintest trace of a scowl across his brutish features. Then he continued in a low, even tone.

"Personally, Chance, I think Howard's just a smart-aleck kid. But he's my wife's eighteenth cousin, or some damned thing like that," Bradley said, drawing a harsh stare of disbelief from his wife as he turned his head slightly to make sure Chance was paying attention.

Bradley saw the same somber, scarred face, that, no matter how grim it appeared, also always seemed to be laughing, as if daring anyone to say or do something offensive. Bradley suddenly realized what it was that irritated him so much about Chance: it was the fact that Chance always seemed to make him choose his words carefully, even if it was with just a brief stare of the lone green eye.

"Kid's kind of rootless and homeless," Bradley tautly went on, turning to face the landscape ahead, which was every bit as impersonal and unfriendly as the man he was talking to "My wife talked me into letting him come along as Jenkins' assistant. I figured it might make something of the boy. But this doesn't mean I approve of what you did to him, even though I was told by some of the others he was going after you in what looked like a fit of rage. And I'm certainly not going to condone any more trouble on your account."

Chance was in the process of rolling a cigarette. "You want me to ride on," he flatly stated.

"No, no . . . I don't," Bradley curtly said. "But some of the others do. They were trying to convince me this morning. It just so happens I was more convincing." The side of Bradley's face screwed up into an arrogant grin which he flashed at Chance, who was lighting his cigarette and listening with the same degree of apathy he'd been showing. Bradley resented this, and his tone look on an edge. "Now," he sourly went on, "the kid's sworn in front of witnesses he's going to kill you. And you had previously threatened to kill him if he ever tried anything on you again. Now comes the problem. I don't know if that means looking at you the wrong way, or spitting too close to your bedroll, or what. Maybe you can tell me. Maybe I haven't made up my mind after all."

"What do you want to hear, Bradley?" Chance asked, with the faint note of a snarl creeping into his tone. "Your meaning is starting to escape me."

Bradley became instantly tense with angry impatience. His face grew hard as he let a few seconds of silence elapse while he formed a response in his mind. He weighed his words carefully. "I want to hear, mister, that you'll go out of your way to keep from getting in Howard's way. I want to hear, mister, that you'll stay clear of the Thornton girl. I want to hear, mister, that you'll cooperate fully with me and my wagonmaster. I want to hear, mister, that that gun of yours won't be drawn unless I ask for it. I want to hear, mister, that I won't have any more trouble out of you in any way, shape or form. I want to hear all those things, mister."

Chance drew on his cigarette, then showed a crooked grin. But there was malice and an anger of his own in the expression. And there was ice in his tone. "That would be a lot of promises from a man not prone to give many in the first place."

"So you're telling me you won't do the aforementioned," Bradley said with disgust.

"What I'm telling you, Mr. Bradley, is that I have no idea what's going to happen," the one-eyed man said with the same degree of displeasure in his voice, fixing both Bradley parents with a cold stare. They, in turn, held his gaze with expectant looks. "I read minds about as well as futures, although I always try to anticipate the actions of man, animal and Fate.

119

"As for the kid, he's easy enough to ignore. As for the Thornton girl, she'd be tough to ignore in anybody's outfit, but I guess for the sake of peace I'll keep my distance. As for cooperating, that's all I've done. As for my gun, I use it as sparingly as possible. As for having trouble out of me, if you believe the worst, then I'll be moving on—though it just so happens you're going in my direction now and I might be hard to shake."

Bradley's face had turned into a brooding frown. He appeared to have lost his voice and he looked quickly at his wife as if embarrassed by the sudden mute state into which he was hurled. But, after recovering from his brief shock, he returned to his usual surly style.

"Got to always play the big tough-guy routine, don't you?" he growled sourly. "Well, mister, I'm just as big and every bit as tough. And don't look at me as if to say that's a matter of opinion." Bradley glanced back and forth from Chance to the land ahead. He had spoken each word as quietly as possible; he seemed to be holding back in uncertainty as to how Chance would react. Now, his jaw jutted defiantly and his teeth clenched, he went on just above a whisper. "I've got the final say around here. I can tell you to ride or I can let you stay. It's up to me and me only—not Thornton, Jenkins, Carlsbad or anybody else. I can handle this outfit, and I can handle you; and if I can't, then you're gone.

"You asked to ride with us. We didn't ask for you. You offered your gun. We didn't hire you. You're a challenge to me and a threat to everyone else—I think that's plain enough to see. Just like it's plain enough to see that everyone's been challenging my authority and questioning my judgment since we stumbled over those bodies. I'm getting sick of the crap, not just from you but from everybody else. Telling me what to do, what not to do; what I should do, what I shouldn't do. I'm going to do what I always do, and that's do what I think is best for everyone concerned.

"It might not be the smartest thing I'll ever do, but I'm doing it mainly to assert my authority—and that is, keeping you on. I want to show some of the grumblers and mumblers that I'm not as foolish as they're all saying behind my back. That said and no more questions, you can get on back to where you were. All right?''

Now it was Chance who appeared to be at a loss for a response. In fact he was biting back the words he wanted to say for the simple reason that he wasn't yet ready to leave the wagon train. His apparent surrender swelled Bradley with false hope and enormous pleasure as he and Chance looked pensively at each other for a brief moment before a thin smile creased the lips of the one-eyed man.

"I guess we understand, then, the kind of ground we're walking over," Chance said, taking one last draw on his cigarette, then flicking it onto the ground.

Puzzled, Bradley silently searched Chance's face for a betrayal of his meaning. But the cold eye and the blankness of his expression only served to confuse and infuriate Bradley more, as he quietly rasped, "What's that supposed to mean?''

"Probably nothing. Probably something," Chance softly replied, looking as innocent as he could. "Just means we're traveling over rocky ground and placing our feet down on unsure soil. And it's best to walk slowly and step carefully, for you never know which rock will twist your ankle when you're not looking. And you'll always have a buzzard over your shoulder and a snake under your feet. Particularly, Mr. Bradley, in light of the trail you've chosen to blaze over the land ahead.''

Bradley's baffled face bordered on a sneer. But before he could open his mouth to respond, Chance touched the brim of his hat in a polite departing gesture to Mrs. Bradley—much to her consternation—and left to take up his position at the rear of the wagon train.

"What the hell is that supposed to mean?" a bewildered Bradley growled, turning to direct his angry tone toward his wife, who shook her head in dismay while looking away from her husband.

"I don't know, Brad," she said wearily, pausing as if making some sort of silent effort to rid the presence of Chance from her mind. But I don't think it's a very smart thing to keep that man with us. I find him quite repulsive and quite frightening. The less we see of him the better off we'll all be.''

"I told you last night almost the same thing I told him," Bradley countered defensively, his tone nearing a whine. His lips curled downward to express his sour mood, but his tone took on a sullen note. "I don't need this grief everyone's giving me about everything I say or do. If you just let me be I'll work things out for all of us." He then shook his head slowly in morose exasperation, explaining, "Last night was just a misunderstanding. You know how hotheaded Bob gets over Dick Thornton's girl."

"Sure," his wife cut in, her voice strong with disgust and accusation, a sudden scowl twisting her sallow complexion and birdlike features. "I ought to know my smart-aleck eighteenth cousin or some damned thing like that!"

"I'm sorry I expressed it like that, Mildred," Bradley quickly apologized with unusual humility, a sigh of frustration escaping. "I was just trying to make a point to Chance."

"What's your point, Brad?" Mildred growled, glaring at her husband crossly. "Like you said, Chance is a challenge to you. And because he's a threat to everybody else, and because a lot of us are disagreeing with you, you want to use him so you can prove something to him and the rest of us here."

"Mildred, listen—"

"No, you listen to me and don't feed me your holier-than-thou, I-know-it-all-you-stupid-bitch attitude."

Bradley's face flushed crimson, but he remained silent out of sheer embarrassment and astonishment. In his twenty-five years of marriage he had never heard his wife speak out against him so sternly and with such menace and venom in her tone. Using last reserves of frayed patience, he was trying to remain calm, for he didn't want to create a scene which would reveal not only his wife's tempestuous outburst, but the reason for it, and the nature of his motives in keeping Chance. Bradley only hoped his wife's soft-voiced harangue didn't travel any further than his children's ears.

Mildred Bradley drew in a deep breath, then expelled the air in a sigh of disgust and anger with her husband. She looked away from him to gaze blankly at the barren terrain they rolled over, and her strength seemed to vanish with the sight she saw. Once again she lapsed back into a state of near despair. "I fear it's a tragic mistake," she solemnly declared. "The most deadly mistake you've ever committed."

Before Chance returned to his end position a number of

conversations had been instigated by his passing. Most notable was a heated exchange developing between the Thornton parents. They spoke in low, almost conspiratorial tones; and, as usual, Dick Thornton wore an angry, menacing expression.

"Just let me catch that one-eyed . . . trash near my girl again," Thornton snarled, "and he'll look ten times worse than he does now."

"You're just looking for an excuse, Dick," Clara Thornton said, trying to sound placating, but her tone clearly filled with bitter frustration. She was several years younger than her husband's forty-five. Even after the many years of helping to toil the farmstead back in Louisiana and raising two children, she maintained about her a happy, healthy appearance. She had a youthful innocence that was prominently displayed by green eyes which always sparkled with life. Her figure was full yet slender underneath her brown hoopless skirt. And her skin was as smooth and unblemished as a fresh blanket of snow— something which never failed to amaze both men and women who knew what life on a farm was like.

"Mary is no longer a little girl. She's a full-grown woman with a mind, body and future of her own. And I think it would be best for you and her if you started treating her as such."

Dick Thornton glowered disbelief at his outspoken wife, then cast surreptitious eyes over his shoulder, looking for any big unwanted ears. Seeing his daughter and son quietly staring out the back of the wagon, he moderated his tone as his expression altered into sullen annoyance at the acceptance of his wife's statement. "I'm well aware of that, woman. But I only want it to be good for her. I want her to have a decent man, and do things right."

"Like we never did?" she insinuated, smirking triumphantly out of the corner of her mouth, feeling unusually brazen.

Thornton's head swung toward his wife, his face showing more surprise than anger. "That was a long time ago, Clara!" he snapped in a low, harsh voice. Then he turned his startled scowl away from her. "Things were different then."

"How were they so different?" Clara asked in a sharp tone. Then quickly she answered her own question. "Nothing was different except you—a boy not quite twenty, full of life,

123

happiness and promises, who used to make me feel like I was something special. I swear to God Almighty I don't know what's become of the man I used to know. Who's Richard Thornton?" She paused to chuckle harshly, her husband grimacing slightly in embarrassment at this sound. "Just a sour old man who has nothing better to do but make his daughter miserable, ignore his wife and boy completely, and make a fool out of himself in the meantime! If I didn't know better I'd say you were jealous of seeing your own daughter near other men."

His anger almost too much for him to control, Thornton flared his nostrils and clenched his teeth under snarling lips. For several painful seconds a tense silence hovered like the heat of flames between man and wife.

"I don't know what's come over you to talk to me like that, Clara," he said at length, a sudden morose feeling placing a restraint on his anger. "I've been a faithful and loving husband, a caring, devoted father. I've worked hard all my life to give my family the best—a family I'm taking far in the hope of finding a better life."

"Trying to convince me or yourself?" she interrupted.

"I'm trying. . . ." Thornton angrily started, eyes blazing. "I'm trying, damn it," he continued in a more relaxed voice, "to take care of the one thing that means more to me than anything else, and that's you three. If it looks as if I'm paying more attention to Mary than I should be, it's because she's at a vulnerable age."

"Like I was when I married you?" Clara sneered lightly.

"Do you feel you've made a mistake, Clara?" he asked, his voice suddenly soft with pain and unconcealed embarrassment, an odd look of bewildered hurt playing on his face. Clara Thornton turned and studied her husband closely for several seconds.

A surge of warm amazement filled her in her shocked state. The sensitivity shown by her husband made her feel not only ashamed of her callous attitude, but deeply perplexed by this strange tenderness exhibited by someone who, she had dreaded, was no longer capable of such a display.

"Of course not, Dick Thornton," she earnestly replied at length, reaching for and holding her husband's right hand with both of her hands. "I just don't want whatever is causing your unhappiness to destroy those who need you."

Both Thorntons remained pensive and searching in the long silence which followed as they stared at each other. Both were preoccupied with their own thoughts, sorting out the reasons for their own emotions and somewhat shocked by revelations of facets of the other's character neither would have believed were there. It was as if they'd awakened in bed to find total strangers sleeping next to them.

"Maybe you're right, Clara," Dick Thornton allowed in a quiet tone, nodding his head solemnly as if a heavy burden of self-admonishment had been lifted from his shoulders. He lowered his eyes briefly. "In fact, you're absolutely right. And I'd be an even bigger fool not to admit it." He looked long at his wife as a sheepish grin enhanced the silliness he felt. "You think there's hope, wife?" he asked in a sort of self-mocking manner. "Think this sour old fool can change?"

"If you want to," she replied softly, gazing deeply into her husband's eyes, her smile sincere. "If so, then I know everything's going to be just fine."

"Think so?" he asked, seeking reassurance.

"Sure," Clara answered in dignified exuberance, the happy shine returning to her face as her husband smiled broadly, reminding her of how he had looked twenty-five years ago. "Just like it used to be."

Thus all went well for the pioneers during the next four days as they rolled over a hundred miles, traversing the high plains into New Mexico Territory without any interruption other than night camp.

There was no distinct trail but rather a broad, flat plateau which guided the wagons across the terrain, sucking them toward the western horizon with the promise of leaving behind the scorched desolation underfoot.

Often they were flanked by buttes and high mesas which marked the treeless landscape. And often the way was led in a seemingly unplanned fashion. Actually the wagonmaster was making allowances by slanting and shifting direction occasionally, hoping to pass through the easiest trails in between the mountain ranges soon to be encountered.

Also, at frequent intervals, and always at the day's end, several men would scout ahead. Not only were they laying out the best possible route for the following day, but they were also in search of Indians who might be hiding in possible ambush points. But not a living soul, red or white, had been seen since their departure from Smiling Sons—other than Chance, who remained true to his crooked promise to Bradley that he would avoid trouble unless, of course, trouble came calling. But the friction had petered out, and Bradley had had no further cause to confront Chance; nor had anyone else.

Even Bob Howard had built an indifferent shield around him toward the one-eyed man. He nursed his wounded pride and bruised face in silence. But, as the discoloring faded, Howard grew into a taciturn, zombielike figure of somber apathy; it was as if the incident with Chance had turned him into another man. He even totally ignored Mary Thornton, who—much to the surprise of those who cared to notice, or those who couldn't help but noticing—was smiling more and talking with a bold alacrity to many of the settlers. And even more surprising was the loosening of her father's austere hold on his daughter.

Dick Thornton's mysterious change of disposition seemed to have a pleasantly contagious effect on almost everyone else. Many members of the other families gradually seemed to be in better spirits in the following days, despite the hardships of travel and the now ever-present threat of Apaches. The despondency and inhibitions which had consumed them since the acquisition of the one-eyed stranger had faded. Even Chance managed a smile or two and several exchanges with some of the men, which was as close to friendly as he could come.

One such exchange occurred on their seventh night out of Smiling Sons. As usual since the incident with Howard, Chance ate his dinner outside the corraled wagons. He was seated on his bedroll, back against a wagonwheel, spooning stew into his mouth.

The new moon cast the terrain in total blackness, but the flickering firelight from the campsite within the phalanx was enough to let him distinguish out of the corner of his right eye the figure of the eldest Deegan son coming toward him.

126

"Mind if I join you, Chance?" Deegan asked, a tremor in his voice. Holding his own plate of stew and a canteen in his hands, he looked terribly uncomfortable, and restless for a quick response he didn't get. His hostile attitude toward the man who had accidentally peeked in on his mother had changed drastically after the Howard incident. Since then he'd found himself begrudgingly admiring the one-eyed man and showing an unwilling deference toward him.

"Don't see my name written on this spot," Chance evenly replied, glancing with mild curiosity at Deegan, who sat down against the rear wheel to Chance's right. "Something on your mind?" Chance asked, picking up a spoonful of dripping stew.

In his early twenties, Deegan had boyish good looks. His lean frame was slightly longer than six feet. The only features about him which possibly gave false impressions of strength were his naturally flared nostrils and husky voice.

"Yeah," Deegan drawled, looking pensive. "I guess a few things are bothering me . . . like, why are you riding with us, Chance?" He then busied himself with eating, as if this action would ease his tension and allow them to fall into a normal pattern of conversation.

Chance gave a curt laugh. "Purely selfish motives, feller," he said in his usual impersonal tone. "And old man Bradley is keeping me on for purely selfish motives of his own. So that's as far as I extend myself to that question."

"Are all your types so touchy?" Deegan asked, in an awe-struck tone. Then, seeing Chance flash him a cynical frown, he shook his head and cleared his throat in an admission of embarrassment, hastily adding, "I meant, are men like you always so hard and mean?"

Chance resumed eating. "You're speaking in generalities, feller. You're going to have to direct your questions a little more clearly if this conversation is to continue."

There was a note of condescension in the one-eyed man's tone, and this, coupled with his rhetoric, baffled Deegan momentarily. "Well . . . gunfighters," he blurted sheepishly. Then as he went on his tone became bright with excitement and his face became strangely lit by a keen gaze of fascination. "Y'know, I used to read about them in papers back home.

Jesse James, Cole Younger . . . I've read your name. You used to have a gang of your own."

"First of all, Deegan," Chance said, his tone hard as he placed the plate in his lap and turned an icy stare on the other, "don't even put me in a category with psychopathic, bush-whacking trash like that. I know all about the James boys, the Youngers, and some of that other lowlife vermon."

"But back in town, you—"

"I'm no gunfighter, boy," Chance growled. Then he moderated his tone as he began eating again. "I'm just a man trying to survive—a man who's often lived by misguided principles, and most probably still does. There's nothing remotely glamorous or heroic about James, Younger or all the other hillbillies and rednecks who imitate what they do. Your terminology is a little screwed up, boy. Jesse James is a back-shooting, thieving psycho. He murders people, innocent, defenseless people. He doesn't go one on one with a man and call him out into the street—that's known as a showdown, boy. That's known as a gunfighter, a man with a gun who fights other men with guns—not a bunch of dirt that clings together in a ball and rolls over those who don't stand a shot in hell.

"I've had the displeasure of meeting this James, and he's nothing but a wimpy, snotnosed kid with floppy ears who probably couldn't fight a cold on his own. And it's the kind of attitude and ignorance you've displayed which will make these vicious chickenshit killers—who would most likely piss in their pants if a gun were stuck in their faces—heroes to be glorified years after they're dead. And stories about what they've done, and will do, will get so screwed up that the reality of it will become fiction which will be held as the truth.

"As for myself and what I used to do, it was a sad mistake caused by a bitter anger and those misguided principles. It could have produced tragic results, but it didn't. We robbed coaches by day and blew up banks by night. Never once did I shoot, or have to shoot, at anyone during that time. I lucked out, I suppose. Maybe keeping a level head and executing plans properly and swiftly made sure no one got hurt. That didn't make it right, though, just because no one got hurt. Maybe it even helped bring about my eventual downfall, for my luck fizzled, and that's when I was beaten nearly to death by those same men I killed in town. Then I was thrown in prison while they rode off feeling damn righteous.

"I'm not saying it was a righteous thing to do to go and kill them, but it eased my pain and loss some. Don't forget there was four of them, boy, and that I have only one eye. By doing what I did I put my life well over the line. I gave them a chance and they lost. But so did I."

"What do you mean by 'so did I'?" Deegan asked, his frown showing intense interest.

Chance stared with equal intensity at Deegan, as if making certain that his meaning would be clear. "I mean I'm just as dead as they are," he said gravely. "My days are numbered."

Deegan shrugged his incomprehension. "But you're alive. And you confronted them like . . . a gunfighter would."

"I confronted them like a man possessed, like a man who's lost his face, eight years of his life, and whatever elements of decency made him feel human and like he belongs as a part of mankind. I'm alienated, partly because of myself and partly because of intangibles which govern our lives at one time or another. I'm a freak because of the way I look. I'm alone because of what I do or what I'm forced to do to save my life and what dignity I have left. And the statement you asked about still stands."

Deegan pondered this for several long seconds, shaking his head in grim bewilderment. It was as if the one-eyed man had read every question in his mind. The younger man didn't realize that men such as Chance, who must often survive by cruel measures, have an uncanny penchant for reading minds, for saying or not saying the right thing at the right time. This ability held him entranced. He didn't understand, for possibly he wasn't quite old enough yet, that there was more to surviving and being tough than talking and acting tough.

One had to think tough and bear his scars in silence.

The scars of the one-eyed man were obvious. And he bore these in silence, along with a great many others. His mind was, possibly, the toughest thing about him. Deegan looked at Chance with a mixture of repulsion and amazement for several more seconds. "You make it sound as if you've got nothing left to live for," he stated in morbid fascination.

"Oh, I've got plenty to live for," Chance quickly replied, a sly smile twisting his lips. "Plenty."

His puzzled look caught between Chance and the darkness in front of him, Deegan grunted. "It's pretty hard to figure you out, Chance," he admitted with a sigh of mock exasperation.

"Talk in riddles, do I?"

"Yeah," Deegan soberly said as Chance poured some water in his tin plate and began scrubbing it clean. "I guess you could say that."

"That's good to hear," the one-eyed man replied, a cheerful note in his voice as he finished his chore quickly and sprawled out over his bedroll. "If you keep 'em guessing, then that makes resting that much more peaceful. Catch my drift?"

"You want to get some sleep?" Deegan rhetorically asked, somewhat irritated. Then he rose to his feet slowly, a bone in his knee cracking in the process.

"That's my basic drift."

"All right," Deegan quietly assented.

But he seemed reluctant to leave, and Chance, seeing this, looked wearily at Deegan. "Something else?" he inquired.

"Yeah," Deegan replied in a low, taut voice. "About Howard."

"What about him?"

"Well, I think he's cooled off since the other night."

"Good to hear," Chance muttered, a wry grin spreading over his face as he pulled the hat down over his eye. "Old man Bradley was worried the kid was going to hurt me."

"What I mean, Chance, is that Bob's got a bad temper at times. But he's harmless; he just got the wrong idea the other night."

"Wrong ideas get people killed, Deegan," Chance said in an easy, even tone.

"I think he realizes that now," Deegan informed, bitter now over Chance's continued aloofness. "And I also think he's going to keep his distance. So there shouldn't be any more trouble."

"That's good to hear, too."

"I'm glad you think so. Because this trip is going to be hard enough without trouble from each other."

"Just remember the riddles, Deegan," Chance said, bringing his hat lower over his face.

"How's that?"

"No answer is certain until it's confirmed by the one presenting the riddle."

Deegan held his ground while he frowned uncertainty at Chance. Then, having no response to give, he grunted his bafflement, shook his head and walked away as a smug smile of enjoyment creased the scarred remains of Chance's face in amusement over Deegan's consternation.

The following dawn brought the same routine: up early, with the men harnessing mules to wagons and forming the column while women prepared breakfast. Then the cracking of encouraging bullwhips and shouted commands of "Roll on!" and "Move on!" to start the train.

Now, as the wagon train traveled further across southeastern New Mexico, the land began to slope away toward the Pecos Valley. They rolled past areas where deep canyon pockets had been cut by streams flowing from the Rocky Mountains in the north. Water stops were made at two streams to replenish barrels and canteens, though this water was somewhat brackish and would be used only as a last resort. By the day's end, as the sun bled beneath towering mountain ranges far to the west, the caravan forded the shallow, turbid waters of the Pecos River.

Crossing the river presented little problem. The heat of May, and of June so far, and the continuous lack of rainfall, had dried the Pecos to nearly half its three-hundred-foot width when the river was flowing at its strongest between the sloping embankments. But the sludge below the foot-deep water caught wagon wheels twice, though they were quickly pushed free without much effort.

At a point more than a hundred yards from the river's west bank the wagons were corraled and camp was made. Animals were herded and children gathered mesquite and sagebrush for fires as Bradley, satisfied that camp was sufficiently organized, rounded up those whose turn it was for evening scout.

Pasted brown with dust and dirt, Jenkins and Howard guided their mounts slowly toward Bradley, who shifted impatiently in his saddle, obviously anxious for his scout party to assemble.

His face on the verge of a scowl, Bradley asked Jenkins in a surly voice, "Where's Thornton, Carlsbad and Bugler?"

But the wagonmaster had no time to reply, as Bradley, seeing the three he was looking for steering horses through the opening in the wagon's circle, eyed them sarcastically and sourly called, "C'mon, Dick! Move your butt, Bugler! Let's get the lead out of them breeches! Want to get this done sometime tonight, y'know!"

Then Bradley, Jenkins and Howard moved out, heading into the setting sun, while the other three, grumbling discontent, urged their nags after them.

"Get the lead out," Bugler mocked in a harsh whisper. "Lardass is sure a good one to tell somebody that."

Chance was making his way around the outside of the wagons, walking his gelding by the reins. He filled his canteen by a water barrel. Briefly he watched the six men trot off and thought nothing of it, until he rounded the corner and was heading toward the circle's opening.

Immediately spotting Chance coming toward her, Mary Thornton held her ground. She had a large towel slung over her right forearm and she clasped a brown satchel in her left hand. Warmly she smiled as the one-eyed man pulled up several feet from her. Her face had an expression of expectant fervor, as if she'd found the very person she'd been anxiously looking for. But her demeanor was casual, as if she had expected to meet Chance at the very spot where they now faced each other.

Chance returned her smile, and realized, much to his own surprise, that he was able to inject warmth into his own. "Miss Thornton," he politely greeted. "Are you—"

"Mary, Mr. Chance," she interrupted, her voice oddly throaty with a sensuality that didn't escape the one-eyed man. She then quickly added, "I haven't had an opportunity to apologize for the other night. And I only like to make apologies if I feel it's personal."

"I don't think there's any need for you to do that," Chance bluntly declined.

"Oh," Mary said, sounding despondent, but favoring Chance with an inviting stare. "Is that so?"

She turned and walked away from a baffled Chance.

"I'll be down at the river," she said softly over her shoulder, then stopped long enough to finish. "If you'd like to hear my apology."

A strange look of surprise swept Chance's face and he glanced about him. But no one had noticed him, nor did they appear to have noticed his encounter with Mary Thornton. Everyone was preoccupied with starting fires and preparing meals.

Chance's lone green eye shone as he watched Mary Thornton strolling toward the river. A dangerous smile formed on his lips. "I think that's one apology," he muttered, "that no man in his right mind could refuse."

Over the bank's crest Chance appeared. The mischievous gleam on his face became a blank stare of puzzlement when he saw no immediate sign of Mary. But, when he discovered her footprints in the soft soil at the bank's bottom, he ambled upstream in the direction indicated by her prints.

After tethering his horse, and when a good ten minutes had elapsed from the time she'd gone out of his sight, Chance casually walked down the sloping terrain toward the river, careful not to betray the urgency he felt to anyone who might see him and whose suspicions might be aroused. It would probably appear to anyone who had seen him leaving alone that he was going to wash or to relieve himself.

At this point the banks on the west side of the Pecos were somewhat steeper than those on the east. The shallow waters were barely flowing in their natural southerly direction, as the river ran a straight course for more than two miles before it bent east and was joined by the Rio Penasco tributary which flowed from the Sacramento Mountains in the west. Both sides were lined in spots with rocks and with cottonwood trees which hung forward as if ready to pitch into the river at any moment.

More than a hundred yards upstream was a cluster of large rocks. It was at this spot that Chance found Mary sitting on one of the rocks, dabbing at her face and neck with a wet washrag. A small bowl filled with the river's brackish water was resting on a rock to her right.

She appeared nonchalant, totally unconcerned, unaware that the one-eyed man was standing several feet to her right staring at her with unconcealed interest. The top two buttons of her white blouse were undone as she began to pat her lower neck with the washrag.

"You must like to live dangerously, Mr. Chance," she opened, her voice devoid of any emotion as she glanced up at the one-eyed man. His face broke into a playful grin. "And wipe that smirk off your horrible face, mister!" she snarled softly, her voice strong with ill will. "You disgust me thoroughly," she growled. "You're the type of man I can't help but despise!"

A confused Chance was finally angered into partial understanding.

But his sudden astonishment outweighed his rising fury. He drew straight and rigid. Then an unexpected calm coldness fell over him, keeping him silent as he became fascinated by the rash change in Mary Thornton's attitude.

As she rose to her feet, an indignant scowl hardened Mary Thornton's beautiful face. The hands which held the bowl trembled in fear, disgust and rage, causing some of the water to spill. With an apparently irrational vindictiveness, she threw the bowl's water in Chance's face. As the water hit him, Chance didn't flinch, nor even close his eye against the assault. It was as if he'd read her intentions by the expression twisting her features and by the mood she now displayed. And had made himself a stone wall.

At length Chance ran the palm of his right hand over the lower portion of his face, wiping away the moisture while rasping a week's growth of bristles. And this rough sound seemed to grate a taunting note on Mary Thornton's nerves, forcing her sudden anger into violence as she lashed Chance across the face with an open palm, the slap loud and distinct.

This action seemed to ease her ill mood. But she drew back in sudden fear, as if it had suddenly dawned on her what she had done, and who she was with, and where she was.

But the one-eyed man's temper remained under stolid control. The only evidence of his burning rage was expressed in harsh words as he said, "Miss, I don't know how much longer I can stand here and let you insult me, throw water in my face, and slap me like I was some schoolkid. Is there any particular reason for this?''

"Is there any particular reason why you'd gun down four men in cold blood?" she rasped in arrogance, once again determined and fierce since Chance hadn't retaliated and she felt he wouldn't. "Is there any particular reason why you hit Bob Howard? Is there any particular reason why you decided to burden us with your charming presence?''

"Yeah," Chance replied with a growl. "But it's personal and a little difficult for you to understand.''

"Real difficult," Mary Thornton shot back with a sneer. "You're a killing, thieving, lying, treacherous, scarfaced, one-eyed pervert who thinks he can take any woman he wants! Well I'll die before I let you lay your filthy hands on me.''

"You might die," Chance cracked irritably, "if your father finds out you were down here alone with me.''

"Huh," she scoffed belligerently. "You're the one who'd be dead, mister. You put a hand on me and every man here will take part in getting rid of you for good. And if you run they won't quit until they've caught you and given you what you deserve.''

"You sure do have an overinflated opinion of yourself, miss," Chance wryly said, changing his mood. The sarcasm was fuel for Mary Thornton's fire.

"No," she defiantly retorted, "you're the one with the overinflated opinion of yourself, if you ever thought I'd let you touch me." She brushed past Chance, then abruptly stopped and faced him from several yards downstream. "How much longer are you going to be making my skin crawl, and everyone else's?" she asked in high indignation.

"If you mean how much longer am I going to be riding with you people," Chance said, "it'll be until I'm near where I want to be.''

Angrily she grunted. "Well, if that 'where I want to be' bit is next to me, you might just as well ride away now, mister.''

"That's not what I meant," Chance replied evenly.

"I'll bet," she sneered savagely. "Well just eat your heart out, Mr. One Eye. Think about it," she suggested with a cruel smile. "I'm a virgin. But I'm certainly not going to waste myself on the likes of you when I can have a real man—any man."

To her surprise, Chance accepted this with a wry grin. "I guess it was too good to be true," he said, his odd tone and strange expression producing a momentary look of disturbance on Mary Thornton's face, since she was not certain what he meant.

A foreboding silence followed as she attempted to cover her incomprehension, glowered with bitter loathing at Chance. But she was a woman who was ravishing even in her unbounded arrogance, though she had become a monster underneath in her vindictive pride. She was well aware of her superior looks, the spell she cast over other men and the humiliation she'd lured Chance into. In this knowledge a vicious creature had been born in the short aftermath of freedom from her father's restraint.

Even in his wounded pride and ill will, and even in the face of the utter contempt she'd shown for him, Chance found her desirable and mesmerizing, holding his eye steady on her untainted physical appearance. He wanted her now possibly more than ever, being able to relate to her savagery and cunning. It had also been characteristic of other women he'd known intimately.

"You're absolutely right about that," she exclaimed impulsively, but with doubt and suspicion. "It *is* too good to be true."

"But then again," Chance went on, a malicious smile blending with his features as Mary Thornton hurriedly stumbled away, looking back in apprehension to catch his soft-spoken words. "It might be true that it's not too good."

This statement was greeted by a sneering guffaw blasted at him by Mary, whose cruel arrogance seemed to intensify as she drew further away from the one-eyed man she'd left cold.

The Fat Man and the Indian
(The Eagle and the Bear)

7

Beginning their third week out of Smiling Sons, the wagon
train rolled across the broad desert basin of the Tularosa
Valley, leaving the Sacramento Mountains behind to the east
while moving closer to the San Andres Mountains to the west.
Between these rugged mountain chains the desert floor rolled
smoothly in spots and stretched out in vast level expanses in
others. Now they were cutting a trail through an ominous-
looking land of jagged rock, high peaks and brown hills. Yet,
as the settlers pressed onward, they found comfort in the
knowledge that the deadly, life-draining landscape could be
escaped. But the sun of high noon which singed the sandy
earth under its relentless wrath could not be fled from, only
compromised with in due time.

Far south of the westward-moving column, Lawrence
Neems studied the dust-trailing train and its occupants from
high atop a rock-stubbled hill. Outstretched flat on his
stomach, he was situated close to the top of the crest.
Scattered rock lined the hill's outer fringes. He had an almost
perfect view of the land for nearly a mile ahead and equal that
to his left and right.

The steep hill touched ground far below the hunter, and
from where he lay it might as well have been a cliff. To his
sides, some flat surface stretched away and rounded down to
other uninviting, rolling hills. Behind him large boulders were
spread over a gently rounding surface. A stark narrow trail led
to the top from behind, like an open backbone. It would be
too brutal to bring an animal up the sharp climb.

At the hunter's fingertips lay a long black telescope. As the caravan began to roll directly in front of him, Neems, grasping and bringing the telescope up to his left eye, changed his squinting gaze to wide-eyed scrutiny.

Looking through the eyepiece and out the convex lens, the hunter swung the scope to the front of the caravan. He saw the hairy-faced Bradley jerking a thumb over his shoulder and barking what seemed like a command to an extremely dull-looking youth, who disappeared behind the north side of the wagons. Neems could see him when he appeared between the break in wagons, though dust veiled his form somewhat.

When he spotted the unmistakable appearance of the one-eyed man, Neems chuckled softly, dropping the telescope from his eye and watching Chance as he slowly passed up the north side of the train.

But suddenly, out of the corner of his right eye, the hunter caught a movement far to the east. His smile of triumph vanishing, Neems jerked his head, and squinted suspiciously at what he believed were four riders more than a mile and a half behind the wagons. Raising the telescope again, he peered in the direction of the brown dust cloud trailing in the wake of the four riders he now saw clearly through the lens. They were galloping their mounts at a steady pace and quickly closing the distance between themselves and the wagons.

Neems lowered the scope, then turned his head to spot the same young man who had gone with a message to Chance now making his way back to the front of the line. A grim, anxious look on his face, the hunter watched the action unfold.

"Something on your mind, Mr. Bradley?" Chance asked, pulling up alongside the lead wagon.

"Just wanted to know when you'd be leaving us," Bradley inquired in an oddly amiable tone, looking briefly at the one-eyed man, then returning his smug stare in front of him.

"After we crose the *Jornada Del Muerto*," Chance replied.

"The Rio?" Bradley countered.

"Yeah," Chance answered, a sudden doubtful look creasing his brow. "I suppose I'll leave at the river." His dubious look continued as he quickly added: "By the time we reach the river we're all going to nèed to stock up on water. This is ugly, arid country. You'd do best to ration as much water as you can. A mule team may be a little faster than an ox team, but they also

138

take more water.''

Bradley curled his lips and his own brow creased. For a second he appeared to be lost in thought. ''I'm well aware of all that, Chance,'' he blandly said, no criticism in his tone. Then he added, ''That's why I'd like you to stay on as long as you want to. We might need you for something other than your gun—who knows? And you've lived up to your word so far, Chance. For the most part this trip's going well and everybody seems to be getting along better; maybe it's because we're getting closer to California, I don't know. . . . If you'd like to,'' Bradley then offered in a husky tone, ''you can stay with us until we cross into Arizona territory.''

Chance gave a declining shake of his head. ''No, I'll be—''

''Mr. Bradley! Mr. Bradley!'' the Carlsbad boy sharply called, nearing the front on the end of his dead run. ''Riders!''

Both Chance and Bradley swung their heads from Carlsbad to stare intensely at each other.

Then, as Chance fixed the panting Carlsbad with a cold look, he snapped, ''How many? How far?''

''I don't know,'' the messenger hoarsely declared in apprehension, caught between giving the information to Chance or Bradley, as Jenkins, hearing the boy's words, moved quickly toward the exchange. ''Looked like four, pretty far back. Hard to tell much else.''

''What's going on?'' the wagonmaster asked, curious and hard eyed.

''Not sure, Frank,'' Bradley replied.

Chance leaped to the ground. Gently he grabbed Carlsbad by the arm and pulled him toward him. ''Get on my horse and take it to the other side,'' Chance firmly commanded. Then he immediately bounded up onto the wagon seat beside Bradley.

''Hey!'' Bradley growled in astonishment. ''What in the Sam frigging blazing hell's going on, Chance?''

''We'll soon find out. You got a good-sized trunk back here?'' Chance gruffly asked. Not waiting for an answer, he peered over Bradley's right shoulder into the wagon, where the three Bradley children sat huddled along the back end, suddenly scared by the unexpected development. Chance saw the large oxhide-covered trunk he'd hoped to find.

''Chance!'' Bradley snarled. ''I want to know what in the

blazing Sam—"

"It's all right, Brad," Jenkins cut in, his tone hard with suppressed anger. Then he looked at Carlsbad stumbling along on the ground, keeping pace with the moving line, holding Chance's gelding by its reins, indecisive as to what to do. "Go ahead and do like he told you, Tom," Jenkins said to Carlsbad, who was every bit as angry and suspicious as the Bradleys.

"Chance!" Jenkins rasped. The one-eyed man pulled his head from inside the wagon opening to face the wagonmaster. "This is exactly the time when you said you'd ride, remember?"

"There's not going to be any trouble," Chance tautly assured, "unless you people keep bellowing my name like that."

After a further moment's hesitation, Carlsbad climbed onto the gelding, scowled his reluctance at Chance, then turned the horse.

"What's going on, Tom Carlsbad?" Bugler asked in his normal whine of a voice. He got no reply as Carlsbad cut between the Bradley and Bugler wagons.

"How can you be so friggin' sure, mister?" Bradley angrily asked, looking up at Chance, half standing and hunched awkwardly over him.

"Forget it now, Brad," Jenkins irritably chimed in, drawing a look of harsh disbelief from Bradley's wife. "It could be nothing. So I think it's best if we go ahead and play the thing out like he wants it—safe. Right, Chance?"

"Exactly what I was planning on, Jenkins," Chance replied, ignoring Bradley while rudely crowding him into his silently outraged wife.

Bradley swung his dark frown back and forth from Chance to Jenkins. "So what now?"

"Girls," Chance said, sticking his head back inside to address the two Bradley daughters. "Help me clear out whatever's in this trunk," he instructed in a soft but resolute tone, his face determined as he hopped into the covered wagonbed.

"Father?" one of the daughters cried, remaining glued to the back of the wagon.

"Go ahead, Cindy," Bradley said, realizing the situation was now out of his control and accepting that with bitter annoyance.

"Just play it real smooth, Mr. Bradley," Chance muttered reassuringly, flipping open the two latches on the large brown trunk.

Blonde, fair skinned, blue eyed and in their late teens, the Bradley daughters were twins. At their father's beckoning they moved with agitated dismay toward Chance and helped him quickly remove blankets, china plates and an assortment of small bags containing various items.

"Frank," Bradley called to his wagonmaster, his grizzled face running with free-flowing sweat caused by the heat and by his doubts and fears. "You let me do the talking."

Jenkins nodded his approval, but remained close to the lead wagon. He looked over his shoulder to see four riders in long gray coats slowing their pace to a trot, now making their way up the right side of the wagons. "Let's just send them on their way without making any trouble," he added in a low voice of concern.

"Pile that stuff in the corner," Chance said, then climbed into the trunk. It was an uncomfortable fit. Nonetheless, he pressed his brawny frame down into the trunk. "Then cover it over with a blanket in case they look back here and figure that stuff belongs in a trunk," he added, before lowering the top to wait in the cramped darkness, his right hand gripped tightly around his Colt.

From atop his vantage point, Neems remained an invisible spectator. He watched through his telescope with high interest, having noted what Chance had done, and the course of action the two men in the front were going to attempt.

The lead wagon stopped, as did the rest of the caravan. All in turn, from back to front, anxiously noted the arrival of Laster and his three cohorts as they made their way to the front, then gathered in a loose semicircle around the Bradley wagon. They were grim-looking, trail-weary men covered from hat to boots in sweat, grit and grime.

"Men," Bradley hastily greeted, making a bad attempt to sound polite and casual. "What can I do for you?" he asked, trying to ignore rifle butts which jutted from saddleboots and holstered revolvers tied down to thighs.

"We're looking for a man, settler," Laster coldly announced. "A man with a black patch over his left eye and a long scar running down the side of his face. We were wondering if you might have seen this man in your travels."

From his position inside the trunk Chance heard Bradley say, "Who's asking?"

There was no reason at the outset for Laster or any of the others to be suspicious of the emigrants, but Bradley's tone and question caused Laster to raise an eyebrow. And his curiosity became cold suspicion. In his momentary study of Bradley, his wife, the Bradley children clustered behind their parents, and Jenkins, who had moved slightly behind the four, Laster's dubious expression, which bordered on a frown, caused a noticeable tension to form in the silence.

The sweat pasting his clothes to his body as if he'd just bathed in a river, Chance listened intently. "Name's Sim Laster," he heard the man say. The name was remotely familiar, but Chance couldn't pinpoint exactly where he'd heard it before.

"You men law or something?" Bradley asked, sweeping a quick gaze over the four.

"Or something, yeah," Mamoreck flatly answered for the group, adding a chuckle as he received a quick glower of admonishment from Laster.

"We're friends of this one-eyed man," Laster lied. Then, although he smiled politely, his tone took on an edge. "We've come a long way in search of our friend. Last we heard he was headed this way. We were just wondering if you'd seen him, settler."

"We've seen the man you're talking about," Chance heard Bradley say bluntly. He snarled to himself, in his mind cursing Bradley vehemently, while tensing and making himself ready to burst forth from the trunk.

Every face around the front wagon riveted expectant stares on Bradley, who remained mysteriously impassive, ignoring the tight masks of apprehension constricting the features of his wife and children, Jenkins and Howard. The latter drew the most rigid with strained nerves, but remained unnoticed off to the right side of the four hard-faced, uncomfortably attired

142

strangers.

"About two days ago, wasn't it, Frank?" Chance heard Bradley ask Jenkins.

It was sheer luck that Bradley knew the direction in which Chance would be heading when he left the settlers. Chance accepted it as luck. But now he figured the man named Laster and whoever was with him as strange newcomers, and a deadly obstacle in his pursuit of his money.

"Yeah," Jenkins blurted, forcing his startled eyes from Bradley to rest them on Laster, who turned and looked coldly at the wagonmaster. "It was back near the mountains. He stopped and bought some supplies from us."

"Last we saw of him he was heading northwest," Bradley quickly supplemented, acting sincere in his pretense. "Isn't that right, Frank?" he rhetorically asked in an easy tone.

"That's exactly the way we seen him go, Mr. Bradley."

"Mind if we take a look for ourselves, settler?" Ridgeway asked Bradley in obvious suspicion.

"Shut your face, Ridgeway," Laster calmly chided. "I apologize for the man's lack of manners, settler."

"Well, if you men would like to take a look," Bradley offered, sounding undaunted, though leery of the four and wanting to be rid of them as soon as possible. "Feel free. But you won't find anything."

"That's not necessary," Laster diplomatically declined. "Ma'am," he said courteously, touching the brim of his hat as he glanced at Bradley's wife. "Sorry to have bothered you people."

"No bother," Bradley replied. "Like to stay for awhile and have some chow?" he offered amicably. "Not too often we see friendly folk out here." He forced an ingratiating smile.

"Thanks, but no," Laster replied, sounding convinced by the sincerity of Bradley's voice as he reined his horse to the left. "Northwest, you said?" Laster inquired, sounding doubtful, shifting his restless expression from Bradley to Jenkins.

"Yeah, that's the way he went for sure," Jenkins convincingly lied.

Laster nodded. "Apologies again if we bothered you people," he called to the Bradleys.

For an uneasy moment the settlers watched the four strangers trot off until they had disappeared up, then over, a rise in the desert floor, heading in a northwesterly direction.

Chance opened the trunk, climbed out, and made his way to the front under the watchful glower of a disenchanted Ben Bradley.

All the anger and bitterness which Chance had caused him had been expelled in the few tense moments with Laster and his men. Now Bradley felt only an exhausted exasperation for the one-eyed man, who was peering in something akin to grim amusement over Bradley's right shoulder, making sure the four strangers were gone, but not until he'd made a mental note of their tall, broad figures and gray coats.

"The river, mister," Bradley wearily said, frowning his disgust, rubbing his right hand over his face. "That's as far as you go."

Breathing relief, Neems slid the five-part telescope into one small unit, his smile of triumph returning as the line of wagons moved out, trundling westward once again.

The clicking of revolvers being thumbed back, the distinct cocking of action levers on repeater rifles being jerked to feed shells into magazines, and the scraping of metal against metal, sounded almost as one. The gloating smile was erased from the hunter's face and transformed into an expression of cold, wide-eyed terror.

With as much professional calm as he could muster, Neems slowly turned his head. Feeling utterly ridiculous in the position he'd allowed himself to be caught in, the hunter swept his stare of disbelief over the five grim, leering faces of Nenz and his motley entourage.

Flanked by Dreyfuss, and Thompson on his left, and by Reynolds and Krupeck on his right, Nenz stood straight and motionless in his dusty gray uniform, the saber in his gloved right hand hanging ready at his side.

Dreyfuss and Thompson brandished large Colt .44 revolvers, while Reynolds and Krupeck leveled Henry repeaters at Neems.

"What's so interesting down there, blondie?" Nenz asked in a mocking tone which struck Neems as decidedly chilling and evil.

"Get up when the general addresses you, boy," Krupeck ordered with low-voiced venom. Neems noticed his own saddlebags draped over this gray-uniformed man's shoulders.

As if he were rising from his own coffin, Neems slowly brought himself to his feet. The general took three carefully placed steps forward, then swiftly placed the tip of his sun-glinting saber against the hunter's stomach.

Nenz matched the hunter's height and weight, but his icy stare and cold grin seemed to wilt Neems' bulky stature. Like a flower without water, slowly dying a shriveled death under an angry sun, was how the lifeless gray eyes of Nenz affected Lawrence Neems.

"Think the general would like you to drop the gunbelt, boy," leered Krupeck. This drew a sadistic chuckle from Thompson and a giggle from Reynolds, who slumped casually back against a boulder, making sure his headband was still firmly in place.

Briefly Nenz eyed the wagon train, appearing amused about something—perhaps the dangerous position in which he held the hunter.

Carefully Neems undid the gunbelt and let it fall to the ground.

"Now," Nenz said, his tone hard, putting some pressure on the saber's handle, pressing it dangerously hard against Neems' stomach. "I'm going to ask you just once more: what's so interesting down there that's made you follow that wagon train so closely for the last three days?"

Dreyfuss and Thompson uncocked and holstered their guns. Reynolds canted his rifle against his shoulder and watched with an amused smirk. Krupeck also relaxed his vigilance, then sat down on a rock and began sorting through Neems' saddle-bags, as Dreyfuss gathered in the fallen gunbelt.

Unable to find a believable lie, and unable to shake himself immediately out of his shock, Neems' mouth hung open. His silence started to infuriate Nenz.

But the hunter was spared the general's violent wrath temporarily, as Krupeck, unraveling several of Neems' reward posters, cried evilly, "Looks like we got ourselves a real live honest-to-bloodsuckin' bounty hunter, Karl!"

"A bounty hunter?" echoed Nenz, his leering expression

lighting his sweaty, grizzled face in evil ecstasy.

"Don't see anybody here we know, Karl," Krupeck quickly informed, sounding disappointed. Then he chuckled as he pocketed a roll of greenbacks, before tossing the saddlebags on the rock-stubbled surface. "Hope you don't mind if I help myself, hunter."

Mockingly Nenz smiled at Neems. "Hunter worth his money wouldn't have let anyone sneak up on him like we did to you, blondie."

Neems gulped hard. "Guess everyone's entitled to a bad day," he said, finding his voice uncomfortably straining forth from a throat parched by fear.

"Well, you may not get your chance to have any more bad days, hunter," Nenz gravely threatened, "if you don't tell me now who's down there that you're following, what for . . . and just how much he's worth to you."

In bitter silence, the trapped hunter cursed himself. The prodding saber encouraged him to reveal all he knew. "A one-eyed man named Chance," Neems reluctantly started.

"What about him?" Nenz impatiently growled. "Damn it!"

"If I tell you about it, what do I get in exchange?"

"Your life, hunter," Nenz quickly answered, though with ominous undertones. "How much is that worth to you?"

"Plenty," Neems replied. "But I might talk a lot easier if you sheathed that sword and let me step away from this edge you got me backed up to."

In an angry gesture of partial agreement, Nenz scoffed while sliding the saber hard into its scabbard, metal clanging loudly as the saber came to rest. "You'll stand right where you are and tell me everything you know about this Chance. And you'll get your life. You have my word."

The hunter had no way of knowing if Nenz was speaking the truth, but he realized he had little choice. So he began speaking freely, but he bit each word begrudgingly as it left his mouth. "The man who's been riding with those settlers is worth three hundred thousand dollars."

They were all visibly impressed by the hunter's fantastic statement. Now deeply intrigued, the general's four men stepped forward and huddled around Nenz and Neems.

"What did he say?" gasped a shocked Dreyfuss.

"Ain't nobody worth that kind of money, hunter," Krupeck intoned in suspicious disbelief.

Nenz remained stolid in the face of the startling revelation, but listened with keen interest.

"It's true," Neems asserted, now sounding defensive. "Just before the war ended this man, Chance, had a gang that robbed Texas, New Mexico and Arizona blind. He's been in prison for the last eight years because of it. But to this day, none of what he stole has been recovered by the law. And the only reason the law let him out was in hopes that he'd lead them to where he's hidden it."

"What law?" Nenz barked. "You mean he's got lawmen dogging him now?"

"No," Neems answered evenly. "I did away with what they sent after him."

"Who'd you kill?" Nenz soberly asked.

"Would you believe, three bounty hunters I sneaked up on?" Neems admitted frankly. His somber expression indicated he was telling the truth. The irony caused all but Nenz to break into a short burst of cruel laughter.

"Seems like I've heard about this man somewhere before," Nenz breathed, his eyes growing wild as he became entranced by his own thoughts, before shaking himself free and directing his fascinated attention to the hunter again. "That's enough money to make a man a god. And I know you wouldn't be following someone through this hell hole for chickenfeed, hunter."

"Sounds like some chickenshit to me, Karl," Reynolds cracked in skepticism.

"Shut your stupid face, Reynolds!" Nenz snarled. "How far do you think he's going, hunter?" he abruptly asked Neems.

The hunter shrugged. "No idea."

"Sounds like we got something here, boys," Nenz flung over his shoulder, continuing to rest his hard stare on the blond hunter.

"So what do we do with him?" Krupeck gruffly inquired, indicating Neems with a disdainful glance, and causing Neems to remember his predicament—but also the general's promise at the same time.

"Let him live," Nenz murmured, slowly stepping aside to make a departing path for Neems, who remained motionless, uneasily searching the laughing faces for hints of broken promise and betrayed meaning.

"How about my gun?" Neems asked, his tone sour, but strikingly brazen under the circumstances.

"I'll kick your gun and telescope down to you," Nenz answered, now unconcerned with the hunter, looking away from him to the caravan.

"And my money?" he added, looking at Krupeck.

"Boy's got some nerve, don't he, Karl?" Krupeck angrily declared.

"Mr. Hunter," Nenz calmly said, staring Neems in the eye. "You're going to live, but you're going to be lucky to get out of here with all the skin on your arrogant ass if you don't move. Now!"

It was difficult for a man like Neems to acknowledge his helplessness and his total humiliation. His angry bitterness was bringing a violent rage to the surface. But professionalism and common sense dictated the better judgment he used. Coming to terms with the utter futility of resistance, he began to brush past the five silently sneering men.

But his caution was no match for the ruthlessness Nenz and his men displayed, though the promise was kept.

As Neems began to walk away from the edge, Nenz gave Dreyfuss a slow, grim nod of his head, a tacit order which unleashed sudden brutality in his four men, and caught the hunter by complete surprise.

Three lightning blows in succession felled the hunter. Dreyfuss drove his left fist deep into Neems' stomach, snapping him double. Then Dreyfuss came down and drove his right fist against the hunter's left cheek, as Reynolds simultaneously brought the butt of his rifle down on the back of Neems' skull. A grotesque mask of wide-eyed agony expressed the state of mind and body Neems was beaten into. While he was pitched forward to the ground by the vicious blows, clutching his stomach, Dreyfuss launched his left knee up into the falling face. The knee slammed into the left side of Neems' mouth, glancing off the side of his head, as Reynolds giggled and

Krupeck joined in by savagely kicking the fallen Neems in the ribs.

The sounds of fists thudding into and bursting open flesh, and of feet being driven into and thumping the hunter's torso, escaped Nenz, who stood along the fringes of the hill, legs splayed, hands clasped behind his back.

He stared in somber enchantment at the wagon train rolling slowly west, away from the barbaric scene of treacherous evil which provided a grim background for the lone general looking majestic high atop the hill.

"Sounds like this Chance," Nenz murmured, leering viciously at the hostile terrain awaiting the settlers, "is an eye-for-an-eye type."

Her foreboding about Chance had begun to take shape with the encounter with the four strangers. Now, two days later, following the nighttime crossing of the white sands desert and passage through the San Andres Mountains, Mildred Bradley's premonition of evil became a stark reality. The one-eyed man would be an indirect cause of the tragedy about to befall the settlers.

They arose from the ground like ghosts from ages past. One minute there were barren rocky hills. The next, the same hills were lined with the terrifying reality the emigrants had so far been able to avert.

The marauding Chiricahua Apaches of Swift Vengeance flanked both sides of the wagon train. It was as if they'd known the white men were coming to cross the desert known as the Journey of the Dead, and had waited behind rocks and in the folds and over the blind side until the last moment before making their ominous presence known to the unsuspecting travelers. Erect and motionless they stood, like tombstones, with death written all over grim, fierce faces which observed impassively the shocked and horrified whites below them.

Within seconds of their appearance, the wagonmasters and Chance met at the Bradley wagon, hands fisted around revolvers. Everyone else remained glued to their seats. Heads poked cautiously outside flaps.

As the silence extended over the stark and shadeless desolation, the sun setting beneath the mountains to the far west was lessening its intense glare over the *Jornada Del Muerto*. Nevertheless, the settlers sweated uncomfortably, for it seemed to them as if there were hundreds of heavily armed Apache braves. Actually there were no more than a hundred in the war party, but more than half their number were armed with rifles and revolvers stolen from dead white men.

"Armed to the teeth, aren't they?" muttered Jenkins apprehensively to no one in particular, turning his head in all directions, noticing their numbers spread over, up and down the hills. Lances, rifles, tomahawks and knives were held firmly. He noticed the dirt-grimed buckskin and breechcloth attire, the sweaty, muscular torsos and arms, the dusty cotton shirts, and the headbands holding long black hair in place.

"Red scum just appeared out of nowhere!" spat Bradley venomously between clenched teeth, his hands wrapped around his Winchester. "Weren't here when we scouted earlier, Jenkins. But they sure as hell got us trapped between these hills now!"

"They're not going to attack us yet," Chance informed in an even tone, sizing up the grim situation himself. "They're waiting to see," he added.

"Waiting to see what?" Jenkins asked.

"Waiting to see where we go," Chance ominously replied.

"What are you talking about, Chance?" inquired a sour Bradley. "We've got to get these wagons circled and be ready to kill these red . . . heathens!"

"You're talking stupid, Bradley," Chance softly chided, but with vicious sarcastic undertones, continuing to assess the situation. "If you don't lower your voice and get hold of your irrational mood, then they just might attack and kill every one of us now."

Seeing her husband on the verge of lashing out, either physically or verbally, against Chance, and aware that Chance was right, Mildred Bradley placed a hand of forceful restraint on her husband's arm.

Bradley turned, angrily facing his wife, but remained silent under her stern glower of deprecation, while both Jenkins and Chance ignored the Bradleys.

"Are you talking about the legend, Chance?" Jenkins asked in a quiet tone.

"The what?" growled Bradley, swinging his head back around, turning his venomous scowl on Chance.

"It's no legend," Chance bluntly answered. "I saw it years ago."

Bradley sighed his frustration. His face flushed crimson with a rising fury he managed to suppress with great effort, realizing there was something wrong about the situation, that there was something Chance knew he didn't. There was a reason the Apaches didn't ambush them at the outset of their passage between the hills. He realized, too, that his authority no longer meant much. Nonetheless he maintained his indignant manner.

"Tell me what you mean, mister," he demanded. "Damn it to hell and back!"

Chance turned and sneered disgust at Bradley. Then he guided his horse several yards away from the Bradley wagon. "It's about a mile ahead," he informed in a deadly serious tone. "Past that outcrop of rock. See where the land starts to dip down into the desert's basin?"

The Bradleys, Jenkins and Howard were all gazing intensely at the faroff desert terrain indicated, as several other males gathered around the lead wagon, armed and looking anxiously about them.

"I told you we should have had an escort," Bugler whined at Bradley.

"Shut up, Bugler," Bradley snarled out of the corner of his mouth, eyes fixed on Chance. Then, taking the edge out of his voice, Bradley turned his head and asked the wagonmaster, "Jenkins, what is he talking about?"

"It's one of the few places I've never traveled, Mr. Bradley," Jenkins admitted with a sigh, looking grim. "The few white men who've seen the place call it 'Hell's Halfacre.'"

"And the Apaches call it 'The Land of the Cursed Warrior,'" Chance supplemented, heading back toward the Bradley wagon. "The Apaches believe it brings them evil if anyone sets foot on or anywhere near it, and death to anyone caught crossing over it. That's why they're waiting to see where we go."

Bradley scoffed. The others were held captivated, faces etched in taut fascination, hardly skeptical of Chance's words under the present conditions, though wondering why they'd never heard of Hell's Halfacre.

"I suggest we head north or south for about four, five miles," Chance suggested. "Doesn't matter which as long as it's not due west."

"I'm not running because of some Injun superstition," Bradley snorted defiantly.

"It's going to be dark soon, Brad," the Deegan father said, eyeing Chance doubtfully in the face of his request. "We're going to have to set the caravan to defense."

"That's what I just said," retorted an agitated Bradley. "We can't go running off on a wild notion—"

"Then I guess you'll see this wild notion soon enough, Bradley," Chance remarked, somewhat caustically. "Because you're going to go ahead and do whatever the hell it is you feel like no matter what anybody else tells you."

"Maybe you should listen to him, Ben," Mildred Bradley murmured fearfully to her husband, who grunted his distaste, either for her request or for Chance, then ignored her totally.

"How can you even be sure they'd attack because of what you tell us?" Jenkins soberly asked Chance.

"He's not," Bradley arrogantly proclaimed, smirking contemptuously, gaining confidence from what he felt was the tide of sentiment turning against Chance. "Right, One-eye?"

Except for Chance and Bradley, the remark caused looks of horrified incredulity to form on the faces of everyone gathered around the front wagon. Here they were, faced with the imminent possibility of death, and their appointed leader was taunting the violent stranger few had wanted at first, but now needed, realizing his fighting violence could be geared in a direction to help them if necessary. It was a time when unity was needed, and all except Ben Bradley seemed to know this. Thus, the skepticism which was now inflicted upon those within earshot of Ben Bradley's words only manifested a growing dissension which could prove the most fatal of all if the situation grew any more critical than it already was.

For a long moment the Apache threat seemed forgotten by those chilled by the look of pure malice sweeping the face of the one-eyed, scarfaced man, who locked Bradley's suddenly vindictive glare with a matching look. Then he heeled his gelding into a walk, passing Bradley and the others without so much as a departing glance as he moved to the back to take up his end position.

"Jenkins," Bradley suddenly called to the wagonmaster. "Fort Bayard the closest military site near here?"

"Seldon or Craig might be a little closer," Jenkins answered. "Any of them would be a three-four days' ride."

Bradley grunted. "Bayard is west, ain't it?"

"Yeah."

"All right," Bradley said, cracking the bullwhip across his team, looking around at the silent, foreboding presence of the Apache warriors. "Let's get out of here and set camp for the night," he ordered in a surly tone. "Tomorrow we start heading for Bayard as fast as we can."

In the San Andres far to the east, Nenz was peering out the hunter's telescope at the now moving caravan between the hills marked by the presence of unmoving Apaches. The five men were huddled together, high in the rocks, their five horses, plus the gelding they had taken from Neems, corraled near an arroyo.

"What do you see, Karl?" Krupeck asked solemnly. "Are those what they look like?"

"Damn," exclaimed Nenz, dropping the scope from his right eye and handing it to Krupeck, who immediately looked through the eyepiece.

"That's one helluva lot of Apaches, Karl," Krupeck quietly supplemented, his expression sour, grim. Then he handed the telescope to Thompson.

His eyelids suddenly cracked to slits, Nenz twisted up the left side of his face, appearing to be in deep somber thought.

"How are we ever gonna get Chance away now?" Thompson asked, handing the telescope to Dreyfuss. "With that many Indians, armed the way they are, none of those settlers will last ten minutes when they decide to attack."

"True," Nenz quietly replied. "But they seem to be holding off for some reason."

"What do you think, Karl?" Krupeck asked.

Nenz shrugged. "Don't know." Then a broad smile of

cunning spread over his face. "But I think I've just solved our whole problem."

"How's that?" inquired a curious Thompson. The men were fast becoming irritated with the general's mysterious mood.

"First of all," Nenz snapped sharply, suddenly, reaching up and snatching the telescope just before a grinning Reynolds touched it. "Wigwam's got to take that stupid thing off his head!"

He was basically a cynical, sneering, arrogant man full of misplaced pride. But when Benjamin Paul Bradley stopped his rig at the top of the inclining earth, he turned into a wan-faced statue of timidity and deference—as did his wife and children, as did many of the others who had stepped forward to rest frightened, curious eyes on Hell's Halfacre, or the Land of the Cursed Warrior.

Like ancient ruins it lay before them. But the expressions of shock, repulsion and fascinated horror clearly indicated they viewed it as something else—as the torture chamber of the Evil One.

Possibly the feeling might have come from the creeping shadow of dusk. Possibly it might have come from a sudden chilly wind which seemed to blow mysteriously at them from all directions. Possibly it might have been the sun-bleached skeletons and scattered skulls and bones—some covered partially by sand, all decayed by time and the elements— which stretched westward for more than five hundred feet on the sun-baked terrain which leveled in with the far-reaching expanse of desert known as the Journey of the Dead. And possibly it might have been the last eroding remnants of weapons used to inflict death on the long-forgotten souls of this great and eerie open tomb.

But it was none of these things which caught the instant attention of all.

"Why didn't you say something, Chance?" Bradley grumbled, startled and dismayed, but obstinate nonetheless, eyes transfixed on the horror before them.

"Tell me what good it would have done, Bradley," Chance said.

"Absolutely . . . ugly," Mildred Bradley softly gasped, looking as if she were going to faint at the sight.

"There must be hundreds of them," Jenkins exclaimed in horrified astonishment.

And indeed there were.

Facing north and south, flanking the area of human remains, were two straight lines of corpses and skeletons roped to wooden crosses each in the shape of an X. Some were naked and nearly decayed to the bone. These provided a trailing stench of putrefaction having long since begun. Others were skeletal figures hanging grotesquely limp under tattered clothing ravaged by vultures. Both lines were back to back, separated by a distance of more than two hundred feet between them. Each line had close to a hundred hanging dead, spaced at almost perfect ten-foot intervals, reaching westward for close to a thousand feet.

"Positively savage," remarked Mary Thornton, drawing a blank look from Chance, which she returned with immediate distaste.

"You're looking at the results of a battle fought years ago. Nobody's quite certain when," Chance said, his tone bordering on sullen, the lone green eye revealing no emotion as he continued staring at the morbid sight. "The remains are of various Apache tribes pitted against their hated enemies, the Comanches."

"How come you know so much about it?" asked Bradley with undisguised suspicion and irritation, adjusting his sore rump on the wagon seat. "And how come you managed to see this place without ending up like them?"

Chance allowed a wry grin. "Maybe I've got friends I don't know about; and others you wouldn't guess."

The remark went over the head of everyone except Bradley, who shot Chance a sardonic frown and was ready to pursue the matter. But Jenkins chimed in quickly, saying, "Now I see why so few people have heard about Hell's Halfacre."

"Only those who've lived to tell about it," Bradley muttered sourly. "Like Chance."

"And led us to stumble on this place, huh, Bradley?" Chance insinuated cynically.

"You trying to say if the Injuns attack us it's my fault,

mister?'' Bradley angrily asked. ''Is that what you're implying?''

''Apaches get spooked if anybody even lays eyes on this place,'' Chance said evenly, fixing a brief look of strange amusement on Bradley, as if he were enjoying Bradley's dilemma. ''Especially if white eyes see it. And any whites who get caught near here end up like those unfortunates—though the crosses weren't here last time I saw this place.'' Then Chance turned his attention on Jenkins.

''As an experienced wagonmaster, who supposedly knows these parts better than any other man around—I believe that's what you told me, if I remember correctly—you should know Indians have vastly different ideas about death and burial rites than white men do. To encroach on sacred Indian burial ground, particularly a place they believe cursed, even though they hold it as some sort of monument for the memory of warriors who died bravely in battle, is a slap in the face to them. Lots of times the soldiers in these parts will make an effort not to patrol this part of the *Jornada Del Muerto*.''

''If it's so sacred to them,'' Deegan said, ''why do you say they call this 'The Land of the Cursed Warrior'?''

''Because,'' Chance said, looking straight ahead, ''they didn't defeat the Comanches here. Story has it that the Apache and Comanche tribes battled here off and on for three straight days, until there wasn't a single survivor. And when the squaws came to claim dead husbands the sun was setting like it is now. You feel the cool breeze that just started blowing, coming from no special direction?'' His questions were directed to no one in particular, but as he paused they became uncomfortably aware of the eerie chill which had started to bite at them moments after they'd amassed on the rise over-looking the gruesome landmark.

''Yeah,'' Bradley mumbled. ''What is that?''

''Seems like the longer we stand here, the colder it gets,'' added a worried Clara Thornton, folding her arms across her chest and pressing her body up against her husband.

''Well,'' Chance ominously continued, speaking louder to be heard over the wind, ''the story goes that when the dead were being claimed, a cold wind blew in on the squaws from all directions. It was so strong that it knocked them down and kept them pinned to the ground alongside the dead bodies for several minutes. Yet this wind stirred no dust, made no tossing of hair, no fluttering of clothes.''

"Like now," murmured Mildred Bradley nervously, as the wind became stronger with each passing second, making the others aware that, indeed, no dust was raised from the earth about them. Nor did hair toss, nor clothes flutter.

"There's no dust!" cried Mary Thornton.

"What is this, Chance?" demanded a frantic Bugler, as if the one-eyed one knew.

"And while the dead warriors' wives were pinned down," the one-eyed man related, "they claimed to have heard in the howling winds the faintest traces of screams and cries—male voices, like someone in horrible pain. They were frantic pleas from these men, wanting to come back to life. When the winds finally subsided the squaws fought their way through the wind and never returned to this place. They claimed that when they were fighting to leave they felt a force, a presence, fighting against them. They said this cold wind laughed at them, mocked them and taunted them with vile curses against them and their dead husbands."

"Let's get out of here!" barked a highly fearful Bradley as several of the smaller children, clinging to their parents, had begun to cry in their fright. "I don't want to spend the night anywhere near this . . . this place!"

Forthwith, the families hurried to their respective wagons, needing no encouragement, as Bradley, not waiting for anyone else, urged his team onward to the left and down the slight incline, Jenkins and Howard quickly following. The other wagons were mere seconds behind.

A grim expression wrapping his face, Chance appeared captivated by the eerie presence of the howling winds, and the sight which instilled terror even in him. He remained rooted to the one spot for several moments and waited until the second to last wagon passed before proceeding with the column.

Just as quickly and mysteriously as the winds had started up, they began to disappear.

The Bradley wagon was well ahead of the others. But the other wagons closed the distance, every bit as anxious to leave behind The Land of the Cursed Warrior as Bradley was. At all times the caravan remained more than a hundred feet away from the line of staked dead which faced them to the south. Few ventured to stare at the grisly remains while passing.

As he reached flat surface, Chance was one of the few to dare a last look. The wind subsiding, he stopped momentarily by the first suspended skeleton, long enough to rake over the long stretch of bones and unwilling guardians of the dead with somber scrutiny.

Then he heeled his gelding onward. But abruptly he jerked on the reins, stopping and swinging his head to the right. His face stark white, with a terrified expression, Chance's lone eye peered out over the darkening terrain.

He could have sworn that he heard cold, mocking laughter.

And, as Chance moved forward again, the laughter returned. He felt cold and hated. He tried to pretend it wasn't there, but he dreaded that there was no escaping it.

"This is crazier than all hell, Karl," muttered a nervous Reynolds as he and the others walked cautiously toward the Apaches.

"Keep that goddamned mouth of yours shut, Reynolds," warned Nenz with a soft snarl.

Having voluntarily stripped themselves of all weapons, except for sabers—and these for last resort—their arms were raised above their heads in a gesture they hoped the warriors would take to show peaceful intention.

Even in the blackness of the night—for their eyes were as sharp as those of an eagle—the Apache sentries spotted the white men coming toward their campsite, which was now more than three miles south of Hell's Halfacre. Several lance and rifle-brandishing warriors stalked off to meet Nenz and his men.

"We wish to speak with your leader," Nenz said in a solid voice to the warriors, who had thrust weapons at them and were directing suspicious hatred at the whites.

Reynolds was the only one who showed fear on the surface. The others realized the importance of remaining calm and brave in front of the threatening Apaches.

"What about, White Eyes?" spat one of the warriors.

"I have words which might be of great interest and

importance to your leader," Nenz smoothly replied.

"Let the white men step forward, Bloody River," called a strong, fierce-sounding voice from behind.

His recalcitrance directed toward the white men, Bloody River hesitatingly stepped aside to give the white party free passage toward the low-burning fire several yards ahead. They slowly walked toward it.

A solemn, grim-faced war council of eight men encircled the fire, evenly divided on both sides of Swift Vengeance, who stared into the flames and didn't bother to acknowledge the presence of Nenz and the others for several long seconds.

"You are not of the travelers," Swift Vengeance declared, his dark eyes raising and holding steady on Nenz, who held a puzzled expression. "You wonder how I know this," he said, noting the baffled faces, and the frightened one of Reynolds. "I know many things, for I have lived long—long before the white man came to our land. And long enough to now see the downfall of Indian peoples everywhere.

"But it is your strange uniform, White Eyes, that tells me you are unlike the others. It is not of the bluecoats. Yet all white skin is alike. But I dare to say all white men underneath are not alike. I have also learned this in my long lifetime. I have also learned that sunlight will shine off the looking glass you were using up in the mountains." Swift Vengeance flashed a thin smile of delight at the general's embarrassment, as Nenz, becoming uncomfortable, shifted from foot to foot briefly. But he knew better than to speak before the old Apache had finished his address.

"You wish to make deal, White Eyes," Swift Vengeance went on in his resonant, assertive voice. "Of this I know also. Do not ask how I know; I know. And I can see you come with empty gunbelts and peaceful intentions. Yet you wear swords. If you trust us, and if you want us to trust you, then why must you wear any weapon?"

Nenz knew beforehand he was taking a serious, calculated risk by walking virtually unarmed into the Apache campsite. He had convinced himself and the others, though, that the risk was well worth the taking. For he had had no reason seriously to doubt the hunter's revelation, other than that men will often go to any extremes to save their lives. But the fact that he had been aware of the hunter's intense following of the settlers, and the fact that he had an innate ability to command men, know their basic character instantly, and judge their capabilities and read motives, made him believe the hunter's words about Chance as the absolute truth. It was a truth he had realized Neems was trying to cover up at all costs, almost even at the expense of his life.

Nenz was a gambler, a man who had faced death many times before in his life and spat back into Death's face— though always, because of the company he kept, with the odds favoring him. He was also a dangerous, violent man, a psychopathic killer who enjoyed killing immensely, and had no control over his mind when gripped with blood lust. But he was an intelligent man and a charismatic force, another trait which made him the successful leader of men that he was.

Nenz had decided ahead of time that he would even lay his life on the line in the face of the utmost extreme to gain approval from the Apaches.

Now that the gamble had been put into play and they had ventured into a dangerous situation there was no backing away from, the general, as usual, set the example. Carefully he removed his saber and placed it in front of the flames. The others were reluctant for a brief second, but imitated his move nonetheless.

"There was no need for that, White Eyes," Swift Vengeance said quietly. "For if my warriors decide to kill you, you are dead with or without weapons. But this tells me your intentions are very serious, and that possibly your words can be listened to with an open ear. Speak, then."

Total silence prevailed over the Apache campsite. All were anticipating the words of Nenz, who appeared at a strange loss momentarily. But when he spoke his words were clear and firm, yet his tone remained respectful at all times. He chose his words carefully.

"We are five men," he opened. "But even if we were a large army with rifles, we would still fear you and your warriors."

This bit of flattery was not lost on Swift Vengeance. He heard sincerity in the white man's voice, and he read the fear in the general's eyes, try as he might to hide it with a calm veneer. Though he became stern and hostile in appearance, Swift

Vengeance was deeply interested in what Nenz would say.

"We saw what you did to the town of Smiling Sons," Nenz went on. "I have no particular love or hate for my people. The lives of the white travelers mean little to me. And I have no love for the soldiers—bluecoats—who war against the Indian peoples all over this land. A land, I believe, you have every right to defend.

"It is to you I come for assistance. And it is we who can assist the Apache nation in their war against white invaders. It is also we who can help you to make the future of your children and your wives a better, more comfortable one."

Nenz paused and raked a quick glance over the war council, as if expecting, wanting them to question his statement. But they remained grim, tight-lipped, unmoving listeners.

"There is a one-eyed man named Chance," Nenz informed, "who rides with the white settlers. He has stolen three hundred thousand dollars of white man's money. We ask simply, if you are to attack the settlers, of whom you would surely kill all, that you spare the life of this one-eyed one for the time being until he can take all of us to the money. Of that we will gladly give you half," he lied, "so you can use it, or we can use it for you to help you buy weapons, horses, food for your villages; whiskey for all your warriors. You could wage war, if you so desire, for many years with this money, on equal terms with the bluecoats.

"We will stay with you if you so desire and help you obtain weapons, horses and food. But it is the one-eyed man, Chance, who is hiding from the law among the settlers, who holds the answer to who will have this wealth. We ask you again, spare this man Chance. You can have half the money, we will have half. That is my deal. I have been honest. We stand before you and your warriors without weapons, without hatred in our hearts for you or any Indian peoples. We are sympathetic toward your fight. Our want is now your want. If you feel I've deceived you, then kill us all. I will not tell you that it is wise for you to believe me. You are wise enough to decide that for yourself, for it is obvious you have lived a long seemingly prosperous life."

A long silence followed the white man's speech. Most of the Apaches looked to their leader, who stared pensively at Nenz. Other braves looked contemptuously upon the white men.

There was no outward sign that Swift Vengeance was convinced by the white man's words.

But Nenz' men were nearly flabbergasted by his humility, and convinced by his performance. Even the general was surprised by the choosing of his words. As hope coursed wildly through them, the whites held steady, with expectant faces transfixed on the withered, hard features of the old Apache. His face was brightened eerily by the firelight.

"Your words sound believable, white man," Swift Vengeance said at length. "It is even possible that I might find truth in them. But the decision is an important one, concerning, as you said, the entire Apache peoples, and it does not rest entirely in my hands.

"I am Apache who has been blessed with many visions in dreams over my lifetime—visions from the Great Spirit, many say. All of them have come to pass during the many suns I have seen set and many moons I have seen rise. The saddest one has been the vision I have seen many times over of the injustice suffered not only by Apaches but by all Indian peoples, at the hands of the white eyes. And within the last three moons I have had visions of my life soon to end. But I have seen one vision in my dreams within these last few moons concerning the fate of the white peoples, and my sad heart has rested easier.

"You return to the hills from whence you came, and you wait. You have not seen The Land of the Cursed Warrior and you will not see it or a horrible death you must die. This is all I say to you. Tomorrow, before the sun reaches its hottest, the matter will have been decided. Pick up your swords and leave."

They felt nothing, except perhaps astonishment. Nenz wasn't certain whether he'd won or lost, gained an ally or formed an enemy. They were a blank-faced group, who, without hesitation, silently picked up sabers, slid them into scabbards and departed, fading into the night.

Swift Vengeance lowered his head and pressed his two index and middle fingers against his nose and already shut eyes. He now seemed a weary and disturbed man who had, seemingly, just aged twenty more years during his exchange with Nenz.

"Kinsmen," he said, when the white party was out of

earshot, the crackling of flames almost equaling his soft intonations. "Let us decide our fate."

For several moments Swift Vengeance coughed violently. Bloody spittle was hacked up from his chest. But he managed to bring himself under control without the assistance or apparent concern of his warriors, who allowed him his dignity.

They knew the Great Spirit had shown him the truth. For they knew the Evil One presided over the Journey of the Dead, and there was no escape. The Great Spirit of Death had drawn together all who would travel the Journey of the Dead.

"They're out there," said Bradley in a trembling voice, drenched in a sweat of cold fear, hands tightly grasping his rifle, staring wide eyed out into the total blackness.

The sky was absolutely dark; they couldn't tell if it was covered over with clouds, or what. They couldn't get a fire started. It was unexplainable. It was eerie. And everyone was wide awake and clustered together in sheer terror, either outside or cowering inside the wagons.

And even in the biting chill of the same low howling winds which had so frightened them several miles back, they all sweated as profusely as their leader did.

It was a darkness so thick it seemed to breathe. Children whimpered to parents, who didn't understand it any more than they did. The animals, herded together inside, cried constantly in panic and were impossible to bring under control. So they were ignored.

But nothing else could be.

Beyond the wagons, in every direction, they could hear what sounded like screams of agony, undying wails of torture.

No one spoke, no one moved, but Bradley.

"They're coming!" he cried, reaching panic. "I just know they're coming!"

"They'll be coming, all right, Bradley," Chance said in a quiet, steady voice. But, clutching his Henry tightly, he was just as scared as the others. "They'll be coming," he breathed into the screaming winds.

And come they did, just after the first gray light of false dawn, every single Apache warrior under the leadership of

Swift Vengeance. From the flat, outstretched desertland to the south, they loomed as small dark figures at first. But then quickly they grew into mounted Apaches, lances and rifles held pointing at the gray sky like fingers of death.

But their approach was slow with no hint of attack. Steadily they closed in on the phalanx of corraled wagons, the settlers now peering anxiously at the advancing warparty.

Exhausted from the long sleepless night of waiting in terror, the settlers, hunched together, silently watched the Apaches from between a wide crack between two wagons which had been pulled apart when the warriors had first been spotted a mile off.

His arm raised high, his palm facing the awaiting settlers, Swift Vengeance stopped his horse thirty yards from the wagons. When the others did likewise, Swift Vengeance pulled several feet away from his warparty toward the whites.

He coughed violently for a short spell before saying, "I wish words with eldest male white eyes. Perhaps there shall be peace between us. For I, Swift Vengeance, leader of the Chiricahua Apaches, speak not only for my warriors, but for all my peoples. We have reached a decision." He spoke slowly, distinctly, uttering each word in an oddly friendly tone, not with the defiance the whites might have expected. There was some surprise on the part of the whites at this.

"Speak your piece from there, Injun!" Bradley nervously demanded, his tone bitter and angry.

"You are leader, I take it," Swift Vengeance called, apparently accepting the circumstance Bradley dictated. "Fat man whose big mouth lashes air hotter than desert sun."

"Why you—" Bradley snarled, his rifle starting to swing upward. But Jenkins came down with a forceful right hand, keeping the barrel pressed against Bradley's thighs.

"Idiot," mumbled a condescending Chance from behind the crimson-faced Bradley. The one-eyed man was standing outside and to the right of the tightly packed group.

"What is the decision you've reached, Swift Vengeance?" Jenkins called, acting as if he'd immediately forgotten the foolish move Bradley had made.

The old Apache appeared unaware of Bradley's attempt, and he was also unconcerned about Bradley's seething fury.

"It deals with five white men who came to me last night, two dressed in gray soldier uniforms I never saw before. And it concerns a one-eyed man named Chance. Him," the old Apache declared, pointing a long bony finger at Chance. All the settlers within the confines of the wagon corral turned dark, puzzled stares on the one-eyed man, who gazed solemnly at Swift Vengeance, ignoring the looks of accusation as he built an indifferent shield about himself.

"What about Chance, Injun?" growled a sour Bradley with high indignation.

"I am Apache Indian, white eyes," Swift Vengeance proudly stated, his tone now edging toward anger. Then he paused, his eyelids slitted, his dark eyes appearing to be lost in a face so old it looked like a leather canyon.

The old Apache was slight of build, emaciated from a long life of hard times and much unhappiness. But when Swift Vengeance drew perfectly straight on the blanket saddle of his black stallion and squared his shoulders, he seemed like a fierce giant to the whites under the present conditions. His jaw was jutting. His lips quivered slightly. He had a strangely wilted look of sadness. But he maintained a tone of dignity.

"I do not like being referred to as 'Injun,' nor any of the other names your people use to make us feel as if we are less than you. It is said that all peoples are equal under the eyes of the Great Spirit, so I've heard. It is sad that you will not recognize us as such. . . . Why is it men cannot live in peace, white man?" he suddenly asked.

"Maybe you should answer that, Injun," Bradley said, arrogantly defying the old Indian, seemingly taunting Swift Vengeance's dislike with the forbidden word he so viciously used. "Just what gives you people the right to terrorize us, Injun?"

"I was not aware that we were terrorizing you, white man," Swift Vengeance said.

"Then what gives you the right to kill white people?" Bradley angrily boomed, further incensed by Swift Vengeance's dignified aplomb, feeling he was being mocked by the old Apache.

"There are no rights to killing, white man," the old Apache replied, his expression becoming suddenly morose. His odd dejection had a soothing effect on all the hostile whites except Bradley. Even Chance found himself greatly intrigued with the baffling dolefulness of an Apache warrior whom he knew was a fierce killer of whites.

Consequently, the tension between the parties eased for the moment, as all, red and white alike, became spellbound by the mysterious compassion emanating from Swift Vengeance. All gave him their undivided attention.

Though he wore a grim exterior, made so by the ravages of bitter time, Swift Vengeance seemed to be a man at peace with himself and those who were his sworn enemies.

"How strange it is," the old Apache leader continued in his peaceful tone, "that your kind often speak of things you try little to understand. Rights? Also I've often heard white men speak of justice. But you use words to deceive, make it seem as if you include much good in your words 'rights' and 'justice,' when it often ends in your using these words only to seek good for yourself.

"Is it right to chase peoples of red skin off their land? Is it right to rape the land you force us off to make you fat and happy, while our babies eat the dirt from the earth to survive? Is it justice that soldiers of blue rape and murder our women, shoot our children? Is it justice, white man, that you should have all while we have nothing? If this is your people's idea of justice, or rights, then you call the wrong peoples savage.

"The treaties of peace you offer? They are like the rights you so freely speak of; meant only to keep the power of the Great White Father. Pieces of paper you burn as easily as you burn our crops and villages. Words too easily used, words without meaning; lies to better yourself.

"Maybe you are poor, but all my life I have seen poor whites gain at the cost of Indian peoples. Why must it be like this? I have spoken with many chieftains of other tribes, and they say they only wish to be left in peace. They want to be able to live as they wish, as their ancestors did. This is their right, not to have everything that gives their lives meaning stripped from them by the greed of your people."

His words were now filled with great emotion, and the sadness in the old Apache's tone was unquestionably genuine. So great was his feeling that it produced a quivering of his lips and a trembling of his voice.

"But you make little attempt to understand us," said he, "because we are different. So you call us your names to ridicule us, to make us feel unworthy. We are something for you to conquer, to get out of your way. But when we are gone . . . then what?

"As my peoples know, I am one who sees the future in visions from dreams. These visions I see have always come to bare truth."

Bradley scoffed softly at this, but the others remained deadly serious. Chance was the most concerned of any, for he was curious about, and somewhat apprehensive of, the five men Swift Vengeance had mentioned. He wondered what their relationship to him was. Since all the attention had been distracted from him and given solely to the old Apache leader, Chance had been going over the entire situation with the knowledge that he was the main attraction for the warparty. The others seemed to have forgotten this. And as he kept his thoughts and reflections fixed on Swift Vengeance and his words, every so often Chance took a cautious half step away from the packed group.

"In these many visions," Swift Vengeance said, "I have seen the passing of the Indian people everywhere as we know ourselves. But I have also seen the death of the white people. We will fight until we as a people are dead, but you will bring death to yourselves. And it will not be a glorious thing. For after you have taken all you can from others, nothing will be left to take. That is when you will turn on each other and kill among yourselves in your greed and pride. Your bloodstained hands you will turn on yourselves. There will be too few men who have too much, and too many who have nothing. And there will continue to be babies forced to eat the dirt of the 'fat man' who takes all and gives only enough to keep the poor quiet. And just as there is no guilt by the Great White Father for us, there shall be none in the future for those who fall in the pathway like red man has.

"But those sick of your justice will some day attain great power, and they will rise up. I have seen this great battle of the future, seen it in the forms of two creatures, the eagle and the bear. And this will be the self-killing of all white peoples every-

167

where. But you shall take many other peoples with you in the battle of the eagle and the bear. For many moons from now this land you take from us will be no more. The white man's land will be swept away by great clouds of fire, and darkness will fall everywhere.

"This is part of the reason I no longer worry over whites. The visions have been much more clear in the time it has taken you to reach this point from where you left. I have seen, too, my own death at hand, but I have not seen how. And I wish to leave my people as much as I can before my passing. It will be white man's greed that will help us survive your justice and rights for as long as we can. We will wait and forget you totally until the sun is near the top of the sky. We will ride and not look back. Whatever is to happen between now and when we return is of no concern to us. But we will return, and then you must hand the one-eyed one over so he can give us what we want. There can be no other way."

The settlers seemed instantly relieved by the Apache leader's demand, and quickly eyed each other in their momentary peace of mind before starting to search the immediate vicinity for Chance.

But their attention was jerked back toward Swift Vengeance as he forcefully called, "Remember, there is no justice among men."

Upon this grim declaration, Swift Vengeance quickly made a way through his warparty and led them south at a fast trot.

"That's easy enough," a relieved Bradley snickered to a somber-looking Jenkins. "Our problems are all finished. We just hand that freeloading troublemaker over—"

"Chance!"

All heads swung from Bradley and Jenkins to the right, and found that the source of the loud cry was Mary Thornton. She was stumbling across the campsite, weaving in and out among the animals. The loud creaking of wood was coming from the far northwest end of the circle where Chance was rolling back a wagon.

"Mary!" cried an anxious Dick Thornton, bolting toward his daughter and the now mounted Chance. The latter was walking his gelding out the opening, causing several of the other settlers to become emotionally unglued, seeing the source of their impending survival leaving.

"Chance!" shrieked a suddenly panicstricken Bradley, moving to catch up with Thornton.

By now the warparty was more than three hundred feet from the wagons. They continued southward, the confusion inside appearing to escape them entirely. With their backs turned to the settlers, and with the wagons between them and the departing one-eyed man they sought, they were isolated from seeing the new development. And even if they did hear the frightened cries, they seemed totally unconcerned.

A look of wild-eyed frenzy on her face, Mary Thornton chased after Chance as he continued steadily walking his horse away from the wagon corral, heading due north for more of the same flat desolation. "Chance! Stop!" she pleaded in near hysterics, reaching the one-eyed man, grabbing at his leg and left arm. "You can't leave! We need you! Stop!"

But Chance was a stone statue of grim determination. He faced straight ahead, ignoring the desperate pleas of the woman who had believed the world would stop for her awesome beauty and beguiling charms. When she drew no response from the one-eyed man who had pursued her with lustful intent several days before, and when the thought of what the Apaches would do to her—not thinking of what they would also do to the others—struck her like a bolt of lightning, she reached hysteria.

"Mary!" boomed her father, caught between fury and disbelief as his daughter suddenly ripped open the front of her blouse.

Bradley reached the opening, raised his rifle and drew a bead on Chance's back. But Thornton cut in front of his line of fire.

"Damn!" he grumbled. Nonetheless he attempted to sight around Thornton's head before Jenkins, for the second time that morning, kept Bradley from unleashing a shot as he brought his right hand violently down, slamming the barrel against Bradley's thighs.

"Are you crazy!" Jenkins snapped into Bradley's angry, astonished face. "You stupid fool!"

"Take me!" Mary Thornton hysterically beseeched under the total disbelief of the watching settlers gathering around the indecisive Bradley and his fuming wagonmaster.

She was torn between attempting to snatch Chance from his saddle, and finishing the shredding of her blouse. "You can have me! Just stop!" Mary Thornton screeched. "Isn't that what you want?"

His grim face set rigidly in front of him, Chance removed his left foot from its stirrup.

"We'll get you back from the savages!" she promised in raving desperation as Chance raised his left leg.

The one-eyed man's bootheel came down hard on Mary Thornton's right shoulder. She toppled backward, thudding to the ground on her rump and back, and her pleas turned into whining sobs as Dick Thornton reached his fallen daughter.

Jenkins was on a dead run for Chance, leaving Bradley slackjawed in shocked outrage. But Chance had spurred his gelding into speed until it reached a gallop. He quickly opened distance between himself and Jenkins, who stopped in out-of-breath, sweating, seething futility.

The one-eyed man was gone without even having glanced back.

Wanfaced and suppressing an emotional outburst, Dick Thornton cradled his sobbing daughter. Quickly she covered her exposed chest, now aware of the humiliation she'd brought on herself in her wild state of blind terror.

"That's just great, Jenkins," growled a spiteful Bradley, his glowering of contempt and anger covering the cold fear he was experiencing. "I could've brought down Chance and saved us all!"

"From what?" Jenkins spat, pulling up in front of Bradley, concerned faces watching the bitter exchange in fright. "That Swift Vengeance is right; you're a fool whose big mouth and stupidity is going to get us all killed."

"I didn't want that man with us in the first place, Jenkins!" Bradley angrily retorted, poking his finger at Jenkins' chest. "You did! You talked me into it, remember?"

"I'm talking about how you were going to shoot that Indian a few minutes ago and get us all killed right then and there. I'm talking about how you were going to shoot Chance at the risk of killing Dick Thornton."

"Well, a helluva lotta good it does us if he runs off!"

"Won't do us any good to turn over Chance with a bullet in his back, Mr. Bradley."

"And it's sure not going to do us any good now!" chimed in a whining Bugler.

"What are we going to do?" cried Mildred Bradley.

"Nothing we can do," Jenkins said tautly, his tone one of sullen anger as he walked away from Bradley, then through the opening. "Except wait. And fight if we have to."

"Fight . . . those . . . red savages!" cried Bugler in sheer terror.

"I said if we have to, Bugler!" Jenkins snapped. "If we tell them what happened they might—"

"No chance of that!" snarled Bradley vindictively, stepping forward into the campsite. "We can't run like one-eye. And they told us we've got to turn him over . . . or else."

"They never said or else!" rasped Jenkins. "How do you—"

"Well, we damned sight better be ready for 'or else,'" Bradley said, lowering his tone to menacing indignation, fixing Jenkins with a cold glare. The tone of his voice and the look in his eyes brought an immediate and total hush between the two men. "Or else."

Several hundred yards south of the distraught settlers preparing themselves for battle, the large Apache warparty was expressing doubts toward what their leader had convinced them of the previous night.

Under the now blazing sun nearing its midday point, they gathered in two nearly equal sides flanking Swift Vengeance. They were a restless group, anxious to pitch a ferocious onslaught against the whites. But they listened with attentive ears, and even though many now disagreed with the peace their leader wanted with the whites, all gave Swift Vengeance due attention as he and the second most respected warrior among them, Wild Eyes, conversed about the matter.

"Your words are strange, Swift Vengeance," Wild Eyes said, his Winchester resting across his muscular thighs, his fiercely blazing dark eyes resting quizzically on his leader's solemn face. "Peace with the white invaders who have seen the cursed land?"

"Do you not believe, Wild Eyes, that the Great Spirit has spoken to me these last few nights?" Swift Vengeance asked.

"Yes," Wild Eyes stammered sheepishly, unsure of his own doubt, but sure of his hatred. "I believe in your visions, as we all do."

"Then why will you not believe that the Great Spirit came to me last night and told me what he did?"

"That killing the white eyes is wrong?" asked Wild Eyes, sounding astonished.

"That all killing is wrong, Wild Eyes," Swift Vengeance softly chided. "No matter who is doing it to whom for whatever reason. And this is what the Great Spirit told me. Did you not listen to my words this morning, Wild Eyes?"

"Of course," Wild Eyes replied on the edge of indignity.

"It was my idea that we seek peace with the whites," the old Apache firmly said. "I have no authority over any of you. But you have always respected my wishes. May I ask why you are having trouble respecting this one?"

"Because," Wild Eyes said, "it was you who told us of the evils the white man brings to us. And we have seen these evils many times since we were children. You have led us to fight these evils as fearless warriors. The Indian peoples will all die, so you have told us from your visions. And those things that you spoke of to the whites, they are all evils."

Slowly, Swift Vengeance turned his head to the right to face Wild Eyes. He wore a strange, peaceful smile none had ever seen on him before. They were shocked by this, as they were by the almost overnight transformation their leader had gone through. But since their massacre of Smiling Sons, all the warriors had noticed this gradual change toward sympathy and compassion.

"Are we without evils ourselves, kinsmen?" he asked, looking from Wild Eyes to all his warriors, who had only assented at first because his strange words and warmth had astounded them into conviction, which soon became half-hearted agreement. "If we do the same wrongs as others to overcome their wrongs, are we not as guilty as they are?"

"It is not the Apache way to sit still and be stomped," Wild Eyes declared, "while those who do us injustice take everything, laugh and spit in our faces!"

"No," Swift Vengeance softly replied. "It is not the way of men anywhere. But I was told in my vision it was the way of the Great Spirit when he walked in body; that is why he walks in strength. It saddens me, brothers, that I've only come to understand this as I near death."

"These strange words make little sense," Wild Eyes said, drawing slight nods of agreement from several of the others.

"Listen to me," the Apache leader said to all. "We of the Chiricahua Indian people are a proud people. We have left our villages and risked our lives to give our people better futures. We face total death as a nation of tribes because of our warlike ways. But do not let your pride blind you. Think not only of yourselves but of your wives and children.

"Last night you agreed to honor my request. I cannot hold you to that. But this one-eyed man of wealth the whites seek may help our people with his money. It is our turn to use what the white eyes have against themselves—but to help us live, not to die. If we take this man in peace we have what we want without losing any more Chiricahua warriors. The bluebellies will soon search for us. But we may be able to help our peoples before we must fight their guns, to the death if you wish. With white money and the help of white men I may obtain what our peoples need before that battle. Will you now agree to ride in peace for all Indian people, and for the Great Spirit who has spoken?"

Vastly reluctant faces stared at Swift Vengeance for a long moment.

"Very well," Wild Eyes agreed with unusual modesty in his voice, as other heads nodded acceptance. "We will see what we will see."

"That is all I can ask," Swift Vengeance said. Then he headed his warparty slowly toward the far-off wagons.

Gloved hands clasped behind his back, Nenz slowly paced back and forth along the foothills. He appeared angry and nervous, looking only at the ground he stalked. His men, sitting among rocks in various positions, were equally restless, dripping sweat, at high tension from strained emotions.

Suddenly the general stopped, looking westward toward the scattering of rocky hills and glaring sand. "Mount up!" he barked, before quickly mounting. "This waiting's killing us all!"

They received the abrupt order with blank looks. In their confusion, the four hesitated briefly. But when Krupeck moved, anxious to comply with the command as if it would help relieve tension, the others immediately followed.

Nenz was already in a gallop while the four were mounting. Seeing this, they angrily spurred already uneasy horses into furious movement. As the gap closed, grim faces were suddenly lit with a maniacal bloodlust.

Clouds of billowing dust folded in their wake.

The Red Death

8

Fear rose so strongly it seemed to reach higher than the glaring sun of midday. But for the white travelers the silence and waiting were even more distressing factors. Frayed nerves were balanced on a dangerously thin line between mild terror and utter panic—particularly among the women and children, though as many as possible were armed with revolvers and rifles. When all within the wagon phalanx saw the warparty moving toward them, horrified stress heightened.

From the morbidly determined faces, and from fingers curled tautly around triggers, it was evident that most expected a confrontation. In the light of Ben Bradley's ravings and barked commands, they had convinced themselves to separate several of the southside wagons, where the better shooters could assume positions on buckboard seats and inside the front and back openings.

Rifle-brandishing males were also outstretched on their stomachs off to sides of the wagon wheels. Other male members of the group assumed various positions around the widened circle. Most women and children huddled together inside the wagons. But some decided that if they must die they'd die alongside their husbands and fathers.

Little did they know that there was actually nothing to die for.

Ben Bradley, who was crouched behind water barrels lined in between his wagon and the Buglers', ran a trembling hand over his sweat-drenched face. He glanced up at Jenkins, who was situated inside the back opening of the Buglers' wagon. Harvey Jacknell and his wife, armed with Winchesters and positioned behind wagon wheels, were close by Bugler and his family of four.

As Bradley looked away from his wagonmaster to study the approaching warparty, Jenkins stared down at Bradley. If it weren't for the seriousness of their situation, Jenkins would have snickered out loud in Bradley's face. The man who always acted so tough and in control of himself was now a jumbled ball of nerves.

But Jenkins caught the wild look in Bradley's eyes too late. As the warparty came to a halt some sixty yards away, and as Swift Vengeance pulled slightly ahead of the others, his right hand upheld, Bradley's entire body quivered with a vehement hatred which twisted his hairy features into crimson-faced fury and panic.

"We gotta get the red devils while we can!" Bradley sharply exclaimed to no one in particular, his voice brimming with raging hatred. He sighted down his rifle on Swift Vengeance, whose face was strangely calm in the face of almost certain death.

It all happened too fast and unexpectedly for anyone to stop the fear-enshrouded Bradley from squeezing the trigger.

"Noooooo!" yelled Jenkins, his eyes bulging in helpless anger and horrified fear, his shriek seeming to echo in the air long after the shot.

In the aftermath of the rifle's sudden crack, all time seemed to stand still and focus on the frail shape of Swift Vengeance as he jerked slightly, but then remained perfectly still and erect atop his stallion.

From the whites, gasps of shock immediately arose. From the warriors, looks of total disbelief swept dark faces, which quickly formed into lines of vindictive hatred.

No one looked at the man responsible. Even Ben Bradley was in a state of shock, though now he realized what he'd done. It was as if he'd been in another world, as if he'd been in a dream, and had now awakened only to find a nightmare awaiting him. He looked in horror at the rifle expelling its deadly breath from the end of the barrel. He thought he heard himself say the words, "Oh my God." But it was only his lips moving, only his mind issuing a grim castigation, much too late to prevent impulsive action spurred by blind hatred—a totally unfounded hatred resulting from a lifetime filled with self-righteousness and criticism of those to whom he believed himself superior.

His disbelieving eyes remaining calm, Swift Vengeance locked his stare on the man who'd shot him. The old Apache slowly raised a hand to the red hole that had been punched in the center of his chest. He covered the blood-gouting hole with his hand, life quickly seeping through his fingers in a steady stream of red. His mouth hung open and he attempted to utter words, but only a dry, choking sound escaped. Then he belched forth a torrent of red from his mouth.

Shaking himself from his shock, Wild Eyes reached forward to grab the beloved and highly respected leader, whose lifetime had given his people much. But the old Indian fell off to the side, eyes wide in death, hands still clutching at the fatal wound.

There was no further waiting. There was no further attempt to make peace.

The thudding of Swift Vengeance's corpse onto the hard earth was like an explosion of dynamite to the ears of all. It was the spark which ignited the rampage, turning his warriors into hate-filled machines of death.

They were all galvanized into action under the eerie warcries of a furious Wild Eyes. Charging the frozen whites, the warriors fanned out to the left and right, while some coursed straight ahead.

At the sound of the piercing warcries, several of the whites became hysterical and began unleashing shots at the Apaches, many of whom were holding lighted matches to cloth-wrapped arrowheads and firing the flaming arrows into the covered wagons. Screaming warriors began encircling the outside of the wagons.

Several of the braves who'd raced madly straight toward the wagons were dropped from their ponies under the initial volley of well-placed shots from Bradley, Jenkins, Howard, Jacknell and even Bugler. Another four charging braves were thrown backward, one right after another, in bloody death under the deadly precision shooting of a calm Dick Thornton. These ponies stumbled violently out from under the dead bodies of sailing braves, and pitched forward headfirst, legs bending and snapping, heads slamming ground and necks breaking grotesquely.

It was during the initial onslaught, in which many braves recklessly attempted to break the circle, that close to forty of them were killed, blasted from their horses, trampled under hooves and rolling mounts. They fell dead between the wagons, their screeching warcries becoming death gurgles, frightened animal cries adding to the pandemonium.

At the outset it looked as if the whites were going to win, but flaming arrows and a swarm of greater numbers quickly changed the battle.

The wildly crying animals inside the wagons became increasingly anxious with every passing second and were milling about in terror, seeking escape from the black clouds of smoke drifting from three wagons being consumed by flames as the occupants of these rigs leaped from within. Several Melton and Smith family members were greeted by bullets and arrows from warriors outside the capsized, fiery vehicles, and flung to the ground in torn heaps of blood-spraying death.

The circling of the wagons continued for a minute more so the braves could dismount. Those who didn't lose their lives in the attempt overturned four wagons. As the Deegan and McMeeley wagons were capsized, terrified screams overrode warcries momentarily. The bodies inside these wagons could be heard crunching on top of one another in the fall to the ground.

Elmer McMeeley and his sons, and Deegan and his sons, fell away from the toppling wagons. Five braves bounded their horses over the canvas and the bones of small children broke under the trampling of hooves. These five Apaches twisted, jerked and flew from their horses under a long, merciless fusillade of rifle and revolver fire, chunks of flesh giving way to red holes of gouting blood.

Before the five dead warriors had fallen on top of the wagons they'd trampled over, a horrified McMeeley bolted to check his other family members. He never saw the ten Apaches who instantly appeared in the opening, nor the three braves on foot who had created the opening, and who also seemed to appear out of nowhere. They leaped on his wagon, two descending on McMeeley and splitting his skull wide open in two spots with simultaneous blows from war axes, before they were ripped to bloody shreds by another volley of shots from McMeeley's sons and the Deegans. Then the latter turned their guns on the ten Apaches penetrating the broken barricade. No one, white or red, had time to grieve over the dead.

Deegans and McMeeleys blasted six braves to death, as the warrior on foot who had escaped injury for the moment, ran for the closest white and swung his tomahawk at the oldest Deegan son's face.

The Deegan boy grabbed each end of his rifle in a hand, thrust it upward and blocked the downward arc of the tomahawk. Metal smacked metal as the war ax deflected off the breech. Deegan senior swung his own Winchester, jammed the barrel into the Apache's ribs and pulled the trigger.

His eyes wide in shock, the warrior spun completely around and away from the Deegans. They could see that the .44/40 slug had passed clear through and out the opposite side of the brave's torso. The warrior began descending to the ground, but not before the white man who'd shot him drilled another bullet into him. This time a red hole appeared in the center of his exposed chest, increasing the momentum which flung him on his back.

As the Deegan men continued to empty shot after shot into the warriors, three other rigs became lit with fire, while arrows continued to whistle through the smoke-filled air from every direction, striking a half-dozen whites, producing blood-curdling shrieks of agony and acknowledgment of death.

"Aaaaah!" wailed Jacknell, an arrow drilling into his left temple.

"You red son-of-a-bitch!" snarled Bradley through clenched teeth, dropping two more Apaches from mounts outside his wagon.

The Bradley twins whimpered inside, cradling their young brother to them as arrows ripped through the canvas.

"Stay down low!" ordered Cindy Bradley in a harsh, trembling tone, pressing the other two hard against the floor near the back of the wagon. Chilling warcries and death screams filled the wagon's inside like the roar of thunder from all ages.

"Oh God!" sobbed Mildred Bradley, tears streaking her

face. ''Oh God!''

More Indians leaped from horses to penetrate the devastated phalanx. But some who attempted to scuttle under still standing wagons were blasted in the face by gunfire from Carlsbads and Smiths.

A brave spotted the cowering figures of the Thornton women inside their wagon and began running toward them, raising his long lance.

Mary Thornton saw the warrior riding toward their wagon. She could do nothing but watch in horror, as the warrior, his face a fierce mask of vengeance, let his spear fly. It just missed the head of Mary Thornton, but thudded dead center into her mother's chest, pinning her to the back of the buckboard seat.

Managing to tear her wild, tear-filled eyes from her dead mother, Mary Thornton stared into the leering face of the warrior who'd dealt the death blow. But his triumphant grin was erased forever.

As the warrior started to reach for the white woman from his pony, hand wrapped around a war ax, Mary Thornton lifted the .12 gauge, double-barreled shotgun from underneath the blanket with which she'd concealed it. The warrior froze, for he saw his own death spat at him from the twin barrels.

Though she whimpered and shook with uncontrollable fear, and though the weapon's kick almost knocked her on her back, the main spread of the buckshot caught the warrior full in the chest and savagely hurled him airborn, huge gaping holes carved front and back in his torso.

Tommy Thornton turned in time to see the warrior his sister had shot flying from his horse. And his father also turned at the sound of the booming shotgun from within. But Dick Thornton turned to witness the death of his twelve-year-old son. Two arrows were shot between the boy's shoulderblades, puncturing his left lung and heart, killing him instantly, lurching him forward face down into the tortured earth.

The warrior named Bloody River rode from Thornton's right, leaned down and swung his war club, crushing Dick Thornton's skull like eggshell, throwing father on top of son in a grim union of horrible death.

Sandwiched between Howard and Carlsbad, Bloody River had less than a split second to gloat over his killing of Dick

Thornton. Bullet holes opened his chest and back, issued immediately from both whites in a simultaneous crack of death, and Bloody River appeared to jolt forward, then back, under the shots before falling from his horse to land by the dead Thorntons.

Elsewhere, Jenkins and Bradley pumped action levers on rifles as quickly as possible, killing braves consistently with at least one out of every two shots. Mildred Bradley hurriedly loaded spent weapons, handing fresh ones to both men when they needed them.

Jenkins fired at passing braves still circling the wagons, the cluster of dead Apaches strewn near his feet evidence of his success thus far.

Bradley shot at those breaking defense and launching offensive blows of death on whites. Both men wore frenzied faces of deadly intent. Both were well aware that death would strike them soon. They only hoped it would be as quick and painless as possible.

The sheer force of numbers would soon favor the Apaches. And the northside barrier, which was a battered hulk of flaming debris, provided an almost unmolested entrance for the Apaches.

But several warriors, insane with the merciless bloodlust which affected them all, made it hard on themselves. On a dead gallop, four Apaches attempted to leap their mounts over capsized wagons. Only one made it. The three others flew from the backs of their ponies as unshod hooves caught in wagon wheels or wooden sides. All three warriors slammed viciously into the ground, two on top of already dead whites. All three horses followed the paths their riders had fallen, and tumbled on top of two unfortunate Apaches, who were crushed into intestine-spewing pulps. The horses rolled off the dead and continued on frightened courses across the blazing field of awesome battle. It was quickly turning into a field of hand-to-hand, neck to neck, death to death combat.

Other braves tried to hurdle overturned, flaming vehicles. One fell and was engulfed by fire. Others also dropped, slammed and rolled. It was a typical display of the mindless chaos which enveloped the smoking battle circle.

Relentless guns blazed death. Vicious knives sliced wounds.

Living people flailed about in flaming shields. The dead bodies roasted after life was already sucked from them.

Thus the inferno raged and mounted, climbing consistently skyward and spreading. It held all the combatants within, knee deep in an ever-growing river of blood.

The whites continued putting up a tremendous and valiant effort, matching the ferocity of the Apaches. For every white killed it seemed as if two or three braves succumbed to death.

Both warring parties were reduced to half their numbers within minutes.

"What the hell kind of place is this?" muttered a grim Krupeck.

The sight of Hell's Halfacre chilled even Nenz and the others. Upon halting their mounts, they gazed in fascination at the scattered bones and flanking rows of roped dead. But then the faintest signs of black clouds of smoke could be seen wafting skyward several miles west, and this threat outweighed the ominous scene before them.

"Is that smoke I see, Karl?" asked Thompson, having trouble keeping his eyes from the suspended guardians of Hell's Halfacre. "The Apaches?"

"Well, you can bet the three hundred thousand dollars they aren't smoking a giant peacepipe," Nenz snarled acidly, heeling his mount down the incline, urging the recalcitrant stallion over the ribcages and assorted bones. Empty eyesockets watched the five gallop between the rows of corpses.

Any morbid enthrallment they had for Hell's Halfacre was immediately lost in the knowledge that the Apaches were attacking the settlers, jeopardizing the only chance they had for a wealthy future.

When the sound of laughter pierced the air behind him, Nenz slowed his stallion and looked over his shoulder at the gruesome sight behind. He turned his head back around, but the mocking, caustic laughter returned. Now he reined his horse to a stop, the others quickly doing likewise. They looked at one another in turn, heads swinging in every direction and faces expressing dark puzzlement.

"Is that you laughing, Reynolds?" demanded Nenz in an angry tone, his sudden fear masked by disgust.

"No," Reynolds meekly responded. "I thought it was you, Karl. I swear."

Since Reynolds had been riding next to him, the general believed that it_ wasn't him. "Krupeck? Thompson? Dreyfuss?"

"Don't think it was us, Karl," answered a baffled, uneasy Krupeck.

Nenz scowled, then quickly looked over his shoulder. "Let's get out of here," he snapped. He raced off toward the rising blackness looming on the horizon.

But Nenz, a worried look on his angry features, dared one more glance over his shoulder, as did Thompson and Dreyfuss, while Reynolds and Krupeck exchanged dark looks.

The general now knew what The Land of the Cursed Warrior was that the old Apache had referred to. And it was then that Nenz remembered the foreboding words of Swift Vengeance.

Like a ghost returning to the scene of its own death, out of the distant northern horizon he appeared as an undistinguishable black shape, trailing great clouds of brown dust in the wake of the furiously pumping hooves of his black gelding, heading toward the wall of flames and towers of black smoke enclosing the brutal scene within.

Bowie held firmly between two rows of clenched teeth, Chance rapidly closed the distance to war. Nearing the wide-open northern side where the wagon barrier lay in shambles, he slid the Henry from its saddleboot and began to disappear into the great clouds of black and gray. From as far away as twenty yards, the smoke carried the smells of death, which cloyed his senses and filled his head with assault like someone clamping a tight hand on his brain. But this only increased the excited fear swelling within him, and lit an even grimmer look of wild ferocity as several Apache figures came into view.

Within the smoky, fiery, body-littered confines, the slaughtering raged at its most intense level. Even though the fight was nearing its last stages, the culmination of battle was reached, with the few white survivors pitted against a greater number of equally determined, maniacal Apache braves.

Chance turned to fire at warriors inside the circle—about

thirty-five Apaches, several wounded, some regrouping in bands of five or six, many seeking shelter behind flaming vehicles as white gunfire relentlessly continued. Jenkins blasted a warrior from his horse, both man and animal pitching sideways to crunch on top of the dead. Then the wagonmaster took an arrow in his left shoulder, and grunted loudly in pain. Near the outside edge of the buckboard seat, Jenkins twisted, lost his balance, and toppled over the side, where he smacked his head against the ground and lay unconscious.

It was then that Chance made his swift entrance. His deadly presence was immediately felt.

With a long knife slash from right shoulder to elbow, Bob Howard was on his right knee, straining against the upright brave slowly forcing the blade down toward the bulging veins in the white man's throat. Probably the Apache would have won the grapple, but Chance, wasting no time, jumped into lightning-fast action.

The one-eyed man moved his gelding alongside the two fighting to the death. Holding the Henry in his right hand, reins in his left, he stuck the barrel's tip against the unsuspecting Apache's eardrum and squeezed the trigger. A fountain of blood squirted out on the other side of the warrior's head, gray refuse and bone fragments paving the way for the man's deathfall.

"Chance!" gasped a disbelieving Howard. He froze in total astonishment at the sight of the man he'd never have thought would return, much less save his own life.

Chance didn't even witness the results of his first kill of the battle. He didn't have time. Two badly wounded warriors who had been lying on the ground close behind Howard began to rise, forcing themselves to forget their horrible blood-gushing bullet wounds.

His horse moving quickly ahead, the one-eyed man managed to drill a bullet into the forehead of one brave. But the other had sprung to his feet surprisingly fast, his rifle coming upward, seeing that the one-eyed white man had no chance to pump another shell into place. So Chance, sliding both hands to the end of the barrel, did the only thing possible. He swung the rifle and clubbed the Apache in the jaw with the Henry's stock. The vicious cracking of jawbone was the only blow needed to pull the Apache's feet out from under him and drop him flat on his back.

A knife-wielding brave leaped from Chance's left side. Chance turned just as the Apache slammed wickedly into him. Both men flew to the white man's right, hitting the blood-soaked earth hard, then rolling away from each other. The Henry was jarred loose from Chance's grip.

Along the flaming northeast side, Deegan and his two sons, wracked with searing agony from arrows stuck in legs and arms, and pumping red in the same areas with bulletholes dotting their slumping, kneeling forms, made one last stand, their faces grim and determined. But their ammunition ran out, and braves closed in on them, pumping bullet after bullet into their heads and chests, others drilling arrows into their backs and groins. The total assault flung their shredded corpses over dead McMeeleys, as all three Deegans were kicked furiously from different directions, now that the murderous Apaches saw the opportunity to vent their wrath further.

The warrior who had jumped Chance rose to his feet, too late. The one-eyed man slung his Bowie and seven inches of steel sank deep into the Apache's stomach. As the warrior's knees buckled and he pitched forward into wide-eyed death, Chance snatched his Henry, pumped, fired, pumped, fired . . . . Four shots immediately opened the chests of four braves who had just participated in the killing of the Deegans.

It was amazing that the cowardly Bugler had survived as far into the fight as he had, though he was wounded by arrows. His wife, daughter and two sons lay dead near him, littered with arrows and bulletholes, wide lifeless eyes staring up at him. He continued pumping his rifle, firing at disorganized warriors both mounted and on foot, who now either sought to leave or attempted halfhearted kills of the remaining whites.

Bugler was indeed frightened. Yet there was marked courage in his determination to live, especially in the state of agony threatening him with unconsciousness.

Several bullets tore up unfeeling flesh as Chance dove and rolled for cover in an area behind a fallen flaming wagon. He had just recovered and sheathed his Bowie.

Two Smith sons dropped three more Apaches before they

were descended upon by death, shot from in front, then their throats slit by braves who'd crept up from behind. In the fusillade of bullets one warrior was accidentally killed by his own brother's mania.

Another brief volley was then concentrated on Bugler, and this one proved to be fatal, now that he had expended his ammunition. While three bullets splintered wood on the water barrels already decimated by a dozen slugs, two more tore into Bugler's face, mutilating his features, launching him on his back.

Three Apaches pursued fleeing horses. They caught the animals and leaped onto their bare backs, but were instantly blown from the running horses by Chance and Howard. These braves somersaulted and catapulted off the hindquarters of the ponies, heads smacking on corpses and hard earth. At the same time Howard was impaled to the earth by a lance plunged through his back by an Apache who'd run up on him from behind.

Hearing Howard's dying screams, the one-eyed man whirled and fired twice at the Apache. The first bullet tore a hunk of flesh and muscle from the brave's right shoulder. But the second brought instant death through the right temple. It was exactly then that Ben Bradley, straddling the bullet-riddled corpse of his wife behind fallen water barrels, took three bullets, two in his shoulder and one in his stomach. Pieces of cloth and flesh spraying his frenzied face, Bradley stumbled against the rig's side, but managed to drop one brave before he caught another bullet in his shoulder.

"Aaaaaah!" Bradley hoarsely yelled, slouching, slapping his left hand over the hole in his right shoulder.

Out of the flames and smoke just to Bradley's right, Wild Eyes charged. His lance was level with the slumping form of the man who'd killed the Apache leader. By the time Bradley spotted the mounted warrior racing toward him, it was too late.

The driving of the lance through Bradley's stomach was done with such tremendous force that it nearly threw the Apache from his stallion. Not only did the thrust snap through Bradley's spine and pin him to the wagon's side, but it shook the entire rig hard enough so that the jolt dropped to the ground both of the corpses of the twins which were slung over the back end.

Wild Eyes gloated over his sadism, and leered evilly as Bradley's hands grasped the lance that held him solidly impaled, then upright in death. But a bullet in the side of his head from Chance ended Wild Eyes' wicked satisfaction.

Through the smoke-filled, scorched air, six mounted Apaches headed along the north side, weaving in and out of flaming wreckage, leaping burning bodies. Meanwhile Chance, sidestepping bodies, Henry in his right hand, Colt in his left, headed toward the east end and one of the few wagons untouched by fire.

The pain of two wounded warriors was ended when the one-eyed man cocked his Colt and painted a red dot in the forehead of one. Then he squeezed the trigger of his Henry and punched a hole in the chest of the other. Both braves flipped onto their backs, one pushed backward and engulfed in nearby flames.

Chance became one with the thick clouds of smoke, but he watched momentarily as the six Apaches began to leave through the wide opening he'd entered. The towering wall of flames masked the immediate view of anything outside the west end, and from around the outside of this wall of fire Nenz and his men made their sudden, deadly appearance.

The unexpected arrival of the white men they'd seen the night before froze the six retreating warriors.

But if Nenz and his men were surprised by the sudden encounter with the Apaches in the smoky opening flanked by burning wreckage, they didn't show it. Quite the opposite. To the horror of the weary Indians seeking escape, the five white men were laughing. Already armed with cocked revolvers and drawn sabers, Nenz and his men made a lightning massacre of the startled braves, a simultaneous, nonstop sweep of death.

Nenz swung his saber and decapitated the brave to his right. The warrior's pony rode on several feet with its headless rider before the corpse toppled to the earth.

Krupeck, both hands fisted around the handle of his saber, drove the blade deep into another warrior's stomach. He literally lifted the wide-eyed, gasping brave from his racing horse, before the weight of the dead body in midair forced

Krupeck's arm down. The body slid off the long, razor-sharp blade and showered blood while it fell.

At less than arm's length from the four remaining Apaches, Reynolds, Dreyfuss and Thompson unloaded a furious cacophany of Colt gunfire, .44 slugs blasting large holes of free-sprouting crimson, hurling warriors backward.

The annihilation had taken less than four seconds, but it took longer for the excitement of the kill to subside. Then dread quickly took over as the ravages of death lying before them told them that possibly they were too late to find and save the man named Chance.

Scanning the area with dark concern, they sat motionless for several seconds, pulling tightly on reins to control the agitated movements of their snorting, uneasy animals. The air inside was parched by extreme heat, and by smoke from thirteen flaming rigs. Clouds of black smoke mushroomed skyward, drifting somewhat north.

Every wagon along the western and eastern parts of the devastated circle was in flames. Wagons along the northern and southern parts were overturned and burning, some pushed in, others pushed outward. Hundreds of arrows protruded from the wagons miraculously untouched by fire, and the close to two hundred dead heaped in piles, slung over the backs and fronts of wagons, draped over buckboard seats and barrels, some roasting in flames. Dozens of dead Apaches lay strewn outside and around the burning circle.

The silence of the five men augmented the sheer horror of the awesome scene of carnage, and the crackling of fire seemed to take on an even more ominous note.

Blood dripping off the tips of the sabers hanging by their sides, Nenz and Krupeck fanned out to search the corpses.

"Let's see if we can find him in this mess," Nenz ordered.

Reynolds, Thompson and Dreyfuss were all in the process of reloading Colts when Krupeck's form became partially lost in gray smoke drifting past a wagon untouched by fire. This wagon had been pushed several yards inside the circle and a dozen feet in front of three capsized, burning rigs along the eastern side. The left side of the arrow-decorated wagon faced the five men milling about in lethargic and despondent search of the deathfield.

When Thompson looked over at Krupeck, as Krupeck stopped beside the wagon and became concealed even more by a thin gray veil of smoke and by the angle he was at in relation to Thompson, the latter thought he heard a muffled grunt. Krupeck disappeared inside the back of the rig.

"Krupeck," Thompson softly called, a tremor in his voice. Then he moved toward the wagon.

The other three remained busy with their search, unaware of what Thompson had seen. They paid scant attention to Thompson when he trotted his horse toward the rig where Krupeck's mount was now standing snorting.

His throat cut, Krupeck lay face down inside the rig near Chance's feet. A pool of crimson was spreading out over the flatbed. Krupeck's scarlet-stained saber in his right hand, the one-eyed man was crouched low, his back nearly touching the canvas concealing him from the eyes of Thompson and the others.

The soft whimpering sounds of Mary Thornton suddenly attracted the attention of ears sharpened for just such a noise. Also the moans of Jenkins caught the attention of Nenz and the others as the wagonmaster stirred into consciousness.

Nenz, Reynolds and Dreyfuss all headed toward the noise cautiously.

But Thompson, anxiety aroused, turned his head back toward the wagon, cocked his Colt, and quickly covered the last few feet. As he reached the back opening, Chance lashed out, striking with a lightning backhand of slicing death.

A cobra of blood-dripping, razor-sharp horror sliced clean through Thompson's neck. His head rolled off and dropped forward onto the ground, where it rested to gaze up at its killer in horrified disbelief. A geyser of blood erupted from the jugular veins. The Colt went off in the reflex of a dead man's trigger finger and instantly attracted the attention of the others, who witnessed the headless corpse of Thompson being thrown clear of his rearing horse.

The moment of shocked silence was broken by the louder sobs of Mary Thornton as she dropped from the back of her wagon, now being lit by fire from the Jacknell wagon in front, to the ground where she sprawled in a fit of wailing delirium. Jenkins, recognizing the gray uniform Swift Vengeance had mentioned, picked up a nearby .36 Remington revolver and staggered upright to rest his elbows on the seat of a wagon. But because Nenz moved out of his immediate field of fire, and because of the cries of Mary Thornton, Jenkins shot the next man he saw, Dreyfuss, in the right side of the head.

This second sound whirled Nenz and Reynolds around in time to see Dreyfuss knocked sideways out of his saddle by the blast.

Reynolds never knew what hit him. But Nenz, out of the corner of his right eye, saw the long blur sailing through the smoky air.

The lance thudded loudly into Reynolds' back, then burst out his chest, violently kicking him off his horse and slamming him downward onto the ground. The protruding tip from his chest snapped off on the hard surface.

For the first time in his life Nenz experienced sheer terror, possibly because a sudden shift in odds now had him cornered to face death. Nonetheless he spun instantly, as soon as the spear killed Reynolds, and swiftly drew his Colt. He thumbed it and triggered a shot at Chance, who had run for cover behind the wagons just in time. Then Nenz turned and fired toward the wagon where Jenkins was leaning over the seat.

But, turning his eyes to Mary Thornton, the general's diabolically evil mind figured how he'd escape the gauntlet of death he faced and hopefully bring Chance out to face him. Nenz could see the girl was beautiful, even in her disheveled state with her face smudged with tears and soot and strands of long black hair sticking to her striking features. He hoped that she would be of importance to either of the men he knew could launch an attack on him at any second—as Chance did when an evilly laughing Nenz spurred his stallion toward Mary Thornton.

But the wild fanning Chance did on the hammer of his Colt sent three shots wide of Nenz. The general fired back at Chance, the bullet missing the one-eyed man but chasing him back behind cover.

Then Nenz stopped by the whimpering woman, reached down, snatched her off the ground and slung her over his lap. "C'mon, fluffhead!" he gleefully howled, his gray eyes filling with evil intent. "You're gonna be lovin' it!" In the short second that he stared into the horrified face of Mary Thornton, something happened to Karl Nenz. As other dark thoughts raced through his head, Chance and his supposed wealth were forgotten.

Hearing Nenz, then seeing him with Mary Thornton hauled into his saddle, Jenkins, arrow sticking from his left shoulder, jumped down from the seat. But he stumbled and fell from weakness due to pain and blood loss.

Chance stepped out again from behind the wagon and leveled his weapon at the general's exposed back, his face twisted in fury and vengeance. But before the one-eyed man could get off a shot, Nenz raced through a crack between the tips of flames nearly touching one another and disappeared around the corner, turning east.

"Mary!" cried Jenkins hoarsely, stumbling quickly outside the circle.

Chance loped quickly to the back of the wagon. He picked up the saber, looking at it momentarily before grabbing the belt and scabbard off Krupeck.

As Chance came through the opening from which Nenz had departed, saber hanging by his side, he watched with grim intensity as Nenz and the prize he'd seized galloped around the east wall of fire. There were reasons, Chance surmised, which were related to himself, explaining why Nenz had sent the Apaches to capture him from the settlers.

But his brief thoughts were broken when Jenkins raced on horseback past him in pursuit of Nenz and Mary Thornton.

After racing his gelding a mile and a half northward over the vast desertland, Chance finally closed the distance to ride beside Jenkins, who looked as if he would slide from the saddle at any moment.

When the wagonmaster appeared as if he would topple out of the saddle in his weakened, anxiety-laden state, Chance reached over and grabbed his right shoulder.

"I'm all right!" Jenkins snapped, his voice booming with sudden reserves of strength.

Chance removed his hand, and both spurred their mounts as fast as they could possible go. But whenever they moved to close the distance to the stallion, still some sixty yards ahead,

Nenz, realizing they wouldn't fire for fear of hitting his woman captive, would turn and fire at them, causing them to drop back. So both men kept the safest distance possible while relentlessly pursuing whatever course Nenz chose.

"Why did you come back?" Jenkins demanded, his tone angry with the contempt he felt toward the man he held responsible for the entire tragedy.

"I wanted to prove something!" Chance shouted back.

"What?"

"That maybe there *is* justice among men."

The White Death

9

Four grueling miles later the mesa came into view, and it was toward this landmark that Nenz violently spurred his white stallion, cutting through a fold between low hills and racing across a long, level stretch of brown desert. He turned and fired at his pursuers as Chance and Jenkins, eating the general's dust and pasted brown from the trailing clouds they swept through, continued to match the furious pace of Nenz, still some forty yards ahead of them. But they refused to fall back any farther.

Aware that he only had one bullet left in his Colt, Nenz holstered the revolver before sliding a Winchester rifle from its saddleboot. Then the general reached the long, high, flat-topped hill and began racing along the western face. He rounded the far corner and went up the northern side until he found a narrow draw that led to the top.

Halting his stallion, Nenz flung Mary Thornton to the ground, then dismounted. He straddled the deliriously sobbing woman, and, as Chance and Jenkins appeared around the corner, some sixty feet away, the general suddenly erupted into wild laughter.

"Hoo-hah-hoo-hah-hoo-hah-hah-hah-hah-hah-hah-haaaaah!" Nenz eerily howled, firing his rifle at the two men. The bullet whined off several large rocks along the hill's base and the horses of the pursuers cried loudly, then became highly agitated, when two more shots were unleashed at Chance and Jenkins as both men jumped from their saddles.

Chance ran for cover behind the rocks. Jenkins stumbled. Another shot from the howling Nenz blasted chips off the rock behind which the wounded wagonmaster fell.

Rifle in his right hand, Nenz reached down and roughly snatched the woman off the ground. The stallion quickly moved away from the laughing madman.

It was as if Nenz had gone through an instant transformation in his short flight across the desert. His diabolical purpose of using the woman as a hostage, for reasons only Chance could guess at, no longer appeared important. His calculating mind had snapped for no explainable reason, other than that he was a half-mad sadist to begin with, and he was now a frenzied figure of total evil. The horrible, shrill laughter was a chilling outlet for the darkness lurking inside the man.

"Hoo-hah-hoo-hah-hoo-hah-hoo-hah-haaaaaaa!" laughed Nenz, disappearing from the sight of Chance and Jenkins, going up the trail. The high-pitched howling continued to fill the hot afternoon air as Chance jumped over the rocks, gun drawn, running for the path, Jenkins stumbling along just behind the grim-faced one-eyed man.

"He's gone crazy!" cried Jenkins, full of fear for the woman captive, now being hauled up the incline. Nenz' forearm was wrapped tightly around her throat as he stepped cautiously sideways, his rifle pointing at Chance and Jenkins all the time he climbed uphill. "He's a madman!" Jenkins angrily declared, teeth gritted vindictively, eyes wild. His revolver was in his left hand; his right held his shoulder as if this would ease the terrible ache.

The wagonmaster was wan from exhaustion and nearly delirious with pain, fear and his feelings for the woman. This made him push himself to use his last reserves of strength. He was near the brink of death, and Chance, looking intently at the raggedly breathing Jenkins, believed the man was about to collapse.

It was a dangerous situation for the three held at the madman's mercy. Chance could have walked away from it, but whatever was inside him that made him go back and risk his life in fighting the Apaches now made him stay and see this hostage situation through to the end, whatever might happen.

Possibly it was a feeling of guilt, for his conscience frequently troubled him and he often fought bitterly with himself. Maybe his return and now his attempted rescue of the woman who had so humiliated him was a means of atonement for ways he sometimes questioned. But an even greater motive, one that he refused to acknowledge, was his desire to appear worthy in the eyes of Mary Thornton. His lust for the woman had gradually changed into something else—which he also refused to acknowledge.

"Hoo-hah-hoo-hah-hoo-hah-hoo-hah-hah-hah-haaaa!" Nenz howled, firing at Chance as the one-eyed man dove across the draw. The bullet sprayed splinters from the rock now covering Chance. "Don't you come up here, Chance!" Nenz warned, his leering face livid and lit with a horribly sadistic glow, holding the woman under his mask of evil, his rifle aimed down the rock-strewn trail at the two cautiously peering faces some seventy feet down the incline. "Yet!" he howled, shoving a yelping Mary Thornton to the right of the two helplessly watching men and out of their sight behind a wall of rock that ran the trail's length.

"Hoo-hah-hoo-hah-hoo-hah-hah-hah-haaaaaaa!"

"It's you he wants!" Jenkins vehemently accused, his pain-filled, worried eyes glaring hatred at Chance. "You just going to sit there while that madman holds her life over us?"

Chance looked away from Jenkins. He was at a loss for words. He felt angry, helpless, foolish, guilty. He was thinking of a plan of action when the laughing madman appeared from behind the rock wall. Now his fully loaded Colt blazed three wild shots at the two men.

"Stay put, one-eye!" Nenz roared in high-pitched, evil glee. Then he placed the Colt against the temple of a trembling Mary Thornton, who was shaking uncontrollably and breathing hard, her eyes bulging in near hysteria at the two men at the bottom of the path. "Or this fluffhead's gettin' it!"

"What do you want?" called Jenkins. "Tell us!"

"Don't come up until General Nenz wants you, Chance!" he squealed in cruel delight, firing at the men, missing purposely, then disappearing behind the wall.

"Don't hurt her, Nenz!" threatened Jenkins in helpless rage, trembling in his state of total misery as the sound of metal scraping metal was heard. Nenz had obviously pulled his saber free.

"No!" they heard Mary Thornton wail hysterically.

"Hoo-hah-hoo-hah-hah-hah-hah-hah-haaaaa!"

"What's he doing?" cried a now seething and deathly worried Jenkins, eyes wide in panic, turning his angry face on Chance whose own face reflected dark concern.

The sound of clothes being torn reached the ears of both men, as did the continued pleas and crying of the woman and the sinister laughing of her tormentor.

His dread now becoming unbearable, Jenkins started to bolt up the path. But Chance reached out instantly, roughly snatching him back.

"What the hell good's it going to do for you to run up there and get both you and her killed?" Chance hissed softly through clenched teeth.

"Then do something, damn it!" Jenkins shot back.

"I will if you don't screw things up first," Chance rasped. "I didn't think you'd be one to break down like an old woman, Jenkins. But I never was a good judge of character."

"You think you're going to have her," Jenkins calmly accused. "Don't you?"

"Can't say that the thought hasn't crossed my mind, Jenkins," Chance replied. "But that's not why I'm doing it."

"Then why are you doing it?"

Nearly face to face, both men locked deadly stares in the brief silence which followed Jenkins' question—one that Chance didn't answer. It seemed as though a personal war would break out between the two right then. But the high-pitched screams of Mary Thornton reached a sudden horrifying crescendo.

"Bitch!" both men heard Nenz snarl as they swung their heads to look up the path. The slapping of flesh against flesh filled the air.

Suddenly, moving the gun from his left to his right hand, Jenkins brought the barrel crashing down on the right side of Chance's head. Hat flying under the clout, Chance toppled on his side. His face was twisted in a snarl of pain which seemed to hold even in unconsciousness.

"Smug bastard!" Jenkins viciously said, looking at the sprawled one-eyed man, blood flowing from the gash on the side of his skull just above his right ear. "If it weren't for you none of this would have happened!"

Then Jenkins, hearing the screams and tearing of clothing continue, cocked his revolver and hurriedly began to clamber up the rocky incline. His left arm hanging stiff and useless by his side, every movement he made touched off a new spark of agony. But raw determination was apparent on a stark white mask of anxiety and desperation.

The mad general straddled the whimpering woman, his saber held loosely by his right side, an arrogant look of evil glee on his face. When Mary Thornton, clutching the torn, tattered remnants of her dress to her trembling nakedness, attempted to squirm from beneath the madman's spreadeagled stance, Nenz raised and violently brought his right boot down against the woman's left shoulder, slamming her into the hard ground. Leering, Nenz then used the saber to further torment her, lightly running the blade's tip down the center of her face, kicking her arms and legs wide, rubbing her nipples, stomach, then vagina lips with the weapon.

Her horror at this bizarre, insidious playing with her private parts, and the saber glinting in the fiery sun as cold metal was run over her flesh, touching, then scratching and drawing blood, instantly aroused Nenz, who unbuckled his belt, dropped his pants and fell atop the woman. Savagely he kissed, sucked, licked and mauled her body with his slobbering mouth and bared teeth, kneading her breasts and buttocks, rasping his heavily bristled face over her smooth skin like sandpaper to wood.

His tongue lapped up the blood he had drawn with his weapon and it was these cut areas of her body that he bit and abused the most.

When Nenz forced his way into her his saber remained in his right hand at all times. Before he climaxed he placed the saber's tip against her pulsating throat, forcing her head back and staring into her wide eyes with his glazed-over look of wild-eyed insanity.

"Pull up your legs, bitch!" he hissed into her face. Mary Thornton tried to turn her face from him, but Nenz pressed the saber harder to her throat.

Before she brought her legs any higher Nenz exploded in her, grunting, panting, clawing her body and tearing skin. He was incensed, a hungry, uncaged beast devouring prey.

Quickly, as if suddenly ashamed, Nenz stood and pulled up his pants, looking at his victim with a great loathing that had instantly welled within. There was something about this woman he had defiled, any woman he had defiled, which overpowered his twisted mind with a sickening terror and shame after his having had their bodies. Was it fear? Envy? What was it that made him lose complete control over his body when near a woman? What provoked the terrible shame and humiliation he felt, could not control, could not understand, upon expending his lust? He hated himself. He hated anyone who would make him feel the way he did, and women always did that.

"I told you to raise your legs, bitch," he growled, face twisted in near rage, eyes crazy.

Slowly, shaking with terror, she brought her knees to her breasts. Nenz, chuckling in wicked delight, his eyes feasting on her exposed buttocks, placed the tip of the saber against the small brown hole shown him and lightly scraped that part of her body several times, poking, rubbing, prodding.

Wincing in pain at each jab, she pleaded, "No, please, don't!"

But her pleas only served to further inflame his imagination as the mad general, laughing sadistically, began to slowly slide the blade up her ass.

Jenkins stumbled several times, falling on rocks, grunting in pain. But he believed the noises from above would disguise his clumsy approach. As he neared the top his breathing became choppier with every step and his fear increased tenfold. When Jenkins was twelve feet from the top he froze in absolute horror as the air was lashed with a sound that dropped his heart into the pit of his stomach.

"Aaaaaa-haaaaa!" he heard Mary Thornton shriek.

"Oh nooooo!" he cried in sheer terror, not realizing the loudness of his voice. "God, no!"

Jenkins could contain his desperation no longer. Wild with vengeance and fright, he quickly covered the last few feet, his teeth locked tightly as he fought a mixture of emotions and the sudden explosion of pain from his wounded shoulder.

Jenkins didn't notice the total silence which prevailed when he reached the top, throwing his right arm, gun in hand, over a boulder. He started to haul his agonized body to level ground, but what he saw caused him to become a statue of repulsion, horror and misery. His eyes went their widest in disbelief. His mouth hung open to let loose a sound that he couldn't quite utter, a scream that lodged in his constricting throat.

The horrified Jenkins heard a movement to his right. He swung his head quickly and started to raise his gun toward Nenz, but it was too late. The last thing he clearly remembered seeing was the razor-sharp crimson blade that seemed to fall straight from the blue sky.

At the bottom of the trail, Chance stirred from unconsciousness under the relentless, maniacal laughter of Nenz. He had been out nearly two minutes. It looked as if blood was flowing from his ear, but it was a laceration above the right ear. Short, sharp grunts burst forth from a mouth filling with the red stream steadily trickling down the side of a face twisted in pain and anger.

Chance began to rise to his knees, but fell on his back, sprawling, head shaking, blood rolling off his bristled chin. But the continuous howling of Nenz pierced his already tortured brain, ending his groans, forcing him to open his eye and become aware of his situation. Then the sound of something being chopped and beaten that produced a cold chill inside the one-eyed man and paralyzed him momentarily.

Focusing his vision, Chance groped for his gun, found it, then staggered to his feet. Under the excruciating agony pounding hot blood through his skull, he dropped on a rock. He breathed deeply for several seconds, then began crawling up the incline.

Nearing the top, Chance felt strength returning and vision clearing as he prepared himself to confront Nenz. Adrenalin coursed madly through his body as the sounds of horror went on and on like an endless nightmare.

Unlike Jenkins, Chance remained silent in his climb, carefully placing his steps, making certain the metal scabbard didn't bang rock, though pain and nausea threatened his balance and wanted to hurl him backward.

A brawny, sinewy hand fell down on top of the boulder. Then the bloody face of the one-eyed man rose over the top.

"Good . . . God," Chance muttered. Raw hatred instantly

swept his grim, blood-covered face.

What he saw was the most chilling, horrible display of inhumanity he'd ever witnessed in a life that had seen many mindless, atrocious acts. He knew he was not only watching a raving madman at work, but something that wasn't quite human. No human being could do what Karl Nenz had done to Mary Thornton and was now doing to the body of Frank Jenkins. But a sick monster could.

Nenz was totally unaware that Chance was watching him from thirty feet behind. The laughing madman was in a frenzy, jumping up and down on the partially dismembered Jenkins. With each vicious blow he dealt unfeeling flesh, his maniacal state seemed to become ever more furious.

"Nenz!" Chance yelled, unable to withhold his revulsion and hatred any longer, raising the Colt.

The chopping blows and insane dancing of Nenz stopped almost instantly, as the general, breathing sharply, turned his head slightly. Then, his startled, grizzled face spattered with the blood of his victims, Nenz showed Chance a sinister grin of pure evil out of the left corner of his mouth.

With lightning speed, Nenz, letting the bloodied saber fall from his right hand, drew his gun from its holster. But it was as if Chance had read his mind. When Nenz whirled, gun cocked, Chance blasted the revolver from the general's hand. The bullet furrowed across the top of the madman's hand, his own gun going off, but well before he'd brought it in line with Chance. The general's revolver flew from his hand and landed several feet behind him. Nenz looked blankly at the weapon, then at his bleeding hand. Finally he turned his glazed-over eyes on Chance as the one-eyed man climbed over the rock and landed strongly on both feet.

"Too easy, Nenz," Chance snarled, holding the gun level with the general's chest. The entire front of the madman's gray clothing was now a dark red, soaked with blood.

A strange smile suddenly rolled over the face of Nenz. It was a smile of pleading, of begging to be understood. But, as he stared into the chilling lone green eye of the scarfaced man, whose clenched teeth were stained red with blood, he knew there would be no mercy, no understanding for the heinous, senseless murders of Mary Thornton and Frank Jenkins. Nenz was gripped by fear, an icy fear of death.

For the man named Chance, this was his moment of atonement.

But Nenz relaxed, and his fear turned to confusion when Chance holstered his gun.

"Pick it up," Chance evenly commanded, his face rigid with malice and loathing as he slid the saber from its scabbard, then held it boldly by his side. "And come on at me," he brazenly taunted in a soft, almost easy voice.

Nenz gulped hard, his eyes fixed on Chance in a trancelike state. Then he turned his head and looked at his saber, lying near the mutilated remains of Jenkins.

"Pick it up!" Chance savagely barked. Nenz swung his head back to glare depthless hatred toward the only man who'd ever caused him to feel naked terror and outright humiliation.

Nenz grabbed his saber, then took three slow paces toward Chance, blood-dripping blade held loosely by his side. The one-eyed man's saber was also held slightly away from his side. For several seconds, each man tried to stare the other down. High above the broad rocky surface of the mesa, two vultures appeared and swam lazy circles in the rich blueness of the dome over them.

If Nenz was frightened, he no longer showed it. Now, legs splayed, a hate-filled, sadistic leer twisting his face, he was prepared to kill the one-eyed man, realizing that he'd ruined any deals which might have been made because of his fit of insanity. A murderous rage which was now creeping back over him.

"You stupid fool!" the madman said, his wide, lifeless eyes staring wildly at Chance. "The money!" he croaked, on the verge of another raving outburst, spittle flying from his mouth.

The response Chance gave was the raising of his saber toward Nenz. Then he angled his body slightly sideways, knees bent, assuming a fighting position. His face was set in hard, vindictive determination.

Nenz snarled with all the hatred and mania he could dredge up from his dark soul. "If I can't have it!" he savagely declared, swinging his sword up, connecting, metal clanging metal, "then nobody will!"

Neither one yielded ground. Both swung blades in unison three straight times, metal ferociously banging metal. They made half circles, jabbing at each other, parrying thrusts. When Nenz swung at Chance's midsection, Chance blocked the attempt. And when Chance lashed back, Nenz instantly shielded his body with his saber.

Relentlessly, both men continued banging metal, teeth gnashing, sweat flying.

Chance ducked a swipe at his head, then countered with a backhand slash at the madman's midsection. But Nenz brought his saber down quickly, wildly smashing his blade near the hilt of Chance's saber.

Nenz became more enraged with every failed attempt. And Chance, feeling the effects of the blow to his head, became weaker with each passing second, the sun's angry glare sapping the life from both men dueling to the death.

Nenz suddenly resumed his mindless insanity. He growled his frustration and launched a series of mighty swipes and slashes at Chance. There was now no skill in his assault; he was simply consumed by his mania to kill.

With every attempted killing strike, Chance moved backward until his back was nearly pressed against a boulder. Nenz took one last tremendous swing at Chance's head. But he missed, his blade slamming rock, jarring his entire body as Chance, dodging under, came halfway up, then lashed his saber deep into the left side of the madman's leg, slicing deep, just above his kneecap.

"*Aaaaaahhhhhhh!*" Nenz shrieked horribly, eyes nearly pressed from his head under the searing agony, dropping his saber, legs buckling, pitching forward. But not before Chance slashed open his left shoulder with another brutal blow.

His piercing wails reaching a crescendo which seemed to echo off in every direction over the *Jornada Del Muerto*, Nenz crawled desperately to the boulder. But Chance, as Nenz had guessed correctly, had no mercy.

Yet strangely enough, Nenz felt no further pain in his last dying moment. For as blackness began to engulf him, Karl Nenz saw several visions which produced a cold chill that replaced the excruciating misery he should have felt.

An arm for an arm. Joseph Sterning's pleading, shame-filled eyes.

A leg for a leg. The mutilated Negro hanging from the Kansas tree.

A hand for a hand. The young Sterning girl being raped by Krupeck.

An eye for an eye. The boy he'd ordered killed.

Through his fading vision, these were the results of the blows Nenz saw Chance delivering. But actually, Chance only struck him twice more, both times to open slices across the madman's stomach.

Sitting partially upright, Nenz slid down the rock. His last vision in life was of Chance leaning over him, the one-eyed man's mouth filled with blood, teeth as red as the saber pointing into his face.

Nenz stared at the face, feeling himself drifting away into blackness. But not before Nenz thought he heard Chance say, "Is there justice?"

Karl Nenz would soon know.

Chance shoveled dirt over the remains of the three new dead. The late afternoon sun was sinking in the west, below the mesa's thirty-foot eastern face. Shade helped ease the strain of his chore, though sweat flowed freely from the one-eyed man's pores. His white undershirt was soaked with perspiration and the sweat cleaned most of the blood off his face. What pain remained from the blow to his head was ignored as if it had never been. The calm composure with which he performed his task would never suggest that he had just survived a day in the face of death.

In the shallow graves went whatever personal possessions each of the dead had with them. Chance kept what food and water he'd found on the horses of Nenz and Jenkins.

There was an odd despondency about Chance's face. He wasn't certain what he felt any more; the tragedy's total horror had drained him entirely. All he now knew was exhaustion. And a sense of misdirection? There was nothing he could do but move on.

Though his guilt had faded a little, Chance was beginning to wish he'd never been let out of prison. He believed he, not Nenz, was responsible for the horror he'd brought the settlers.

And briefly he wondered why he was alive when everyone else had died.

There was, indeed, something ironic about his life. And his destiny? Something lurking deep within made him believe that what awaited him would be even more ironic and even more deadly; that by surviving he had only created more trouble for himself.

When he finished covering the remains, Chance stepped back. Solemnly he gazed on the three mounds. Then he picked up both sabers used in the death duel with the mad general, one in each hand.

Gloomily he looked at the grave of Karl Nenz. The whole maniacal escapade with Nenz still held Chance astonished and somewhat horrified. He remembered his death duel with Nenz as if it were a dream—or a nightmare. Clearly, he knew that he would remember the sheer horror of this day for the rest of his years.

There was no explanation for what had caused Karl Nenz to do what he'd done. But Chance knew that whatever darkness dwelt deep in the hearts of men often produced such unexplainable atrocities, and acts that were unforgivable in the eyes of others. This darkness often caused him to act in similar fashion. He recognized himself as just a man living in a world of men. He didn't put himself above the human condition, he only tried to survive in it with whatever it took. And he was a man who learned from his mistakes.

As if it were some sort of burial rite, Chance consecutively dropped the sabers in the mound of dirt covering Nenz. He did it without malice, but softly, almost religiously.

His lips parted slightly, he swept a disconsolate gaze over the three graves. Then he bent down, picked up the short-handled shovel, and took several steps from the dead. But he stopped, looking out over the vast expanse of desertland which had been the site of so much misery.

Every person he'd known, every dream and aspiration he'd ever had seemed to fill his mind in one enormous collage of fleeting images. He wondered about what awaited him on the trail he would take north to the site of what had started it all. Momentarily he stayed rooted in his daze, as if the enormity of the suffering of this day were being lifted from his shoulders.

"Was it worth it?" he murmured to himself in near despair. The far-reaching land seemed to suck the lone man into nothingness.

More than three hundred miles and six days later, Chance was about to discover the truth.

The sun was setting in gray sky of dark, broken clouds over northeastern Arizona territory when Chance, nearing the Puerco River from the south, quickened the steps of his gelding. The horses of Nenz and Jenkins, tied to his saddle-horn with a lead rope, were also encouraged to hasten their strides.

After he led the horses through the sludgy, nearly dried river, he guided them several hundred feet southwest down the bank, where the river began to curve northward through the valley. He went up the steeply sloping north bank, then dismounted and tethered the horses to a creosote bush.

A sense of wild hope raced through him as he stared at rocks piled in front of a boulder. Underneath lay what he'd traveled so far and put himself in grave danger for—and what so many had died for, directly and indirectly.

Almost frantically, he dug in his saddlebag for the short-handled shovel, then stood still for a long moment wondering. The rocks were arranged just as he remembered having left them but somehow they looked different. Maybe it was because it had been so long. Maybe. . . .

With swift strides Chance loped the several yards to the rocks, stuck his shovel in the ground, and began tossing the stones away until he'd reached soil.

In less than five minutes, his thickly-stubbled face dripping with perspiration, he had uncovered the large black chest lying more than a foot under the hard ground. He had never locked the chest because anyone who knew what was in it would find a way to open it, regardless.

Quickly he cleared away an area in front of the two latches. For frozen seconds he stayed rock steady, his breathing ceasing, his lone eye resting hard on the chest which held a rich prize. The moment had arrived. He felt lightheaded in his state of total exhaustion and anxiety. Then he reached down, flipped the latches open, and took a last long look at the chest, wondering.

The lid came up. And the look on the one-eyed man's face became as dark as the horizon behind his head. The longer he looked inside the chest, the more livid he grew.

For there was something in the chest, but it wasn't money. It was a cruel joke, a joke that burned hellfire inside Chance.

Looking up at the one-eyed man, the skull, resting on a black pillow, seemed to mock and taunt the fury growing rapidly inside Chance. But what was an even more vicious blow was the black eyepatch over the skull's left eye socket. A cruel joke indeed, a devastating, traumatic blow. But there was no way of venting the violence and horror expanding his soul, making his body balloon with boiling blood.

There was only one thing he could do.

The sneering skull was covered by a lid slammed so hard the whole earth about Chance seemed to tremble.

"Godddddammmmmmmiiiiiiiiiiiiiiit!"

His vehement roar of despair and futile rage echoed throughout the valley. To the sky. To the living. To the dead. The shock was a further taunting blow to his ears, to his eyes, to his life and the tragic marks he bore.

Today there was much happiness in hell.

The Judgment Day

10

Easter Sunday morning in the town of Calvary came with ominous black clouds rolling in from the west. But this did not stop the throngs from crowding into the large white church as they drifted toward wide-open doors where soft, melodious pump-organ music flowed from inside. In fact, it looked as if the men, women and children, all attired in their Sunday best —dark suits, flowing white dresses, men with pomade-slickened hair, women with sweet-smelling perfumes, every child polite and with happy smiles—were anxious to find refuge from the threat of the impending storm which had been building steadily the whole night.

To an outsider, the obvious display of the town's religious zeal might immediately strike one as curious, or odd, or appealing. But the cleanliness of the town, because every building was a spotless white, for the townspeople were fanatics about cleanliness, and the good will and carefree happiness which seemed to emanate from all sides, might ease the troubled conscience of worries of almost anyone.

It was not to be for the man named Chance.

Here, where there was no hostility or violence, Chance made his slow approach from the south. And if he felt anything toward the unusual sight, he didn't acknowledge it. His face remained blank, his manner stolid.

The town was in the shape of a crucifix, with the white church at the highest point of the cross. A narrow street ran in front of the church. With a large marble crucifix atop the steeple, the church was situated at the bottom of a high hill that rolled out in southeast and northwest directions and faced to the west, where a wide street divided two rows of the white buildings. Atop this high hill, directly over the church, were three crosses, the center one the tallest and painted white, the two flanking crosses much smaller and barren of paint. North, south and west, two tall crucifixes, painted white, at each of the three entrances, upheld long white banners.

It was up the southern arm of the cross-shaped town that Chance passed under a banner that proclaimed: CHRIST THE LORD IS RISEN TODAY, ALLELUIA! To the west, thunder rumbled and sheets of lightning lashed down at canyons and hill-marked brown desert.

Father Al Aspane was well over six feet and two hundred and ten pounds. Though his smile was broad and friendly, he wore a stern exterior, and underneath he was all fire and brimstone. He had hair as white as his cassock, a voice which rolled like the distant rumbling of thunder, and large blue eyes which seemed to welcome but at the same time search and warn. They were eyes from which you could have read the Ten Commandments. Also he had thin, mean lips from which severe lambasting haughtily condemned the evils of the world with selfrighteous indignation. Large, rough hands wrung the hands of worshippers with unnecessary vigor, touching the souls of the citizens with his drawing presence, sensing for sin. All in Calvary were avid churchgoers, many coming as regularly as twice a week.

Along the street in front of the church, several horse-drawn carriages deposited women and children. The drivers then parked and secured the teams in stables down the north end of the street.

"Mr. and Mrs. Schmidt!" Father Aspane exuberantly greeted, wringing hands with a paunchy man who sported slicked-back dark hair. "Looking dapper! Looking dapper!"

A faintly sarcastic grimace from the reverend. A slightly embarrassed grin from Mr. Schmidt. A chuckle from both men. It was a private joke between the parties. The Schmidts hurried away, as if such a remark, heaven forbid, could not be permitted on Easter Sunday.

More hand crushing. Perfunctory exchanges. Curt nods and solemn faces.

There were a few who disagreed with the town's policy of

holding Easter Sunday on a hot June day. But the reverend, who saw signs of supernatural forces working in everything, liked the idea of celebrating the resurrection on the day Calvary had been officially founded. The town council liked the idea, also.

It was not until the last family was ushered inside that the reverend took notice of the one-eyed stranger who was trudging his weary gelding toward the church. The stranger was now less than thirty feet from the reverend.

Father Aspane studied Chance for a long moment. Immediately he decided that what he saw he didn't like. His eyes became suspicious, and his face showed concern, noting the grim marks of obvious violence, the tied-down holster, the heavily bristled face, the unwashed body and clothing.

"Would thou care to join us for Easter services, stranger?" he tautly asked, forcing the reluctant invitation when he could think of nothing else to say.

Chance came to a halt several yards in front of the church steps. "Kind of late this year, aren't you, Father?"

The dour, exhausted expression on Chance's face, and the note of dejection in his voice, relieved the reverend's anxiety. He nodded his head, as if in appreciation that this man, who was obviously a heathen, was familiar with Christianity. And now that he could tell this was a troubled mån with most likely a sordid past, Father Aspane's face became hard but his tone was somewhat compassionate. Nevertheless he injected a reproaching quality to his voice as he said, "I am never too late to help ease thy troubled conscience, son. I can tell thou are a great sinner," said he, "for thy past is obvious. Thou hast been living without the Lord, son. But," he said forcefully, "the mercy of Christ Jesus Almighty is open to those who seek, son." Then he swept a glance over Chance's attire. "Will thou join us, son? Thou can sit in the back."

"Thanks, but no, Father," Chance declined. "Just point me to the nearest saloon."

"There are no saloons in this town, son," the reverend distastefully said, an edge of indignity in his tone. "Drink is the blood of the devil, loose women the damnation of many a good man."

"You mean to tell me," Chance said, his sullen tone now

209

taking on an edge of its own, "that there isn't one bottle of whiskey in this town?"

Rankled by the interruption, Father Aspane pointed a finger of reproach at Chance, then dropped his arm by his side. "There are some of my brethren who must partake occasionally. For those few who indulge we have a recreation hall," he admitted with some embarrassment. "But all are now attending service celebrating the Risen Lord, heathen."

"I think I'll forego the celebration this year," Chance said, then guided his mount away from a cross Father Aspane. "Wouldn't want to dirty any of ye brethren, Father."

Grunting his dismay, the reverend shook his head as Chance moved off down the center street. The sky was now a thick black blanket directly over the town, with thunder booming, lightning striking down from the heavens. "I fear thou are a man that the Lord strongly disapproves of, heathen!" the reverend called after Chance.

"Yeah," Chance flung over his shoulder, his head turned sideways, the words coming out of the right corner of his twisted mouth. "I know damn good and well that this is one feller they've got a big list drawn up for."

"I trust thou to keep hands to thyself, heathen!" Then, receiving no response from the one-eyed man, Father Aspane vented a low sigh of disgust. He glared briefly at Chance before stalking off to the church to begin services.

Chance pulled up at a trough in front of a general store on the north side, dismounted, and tethered the three horses tightly. Then he slid his Henry from its saddleboot and stepped up onto the boardwalk. As he went into the store and took various items, leaving the appropriate amount of money, the opening hymn of "Christ, the Lord, is Risen Again" reached his ears.

Chance plucked a fresh bottle of rye whiskey from under the counter. A strange, wry grin then came to his lips. He heard wood creaking behind him and turned sideways with a smooth swiftness that frightened the woman standing in the back doorway.

She was a tall, black-haired, blue-eyed woman in her late twenties, and perhaps she had once been beautiful, striking. But hard and bitter times had carved a permanent look of gloomy sadness on a face that had grown too old too fast. It was a type of face with which the man named Chance was all too familiar. Except for the physical scars of violence and brutality, it was a face like his, one that had seen the same harshness and ugliness of life, a face of the cheated, the betrayed, the mocked, the hated. And as Chance coolly appraised the woman's long, slender and still tender body beneath a tight-fitting black dress, he came to an instant understanding, in light of his knowledge about Calvary, of her troubles and why her bitterly sad demeanor was such as it was.

"Ma'am," Chance greeted. "You're not at services. Thought everybody in the town was a devout Christian."

She shook her head. "Devout Christian, mister? No." She sighed wearily. "Everyone in this town is not a devout hypocrite."

Chance made a wry face. "If you'll excuse me, ma'am. My number's soon coming up."

He turned and made to leave.

"Wait!" she cried, sounding almost desperate, her plea cutting through the strong church singing. Chance slowly turned his body around to look long and with hard puzzlement at the woman with the mournful eyes; she swallowed hard.

"I saw you ride into town," she said in a timid yet somewhat brazen voice, before taking several steps toward Chance, who now completely turned to face her approach. She stopped in front of the one-eyed man. Suddenly her hand reached out and gently touched, then traced, the livid scar on Chance's face. A look of strange warmth, of pleading, and perhaps of compassion, came to her eyes. "I. . . ." she stammered, "I feel as if you're someone I've known all my life. Or maybe somebody I should have known."

And strangely, Chance likewise felt a heat of mercy growing within him. "I'm not a man anybody should know, ma'am."

"Kathy. Please." A brief pause; she left her hand on Chance's face. "They're coming after you, aren't they?"

Chance nodded shallowly.

Kathy drew a breath and again swallowed hard, as if speaking was putting a great strain on her. She then touched her lips with the tip of her tongue, a look of pain in her eyes. "How long's it been since you had a woman?"

A pathetic half smile formed on the one-eyed man's lips. "Too damned long," he said.

The sad-faced Kathy smiled. "You've had women," she slowly went on, her tone soothing, tender. "But you've never really had a woman. You thought you had a woman once. You've led a troubled life—a horrible one, in fact. The pain's there; I can see it."

As if mesmerized, Chance listened. A choking anguish welled in his gut. He fought it down, told it to go away.

"You're like me in many ways," she said. "Outcast. Shunned. Despised for being what we feel we have to be in order to live with ourselves. Have you ever known any Kathys?"

"Yeah," Chance said. "That was the once."

"Take me," she said in a low, soft voice. "Upstairs."

She turned and led Chance upstairs to a small room with a dresser, mirror, bath and single brass bed. Without further talk they embraced and kissed each other with an understanding and tenderness they savored for long moments.

The Easter congregation went through two more opening songs in fervent celebration of the Lord's Day while Chance and Kathy undressed each other, touching, kissing, looking.

"Blasphemous, aren't we?" Chance said, smiling, touching her smooth-skinned, tender nakedness and easing her down onto the bed.

Hungrily, she kissed him, her hot tongue and fiery breath filling his mouth as Chance gently cupped one of her smallish breasts, teasing the nipple, producing a soft feminine moan of mounting excitement, rubbing one nipple, then the other, until they stiffened like hard rubber and he could feel her wetted womanhood sliding against his thigh, slippery, soft, heated and wanting. She opened her legs, eyes rolling back in her head while Chance softly kissed her face, neck and ears, stroking her sensitive parts, teasing her entire body with caresses which made her rub herself over Chance in crazed ecstasy, her musky scent filling his nose. The one-eyed man took one breast, then the other, into his mouth, licking, kissing, sucking, rubbing, taking his time, readying her for the right moment, worshipping her body with a gentle tenderness that, given the kind of man he was forced to be, seemed extremely unusual.

And when he began teasingly rubbing the now inflamed knob of her desire, she wrapped and squeezed her long, beautiful legs around his waist in impatient desire.

Unable to control the raging fires inside her any longer, the woman grabbed Chance's stiffened member and slid down on it, gasping softly as it was slowly thrust deep into her, filling her, pressing her clit. She then brought her knees back to her as far as possible, rocking up and down, Chance trying to pace himself to her furious motions. She bit, clawed, cried, lost in a frenzy of pleasure, riding Chance hard, relentlessly seeking release. This was not the kind of woman welcomed with open arms in a town like Calvary. This was a woman who had raw, violent sexual needs, and Chance could imagine how she had been made to suffer—scorned, shunned, branded impure and a whore, for being human.

Suddenly she slowed, pushing Chance as deep into her as she could, her body tightening, her hands digging, clutching Chance's buttocks. Then wildly she squirmed up and down him like a maddened animal, crying, her climax shrieking through her whole body, lasting, touching every nerve ending, exploding throughout her trembling flesh, threatening a swoon, filling her with an intense joy she wanted to last forever. At great length she calmed, breathing heavily, still crushing Chance to her.

Pushing himself away from her heaving, sweating body, Chance slid his swollen cock out of her, not having spent himself. And at this, Kathy seemed amazed. She grasped his glistening wet spear as Chance stood beside the bed. Then she sat up on her haunches and, feeling her loins tingle, she took Chance in her mouth, tasting, smelling herself on him. She kissed his manhood with tender and teasing caresses for what were to Chance several irritating moments of anticipation, the fire having built deep in his scrotum, demanding explosion. She had not had him in her mouth, sucking and stroking, fully ten seconds before Chance's seed burst forth and filled her mouth. Greedily she tightened her mouth, swallowing Chance, relishing the taste, the streams of semen shooting down her throat. Nothing short of biting off Chance's cock would have satiated the sudden burning she had to take him that way forever.

Upon going limp in her mouth, Chance withdrew. Kathy sighed and dropped back onto the pillow while he dressed quickly and quietly.

She wiped her lips, watching Chance. Pants and boots on, he sat down on the bed. The singing continued and filled the silence between them. Chance sat and stared grimly at the wall before him.

Kathy reached out and touched his bare back. "They're here, aren't they?"

There was a pause before Chance answered, "They'll be here."

"Death," she said gravely, the sadness once more returning to her face. "It follows you, haunts you. It will always be with you, won't it?"

Silently Chance slid on his undershirt, then put on his shirt and buttoned it. Grimly he stood and fastened on his gunbelt. He picked up the whiskey bottle.

"We could have been something," Kathy softly said, eyes hurt and pleading. "Me and you. We could have."

Somberly Chance shook his head. "You wouldn't want me, ma'am."

"Kathy," she corrected.

"Kathy," Chance said, sighing. "I'm a dead man. I have no future, no hopes, no dreams."

"But why?" she cried, her voice a soft, uncomprehending whine. "It could be different, damn it."

Chance said nothing. Perhaps, he admitted to himself, she was right. But then again, he was not the kind of man who needed company with his misery.

"We could have been something good," she insisted at length, looking determined. "It would have been good."

Chance looked at the bottle in his hand, then set it on the dresser next to the bed.

"That's a comforting thought," he said in solemn sincerity. "I'll take it with me into hell," he added, turning and heading for the door.

"I won't watch," she called after him, a mournful pout of defiance on her face. "I can't."

"That's why you'll need the bottle more than me," he said levelly. A pause. "And I don't want you to watch, ma'am."

After he had placed the supplies in his saddlebags and stepped back onto the boardwalk, Chance rolled a cigarette, his left shoulder leaning against a beam.

A thin smile wrinkling his lips from which his cigarette dangled, Chance turned his head, looking up the street to the church.

It sounded as if everyone in Calvary were skilled singers. Every note was sung precisely. The combination of high-pitched feminine and deep male voices made for a beautiful melody. So loud was the chorus that it seemed to drown the pump organ, the rumble of thunder and the occasional violent cracking of lightning as the singing reached out through the valley. Over the flat desolation to the west the voices of joyful song echoed, drawing the four riders toward the town like a sucking wind.

Puffing leisurely on his cigarette, Chance listened to the resonant, solemn voice of Father Aspane as he greeted the congregation. A cool breeze began to stir while the reverend continued his opening address. Horses snorted and cried softly throughout the town, the angry sky boomed more frequently and lightning ripped across the darkness above more regularly.

When Chance turned his head right for no particular reason, he spotted the four riders slowly moving in on the white town. The one-eyed man intently watched the four riders, now a half mile in the distance, clouds of dust being swirled about their figures in the winds which steadily picked up strength from the west.

"This is the day that Christ, the Lord, the Son of Man, overcame Death to give the lives of men everywhere a special meaning." The reverend's opening words continued, with brief remarks about "the heathens of this land," and how the town "seeks to escape the evils of this world."

Chance flicked his cigarette butt into the street, then went to his horse. As he removed a black slicker from underneath his bedroll, the skies opened up and the rain began to descend. At first the downfall was light; but then, as he stepped back up onto the boardwalk and under the canopy, rolling another cigarette while the congregation sang the Acclamations, the downpour became so heavy it looked like a thin gray sheet. The four riders seemed lost in the distance under falling curtains of water.

With his body Chance shielded his rifle behind him, the weapon canted against a beam. Contentedly he puffed on his cigarette and waited, as the congregation recited the Glory to God. Then, as the gray-coated figures of Laster and his comrades became discernible as they closed the gap, the Easter readings began.

With the rain violently pelting the roof, and the crash of thunder resounding outside, the reverend finished his reading of Luke 24: 1-1. "Then he went back home wondering at what had happened."

The reverend paused and the tightly packed crowd inside the large church expectantly awaited the sermon.

The large priest was hunched over his pulpit. He looked down at his notes briefly, sniffing and wrinkling his nose, assaulted by the combined smells of perfume, hair tonic and body oil—odors so strong in the packed space that it was nearly nauseating to the priest.

A baby in the back began to cry, but the mother quickly silenced it. Undivided attention was always given the Reverend Aspane, for nearly all in the congregation enjoyed his dynamic sermons. They loved the fierce speeches he threw at them about the consequences of sin and what God would do to the wrongdoers of this world. And since his critical words were almost always directed toward people outside of Calvary, they reveled in a sort of selfrighteous fascination during these weekly harangues.

The reverend looked up and drew a deep breath, his solemn face sweeping over the intensely silent crowd. "Brothers and sisters in the Risen Christ Jesus Almighty," he began, his voice loud enough to be easily heard over nature's disturbance beyond the church walls. He was always deadly serious during his sermons. Never did he lighten the mood, or begin with a joke, for he held that sort of thing in contempt. "This is a day of triumph immortal," said he, waggling a finger at the large crucifix to his far right, as if to emphasize his point.

"Let us forget, for a moment, the wealth which let us form our community away from the heathen of this land. Let us forget, for a moment, the trivial problems of our everyday existence. Let us forget, for a moment, our spouses and our children. For if your hearts are solely concerned with the things of this life, then you," he declared icily, teeth clenched momentarily, grabbing at an invisible person before him, "have no place in the heart of Christ Almighty. It is a sad day when men forsake the gift of God's Love—an unbounded, endless love that wants—'that wants' I repeat with adamant feeling—every man, woman and child under the skies above to share in an endless life of joy which we can't even begin to conceive of."

"Not another fire and brimstone," Schmidt growled softly in exasperation to his wife. "And on Easter Sunday, for pete's sake."

"Sssshhhh!" his wife scolded, as several people around them cast them glances of admonishment. Schmidt rubbed his face in disgust, shaking his head.

"Though I can commend ye heartily, by God as my witness!" the reverend enthusiastically proclaimed, his gesticulating nearly frantic. "Though I can look each and every one of ye in the eye and honestly declare that this is a Godfearing, devoted Christian community. Though I say this," said he, eyes intense, nostrils flared, "may I also point out that there is room for improvement in all thy lives, by God as my witness."

Though the reverend was an excellent speaker in many ways, he had a bad habit of repeating himself often. "For is this not somehow related to the death and resurrection of the Lord? For was not His life given to exemplify the meaning of a perfect love? Would not improvement in certain facets of our lives help us grasp and lean toward a better conception of Christ Almighty, Son of God . . . His perfect love, exemplified in His death on the cross.

"Do not be influenced or concerned by the ways of heathen savages throughout this violent and immoral land—though if a savage should pass through our holy town, may we impress upon him the ways of the cross. This is for the most part an untamed and uncivilized land, as we well know from those of ye who lost family on the journey westward.

"Tired of savagery, were ye?" he boomed, pointing directly at a man in the front, the reverend's eyes blazing at the cringing, slightly embarrassed man. "Tired of the immorality of thy heathen brother, were thee? By God as my witness, thee had every right to be! Though you tried, brother. Though you tried. And I commend thee heartily. For this is a sacred town that the Lord smiles upon, always. Devoid of liquor, for the most part. Free of painted women, who are the scourge of mankind everywhere . . . else! Loose women who flaunt their bodies and cavort about half naked. I have seen this, brethren, elsewhere, by God as my witness! Modern-day Sodom and Gomorrah is in this land!

"But let them play, brethren. Do not let their wickedness stain ye. For their day will soon come, and there shall be much wailing and gnashing of teeth before the Lord, as the Good Book says. The Lord, your God, who shall hurl the wicked into Gehenna forever! But when the wrath of the Lord's hook sweeps the stage of the human garbage pile, ye shall not desire in the least even to see it. Mighty and awesome is the Lord's vengeance. Mighty and awesome!''

The preacher had a full head of fire now. His jowls were flapping, his body shaking, occasional drops of spittle sprayed those in the front row. An elderly man who had the misfortune to be just below the pulpit would have no cause to bathe for weeks to come.

Dry underneath the protection of the canopy, Chance puffed the remainder of his cigarette to a butt, watching the four men steering their mounts under the high white banner at the western entrance. Casually he reached behind him, grabbed the Henry, then raised it and canted it against his right shoulder.

The two crosses which held the banner greeted Laster and his men with: WELCOME TO CALVARY. And the banner overhead proclaimed in bold black letters: JESUS CHRIST IS RISEN TODAY! To this there were low snorts, grunts and guffaws from the four as they quickly read the words. Then they focused their undivided attention on the stolid figure of the one-eyed man as they reined their mounts to a halt more than thirty feet from Chance. Rain cascaded relentlessly, though the wind had subsided. Thunder and lightning were louder than ever over the valley.

Yet nothing prevented the tirade raging inside the white church from lashing the ears of the five men more than two hundred feet away.

"And the elderly? By God as my witness, how sad have I witnessed mistreatment of the elderly. Sad but true, we shun the elderly, mistreat them. And do ye know why? Because we see death in them; our fear of dying manifests tenfold as we come into contact with those who are fast approaching it."

"Loudest damned preacher I ever heard," grumbled Stanley with sardonic vindictiveness. "Ain't he, Sim?"

Laster didn't respond. All held their hard gazes steadily on Chance, who remained unmoving and impassive.

"Don't know how you figured it, Sim," Ridgeway remarked with a note of pride and astonishment in his voice. "But you hit the nail on the head," he drawled, voice a dim murmur in the downpour, "when you figured him to show here."

"Why is death such a dirty word?" they heard the reverend ask. "It's the most personal, yet, dare I say, the most selfish and dreaded area of human existence."

"How about it, Chance?" Laster mumbled.

"Laster, I take it, dude," Chance said.

"For are not each one of us concerned—and justly so to an extent—with our own deaths?"

"You presumed right, one-eye," Laster replied, his soft tone arrogant, with an edge to it.

"Who you friends with?"

"Bradbury knows you," Laster answered. "Just so happens he couldn't make it."

"Good friends?"

"I believe you could say that," Laster replied.

"I like it when it's personal, dude," Chance said flatly, flicking his cigarette into the muddy street.

"Pray, brethren, that we find consolation and love in Christ Almighty. Death is only a step into a beautiful beyond. Fear not death!"

"Turn over the money," Laster said under a roar of thunder and a flash of lightning, "and it don't have to get personal."

"Fear not the power of the Evil One! Fear not the agony of eternal damnation—everlasting, horrible punishment! Fear it not!"

"There is no money, Laster," Chance firmly stated.

"You're lying!" Stanley angrily accused.

"Then let us see your bags, one-eye," Laster demanded.

"It's not in there," Chance evenly replied. "So why don't you just turn yourselves around and—"

"You've hidden it?" asked Mamoreck irritably.

"I have no idea where it is, feller," Chance said, his answer a half truth.

"It's in his bags, Sim!" Stanley said, his tone solid with conviction and disgust.

"The heathen of this land have succumbed to the powers of the Evil One! They kill!"

"Preacher says not to fear death, boys," Chance grimly intoned, a slight grin forming on the corner of his mouth.

"They indulge in lewd conduct with painted ladies, and other men's wives!"

"Think you can afford to take the chance?" the one-eyed man said. He stood upright, then moved a half step away from the beam. The four watched him with somber concern.

Stanley scowled darkly. "I'm telling ya it's in his bags, Sim."

"What if it ain't?" Laster growled.

"You figure he's going to let us take a look any other way?" Stanley posed rhetorically, his tone challenging.

Laster grunted irritation, realizing that a violent conflict was inevitable. Neither party was willing to yield ground. Laster and his men had come too far, and Chance, bitter and despondent, wanted to end the hunt here and eliminate the last of the hunters he knew about. He was aware that his own trail might also end in the lashing downpour which drenched the white buildings of Calvary, for the four gunmen were prepared to kill him if they had to.

For some reason he thought of the mad general's last words: "If I can't have it then nobody will!" And that was exactly how he felt as he stared down the four who had tracked him hundreds of miles, and by a lucky guess and a last breath of hope had found the man they had so desperately tracked.

"You want to reason about this, Chance?" Laster asked gruffly, though his tone had a note of pleading in it.

"Preacher would say there's no reasoning amongst heathen," Chance said, his legs splayed, face grim and hard with challenge. "And I don't need to catch a bullet in the back after your reasoning gets you what you want. So you reason that out for yourself, dude."

"I told you he's got it in his bags!" Stanely vehemently declared. Laster was reluctantly convinced by his comrade's belief.

"No reasoning, one-eye," Laster solemnly said, turning his animal to the right. The others did likewise. "There's no reason at all for you to catch a bullet in the back when it'd be just as easy for me to put a bullet in the front of you," he evilly boasted. "Unless you plan on helping us to what we want."

"No chance of that," the one-eyed man icily declared.

At this, the four dismounted and tethered their horses directly opposite Chance, some seventy feet on the other side.

Inside the church, Father Aspane, his face flushed crimson, ended his sermon.

"Brothers and sisters in Christ," said he, now calm and dignified. "Let us rise and, before we profess our faith, let us sing—with as much love as we can bring forth from our hearts —'Jesus Christ is Ris'n Today.'"

Instantly, as if he'd read the reverend's mind, the organist launched into play, preparing the crowd by playing through the first verse. The congregation rose to their feet, hymnals held before faces with various expressions in the aftermath of the preacher's words—enthusiasm, concern, mild dismay, appreciation, acceptance.

Outside, the four took several slow steps toward Chance, spreading themselves out in opposite directions on both sides of the one-eyed man. He remained under the canopy, rifle still leaning against his shoulder.

Inside, the organist paused after his warmup. Then both music and singing began in perfect unison, the reverend exuberantly leading the congregation.

Laster came to a halt forty feet in front of Chance. Ridgeway and Mamoreck were to Laster's right, rounding a semicircle. Stanley backed off to Chance's right. The angelic voices filled the air on the scene of impending death.

"Fitting place to die, Chance," Laster said evenly. His men were now standing still, spaced to the left and right of Chance, their legs splayed as they unbuttoned their long gray coats.

Chance agreed, his tone easy, and for some strange reason he was not even concerned with the thoughts of dying—though he had every intention of killing these four, convinced that he could take them. The ordeal he had lived through had convinced him that almost any odds, even those which at first glance seemed insurmountable, could be beaten.

"Isn't Calvary where some guy who said he was the Son of God was nailed to a cross?" Ridgeway growled cynically, irreverantly. "Called Himself Jesus Christ?"

"That's the feller," Chance replied.

Ridgeway grunted mockingly. "Always thought it served him right."

With sharp viciousness, Chance looked at Ridgeway. "Then tell your problems to the Lord, moron," he said, acid in his voice.

Inside, the chorus of joyful singing grew louder and more enthusiastic under the direction of the reverend.

"But I don't think any of us are going to see the resurrection," Chance grimly added, stepping down into the street as Laster and the other three drew their coats back to hang them behind their gun butts. For several stretched seconds, Chance looked at Laster, his head tilted slightly to the left, barely able to keep the tall, broad figures of the other three in his vision. But he knew the course of action he was ready to spring into.

Then, the thunder pounding out a deafening salvo, lightning seeming to rip continuously, the singing peaked at its highest pitch. Chance swung his rifle down and leveled it at Laster, just as Laster and the three others slapped leather, beginning to cock and draw their weapons. Ridgeway and Mamoreck had trouble gripping their rain-slickened revolvers; this was an advantage Chance had counted on. He drilled a bullet into Laster's right shoulder, spinning the man halfway around. Laster's gun flew from his hands as his face locked in pain and a silent scream lodged in his throat.

While Laster dropped into a large puddle, great sprays of water and mud bursting out in all directions, Chance pumped the Henry, whirled to his right, and blasted Stanley in the chest. As Stanley was knocked on his back, instant wide-eyed death sweeping his horrified face, Chance pumped another shell into place and dove ahead, slightly to his right.

The blanket of rain thickened. The thunder pounded raging fury, drowning the sound of gunshots as Ridgeway and Mamoreck finally drew and began fanning their guns wildly, panic flooding faces lashed by rainfall.

"Sing we to our God above, Al-le-lu-ia!"

A bullet from Mamoreck furrowed Chance's right thigh. Mamoreck's other slug flew wide as the one-eyed man, ending his short water-splashing slide in the mud, fired, painting a red dot in the center of Mamoreck's forehead.

Mamoreck's head snapped upward and back grotesquely. His mouth hanging open, the dead man was kicked backward and landed hard on his back. Great splashes of water and mud shot outward when he hit the street.

Instantly Chance rose to his right knee, slipping slightly. A bullet from Ridgeway landed in front of him, spraying his face with muddy water.

A muffled moan of torment escaped Laster's mouth as he crawled desperately for his revolver. Another bullet from Ridgeway ripped a hole across the side of Chance's slicker, and a slug had also whistled past Chance's ear, before Ridgeway got two bulletholes in his stomach. Ridgeway snapped double, nosediving into the muddy street.

Laster snatched his revolver just as water and mud exploded from underneath Ridgeway as he hit the ground.

Lying on his right side, Laster twisted himself around to face Chance, cocking his gun. But the one-eyed man seemed to move faster than the flashes of lightning, sensing victory over death once more.

"Praise him all ye heav'nly host, Al-le-lu-ia!"

The last crack of death spat forth from Chance's rifle. The slug punched in o the center of Laster's chest, flipping him onto his back, ₅ in flying from his hand—for good this time.

Inside, the townspeople had no idea death was blazing with relentless greed and playing a brutal part in the celebration of the resurrection.

"Once again!" bellowed an exultant Father Aspane as the singing ended. "First two stanzas!"

Without hesitation, for they were as jubilantly enthralled as the reverend, the church blasted forth with more song. The repeated verses reached the ears of the lone one-eyed survivor as he brought himself erect and picked up his hat, drenched with water and plastered brown with mud.

Somberly Chance surveyed the dead being pelted by the downpour, their flowing blood diluted by rainwater as it spread out from underneath their motionless forms, lifeless eyes staring at the blackness above.

"It wasn't worth it, Laster," he solemnly said. "But you'll never know."

Then, as the singing once again rose in fervor, Chance ambled toward his horse. He slid the rifle into its scabbard, unhitched his gelding, mounted. Under the steadily beating rain, the blasting of thunder and ripping of lightning, he headed up the street toward the church, leaving behind the sprawled dead. He neared the church at a walking gait.

"Sin-ners to re-deem and save, Al-le-lu-ia!"

The last verse echoed throughout the valley. And Chance disappeared around the corner.